44 100

Previous Books in
The Unspoken Series
by Marilyn Grey

Book #1
Where Love Finds You
Ella & Matthew

Book #2
Down from the Clouds
Gavin

Book #3
The Life I Now Live
Heidi & Patrick

Book #4
Heart on a Shoestring
Miranda & Derek

BLOM

MARILYN GREY

WINSLET PRESS

Bloom
Copyright © 2014 by Marilyn Grey

To learn more about Marilyn Grey, visit her Web site:
www.marilyn-grey.com

ISBN-10: 0985723556
ISBN-13: 978-0985723552

This novel is a work of fiction. Names, characters, places, and incidents
either are the product of the author's imagination or are used fictitiously.
Any resemblance to actual events, locales, organizations, or persons living
or dead is entirely coincidental and beyond the intent of either the author
or the publisher.

Cover & Interior Design by Tekeme Studios

Printed in the United States of America

First Edition: May 2014
14 12 11 10 9 8 7 6 5 4 3 2 1

To:
Candice Joy

For:
showing me what real beauty is

extended version:

Oh, Can. On one hand, it's hard to believe it's been over ten years. On the other hand, it's hard to believe it's *only* been a little over a decade. There are friends that come and go ... even family members that come and go ... and then, there are those rare few who become a part of your very existence. The friendship in this story is very close to our own. Ella and Sarah are opposites in many ways. Not that we are exactly like these two girls, but we are opposites for sure. We used to think music was the bond that kept us together, but now that music is history in our friendship ... what is it? Was it ever music? I don't think so. It was us, Can. Just us. Two people who love each other like real family. That's what we are. It's not like a marriage where two people fall in love and choose to marry the other person. It's different. We didn't choose each other. We crossed paths. And although we've had tough times, we've never stopped holding hands. Cheesy as it sounds, that's what sisters are. Real sisters. They are different, but there's a bond there that can never be broken. A love unlike any other. I have never had many friends and doubt I ever will, but why would I need them when I have you? The rose. My rose. Whenever you feel misunderstood, just remember that there's at least one person out there (crazy as she may be) who not only understands you ... but loves you for every little piece of beautiful that you are. You are a shining example of what this book is all about. Real beauty.

The best and most beautiful things in the world cannot be seen or even touched. They must be felt with the heart.
Helen Keller

Strange, isn't it? Each man's life touches so many other lives. When he isn't around he leaves an awful hole, doesn't he?
It's a Wonderful Life

Everything has beauty, but not everyone sees it.
Confucius

People are like stained glass windows. They sparkle and shine when the sun is out, but when the darkness sets in, their true beauty is revealed only if there is a light from within.
Elizabeth Kubler-Ross

 *prologue*

J ames and I made s'mores by the fire. Always a careful person, I stayed three feet away from the crackling flames as I roasted my marshmallow, then smothered it between chocolate and crunchy graham crackers. James wiped my face and kissed the side of my mouth. We spent an hour talking about life. Our goals. Our future.

Near the end of the conversation I yawned. He got down on his knees to clean up the boxes and trash. At least that's what I thought.

Staring up at me, he took something out of his pocket. I straightened my back as I sat on the log and a smile wrapped around my face as he took my hand.

"Sarah, we've both been through a lot. I know I'm not like all of your friends. I'm normal. A mechanic. Not artsy like you and all of them. I've argued with myself constantly. Had this ring for a while, you know." He spun it in his hands, looking down. "I didn't know how to make this romantic and over the top. I didn't want to ask for help either because, to me, that's a lie. This is who I am. I may not be the most romantic guy in the world, but I need you. Forever. So ... what do you think?"

I covered my mouth as he slipped the ring on my left hand. "Of course, James. You know my concerns about leaving Abby though. She can't lose a mother figure twice. It would be unbearable."

"Your cancer is gone. Doctors say there's a good chance it's gone forever."

I nodded, part of me nervous to commit to someone.

11

He stood and pulled me into his arms. "How does it feel? To be my fiance?"

"It feels ... normal."

We laughed. He carried me into the tent and flopped me onto the pillows. We had a ton of cheap three-dollar pillows stuffed in the tent. James surprised me because I once told him I wanted to sleep on a cloud.

"Can you go put out the fire?" I said.

He smiled. "Yes. Right after I kiss my future wife."

We kissed as the moonlight lit our faces.

I stopped him and said, "I'd feel better if you put out the fire."

He pulled me into him and held me there. "I'll get it in a minute."

That's the last thing I remember before waking up to James screaming for me.

By the time I opened my eyes the tent was orange and a horrible scent clung to my nose. I screamed and backed into the corner of the tent, looking for James as the bed of clouds engulfed into huge flames. I closed my eyes and covered my face with my arm as I clawed at the tent, trying to rip the cloth and bite my way out of the fabric. The flames licked my skin, inching closer.

I looked down at my legs and hands. Didn't take long to realize. The ghastly smell was my own skin melting off. Sharp bursts of pain seared through every inch of my body. Skin, black like the marshmallow I burned a little while ago, flapped off my arm and I could see the bone in my left hand, where the ring he gave me no longer resided.

James screamed my name again. A haunting chill swept over me, cooling my inflamed body. I collapsed in the corner of the tent like a parachute falling to the ground and asked God to take me quickly. A rush of sunny memories terrified me. I'd never see them again. This was the end.

Then each memory vanished and the world turned black.

 *one*

My room smelled of buttery pancakes and pumpkin pie. I turned on my phone. 9:32a.m. September 15th. I no longer needed help taking off my burn mask. Thankfully. No need to wake Cheyenne this morning, who was still sleeping peacefully in the twin bed beside mine. Ella had been an angel. Not only allowing me to stay in her home, but allowing my cousin Cheyenne to stay with me as well. Ella worried that she wouldn't be able to help me after she had the baby, but Adelaide Kessler was four weeks and two days old and Ella spent four weeks and one day out of those first weeks of her daughters life checking on me every three hours. At least.

I stayed in the hospital longer than most of the other burn unit patients. Partly because I had a lot of infections along the way, near death experiences, and trouble learning to walk again. And also because I wanted to. I feared coming home and burdening others. I feared being needy and, most of all, I feared that I'd no longer be able to hide my tears. When someone visited me in the hospital I had enough warning to dry my eyes and put on a happy face. In the world I'd need to hold it in or let it out. And let it known.

Cheyenne stirred and saw me standing without my burn mask. "You're getting quite ambitious, aren't you?"

"Funny," I said. "Gone are the days when ten mile runs were ambitious. Now getting out of bed myself is an accomplishment."

"You've come so far since the accident. Imagine how normal life will be by this time next year."

I toddled toward the bathroom. Ignoring her optimism. I knew the heart of an optimist well. I used to be one. My entire life. Until now. But

13

normal wouldn't exist for me ever again. A new normal, maybe. But not my old normal.

Cheyenne closed the bathroom door behind me. "Let me know if you need help."

I stood in front of the mirror. Someone's face stared back at me. Red, swollen, and disfigured. The right side of my face remained somewhat normal, but the left side ... I looked away and positioned myself on the toilet. Took ten minutes to do something I once did in two. I washed my hands and avoided the mirror.

Throughout my life people complimented my beauty, but honestly, I never thought much of it. I didn't get too into my looks like some girls. Wasn't important to me.

Every time I saw my reflection in a mirror I couldn't help but realize how important it actually was to me. I just didn't realize it until it was gone.

Life with a different face is a new life altogether. People treated me like a child now. They talked to me with loud and slow voices as though my ears melted away in the fire. Strangers stared and kids pointed. Men, who once turned their heads to watch me walk away, now turned their heads in disgust. I never needed attention. And I still didn't. Maybe that's why it upset me to be looked at so much.

Cheyenne knocked on the door. "Everything okay? Ready to change your dressings?"

I opened the door.

"And here are your pills."

She placed them in my palm on top of the cloth surrounding my hand. I put them in my mouth one at a time and gulped the water she gave me.

"Well," she said. "Ella made baked pumpkin oatmeal for breakfast. Would you like some?"

"No, thanks."

"You need to eat more, Sarah."

Cheyenne was not only my cousin. She was a nurse. And sometimes I wished she weren't.

"Let's change this stuff," I said. "Get my ever dreaded shower and get through the morning routine. Maybe after that I will eat lunch."

Cheyenne entered the bathroom and closed the door. Ella and Gavin chatted downstairs. I could hear them discussing work and lessons as silverware clanged in the sink. I imagined Adelaide snuggled against her chest in the baby wrap and Gavin's arms around them both, wondering if I'd ever be able to have children. If so, I wouldn't be able to nurse them. My flat chest with weird skin caught my eye as Cheyenne helped me undress. Mirrors insulted me, especially when unclothed. So I stepped aside and closed my eyes.

The pain, still intense, seemed as though it would remain with me for the rest of my life. "Poor James."

"Not poor James. He loves you."

"Did I say that aloud?"

She nodded as she completed her task and I took slow steps into the shower. I so dreaded the shower.

"Looks aren't everything, Sarah. They aren't even close."

Easy for her to say. She still had her beauty. I didn't even have breasts to nurse a child with. The doctor mentioned plastic surgery, but the thought appalled me.

"I'm like a child," I said. "He needs a wife. Not a child."

She turned on the water and I flinched.

"He needs you," she said. "Period."

Cheyenne helped me finish my painful morning routine in silence, then she asked me if I'd be okay with her leaving for a while. I nodded from my bed. Sleep called for me. Especially after those torturous showers.

MY DREAMS EITHER INVOLVED BEING TRAPPED IN A BURNING building or a mangled car. So I didn't sleep much, but this time I dreamt of James and Abby with a woman who could take care of them. When I awoke James was sitting beside me smiling. "Morning, beautiful."

"How can you say beautiful?" I said, closing my eyes again.

He didn't respond. I looked at him again. His smile disappeared. Replaced by two serious eyes and turned down lips.

"Abby deserves better, James. So do you."

He unhooked the necklace around his neck and placed it on the table by my bed. The ring clanked as it hit the wood. James touched my shoulder.

"I'm sticking by you until that ring goes back on your finger with a wedding band."

"James."

"Sarah."

"You don't have to feel sorry for me. Don't do this out of pity or guilt. I'm a big girl."

He stood. "Every time I visit. Every single time you try to get rid of me. I'm doing the best I can. What do you want from me?"

"You don't want to marry me. Admit it. If you met me now you'd never think twice about putting a ring on my finger." I held back tears. "You're worried about Abby. I get that. Since your brother died and Abby lost her parents, you feel like you need to protect her. That's true. You're her daddy now and she needs you. But she also needs a mother. A real one. Let me go, James. Just let me go. I don't want pity."

His eyes narrowed. "I've been by your bed every moment possible since this happened. Is this your way of saying thanks?"

"I am thankful." I looked down. "You're a wonderful person. You've been good to me. But I'm okay. It wasn't your fault and you can walk away without hurting me. I'll be okay."

"What would you have said if we were already married and this happened, huh? What then?"

I stared at my bare chest. The chest that was meant to nurse my children during sleepless nights. Gone. My dreams of motherhood went up in smoke. I'd failed my children before giving birth to them.

I loved James too much to see him settle for me just because he loved the person I was before all of this. Maybe one day he would understand it was my love for him that helped me let him go.

He stood in the doorway. "You know that scene from Titantic?"

I shook my head.

"Come on, you've made me watch it six times."

"Which scene?"

"The one."

"Please don't, James."

"I've been by your side since this happened. You almost died twice and that kind of thing makes you realize a lot. Made me realize that I may be able to go on living without you, but I don't want to." He closed the door. His footsteps trailed off. I heard the car door close and the engine rumble. The door opened again.

Ella sat a few scones and a steaming cup of my favorite tea on the table beside me.

"I know what you're going to say," I said. "Don't say it."

She smiled. "What am I going to say?"

"That I need to be nice to him, but you don't understand. I need him to let go. For his own good. If I'm nice he'll hang on."

"I don't know what's going on between you two. You never say anything and he's as private as you are." She handed me a blueberry-orange scone. "I was going to reprimand you for not eating. You have to if you want to get better. English breakfast tea four times a day doesn't count."

I picked off a piece from the scone and chewed it. Pretty good actually. "Change of pace, huh?"

"What do you mean?"

"Me, depressed. You, cheery." I laughed. "Tables have turned."

"You remember what you said to me once?" She tapped my foot. "My dream is every day. When I wake up, I want to find something new. Something beautiful about each day I'm given. I want to take the cards I'm given and play them with a smile, not to win, just to play."

"Yeah. I said that when life's biggest disappointment was losing a job or being single."

"Well, try it." She stood, left, and returned with the baby. "Find something beautiful."

"It's hard, Ella. I see negative in everything. There you are holding a baby and instead of seeing her beauty and your happiness all I see is my inability to have children and it makes me not want to be around either of you."

"Doctor never said you can't have children."

"What kind of man wants to marry a woman with a shriveled up chest?"

"The man you have." She glanced at the glistening ring on my night stand. "He wants you."

I closed my eyes and remembered the first time I opened them after the accident. I didn't know where I was and when I did I wished I had died. For months after that, wrapped up like a mummy, I kept wishing I'd close my eyes and die of an infection. People came in and out of my room. Checked my catheter. Did my excruciating physical therapy. Had conversations about their boyfriends and girlfriends and lives outside of the hospital. The life I wanted to crawl back to.

Being strapped to a hospital bed has a way of changing your perspective of life. Before the fire I loved my iPhone, e-books, and having information right at my fingertips. I could think of someone, text them from across the country, and get a reply instantly. All those nights and days in that bed, listening to nurses talk about trivial things, watching them check their phones, seeing them obsess over what to wear on a date, all of it made me realize how much life I missed while glued to my own screens and obsessions with instant information. I dreamed of a simpler time where sending a letter to someone took time, a lot of time. Then, someone on horseback trekked across the land in honor of delivering your well thought-out words to the recipient. I dreamed of life, true life, where I'd marry for love and passion, not duty and sacrifice.

But I was stuck in that bed, forced to listen to people arguing about whether it was okay to wear white in October, and I longed to close my eyes and never open them again.

To be done. With the pain. The fast-paced, trivial conversations. All of it.

I wanted to be done.

I should've never went camping. Should've made him put the fire out. Shouldn't have fallen asleep. Endless regrets always ran through my head.

I tried to remain positive. That's what people expected of me. Always the sunshine in the room. I didn't want to let people down. Or maybe I didn't want to let myself down. Why is being fake easier than being real?

I opened my eyes. Ella smiled, sat in the chair across the room, and nursed Adelaide.

Knife in my non-existent chest.

I winced. "When you're finished could you give me some pain medication?"

She nodded.

"And do you mind not nursing her in front of me?"

A tear slipped down her face. "Sarah, I love you, but I'm not going to hide life from you. Yes, I can nurse a baby and you may never be able to, but there are many things you can do that I will never do. Think about who you are and how this can be turned into something good. So, you can't nurse a child. Adopt one. Do something. Think of others. Count your blessings."

My phone made a sound. I picked it up with the hand that didn't get burned. The hand I could still type and write with. A notification. Physical therapy in two hours. Great.

Ella already knew. She nodded when I looked at her and said, "Let's get you ready to go."

"Where's Gavin?"

"In the studio. Today's homeschooler day. He's teaching a few art classes and I have a few private violin lessons later. It's fine. I can take Adelaide."

"I can get Cheyenne."

"Sarah Jordan, I'm taking you. Soon you won't need help anymore and you'll be so busy that you won't have time to read. Enjoy this while it lasts."

I inched myself into a sitting position and sat on the edge of the bed. "Maybe I'd enjoy it a little more if I wasn't in constant pain."

"You've made it this far."

"This is so hard, Ella. It's so hard. I felt okay until I came home. Or to your home. Now life is going on all around me and every time I look in the mirror I want to cry."

She placed Adelaide in a baby wrap and put her arm around me. "I've always admired you, Sarah. And I still do. Throughout all of this you still manage to laugh and smile. You don't tell everyone how hard it is and you put on this positive mask, but underneath you really are that person. These moments of sadness are normal. What I admire is that you still smile more than you cry."

"Thank you for that." I smiled. "Let's go."

two

Ella waited in the hall as a young nurse led me back to a large physical therapy room. She helped me fill out a few papers, then left. A few minutes later my therapist walked in. "Sarah." A smile lit up his tanned and handsome face. "Nice to meet you. I'm Dr. Koursaris, but you can call me Vasili."

His accent mixed with his dark and exotic features embarrassed me. Of all therapists? They had to give me a young attractive man. I shook my head.

"I know this is hard, Sarah. It's painful and lonely and hard. So much time spent sitting in one place with only your thoughts. You're doing great. It's going to get better. I promise you."

"How can you promise that?" I snapped. He barely blinked. Not phased by my outburst. "Sorry, but how can anyone promise that? I've lost so much." I looked down at my bare chest as a tear slid down my gross face. "I look like a monster. My fiancé's daughter refuses to even look at my face. I'm disgusting to strangers. How? How can you promise that?"

His eyebrows dropped and he cleared his throat.

"Sorry to unload." I brushed the hair from my eyes. "I just don't see how you can say that. You don't know how it feels."

He nodded, clicked his pen a few times, then looked at me. "How about we begin?"

Half unwilling, I conceded. Since he wasn't familiar with me yet, we went through the basic exercises first. When our time was up I stared at him, confused.

"Just wanted to get a feel for things," he said. "We can save the more painful stuff for next time."

I glanced at his hands. No rings. "Where are you from?" I said. "Obviously not America."

"Chios." He smiled. "I'm Greek. Parents came to America when I was ten. My grandparents still live there."

I smiled. "Well, thanks for putting up with me today. I won't be so crazy next time." I stood and looked at the door, then hung my head. "I have to admit, this has been extremely embarrassing."

"Don't worry about it."

"Your accent is pretty thick, considering you were ten when you moved."

"My parents home-schooled me. I didn't learn English until seventh grade."

"Wow," I said, suddenly feeling like a normal person again, having a normal conversation. Except I was ugly and he was gorgeous. And that made it not quite as normal as it could've been in the past.

We stared at each other for a few seconds. Not an ounce of flirtation in the moment, but there was something about the way he looked at me that made me wish I were pretty again.

"See you in a few days, Sarah." He held the door as I walked through. Ella stood when she saw me, then she saw him and froze.

We drove to her place in silence and after we settled down inside she finally said, "So, you do realize that you're still engaged to James, right?"

I sighed. "Ella."

"What about the physical therapist guy?"

"Call him Vasili. And in case you failed to notice ... he is quite lovely on the eyes and I am, well, look at me. Even if I wanted to burst your little idealistic noggin by ending my engagement for my physical therapist, it's not gonna happen. What kind of guy would actually want me now?"

"I didn't realize how shallow you were." She adjusted Adelaide in the baby wrap. "Since when is love based on perfect bodies?"

I raised my eyebrows. Gavin walked in through the back door, entered the living room, and wrapped his arms around his wife and baby. Bliss. They always seemed so content. Like they never argued at all. So opposite of James and me. I watched them talk about their business, groceries, and Adelaide. Eventually Gavin realized I was in the room and greeted me. He sat on the couch next to Ella.

"We were having a little debate," I said to Gavin. "Care to weigh in?"

He turned to Ella. "Do I have to?"

She laughed. "Sarah here thinks that men only date perfect women."

"What? No. That's not what I mean," I said. "I'm just saying if James and I end things, which I'm pretty set on doing for his own sake, then I am looking at being single for life. And since I can't have children anyway I guess it doesn't matter."

"Doctor hasn't said you can't have kids," Ella said.

"Sarah," Gavin said. "James loves you. Don't push him away."

"I want better for him. For every man."

Ella stood and sat next to me. "You can't think so low of yourself just because you have some scars."

I faked a laugh. "Some scars? Is that what you see? My entire body is altered. This isn't me anymore. I'm not just an average looking woman, guys. I'm ugly. Do you hear me? Do you even see me? I'm not depressed about my looks. I'm getting used to this new life. But it's really starting to make me want to flip out when everyone around me pretends I'm still the same old beautiful Sarah. That's not me anymore."

Gavin spread his legs and propped his elbows on his knees. "That's not how we see it. We understand where you're coming from and I guess we can respect that, but try to see what we see."

"What? That true beauty is within?" I mocked.

"No," he said. "That you are still the same old Sarah and if you're getting uglier it has nothing to do with your skin."

I stood and took a deep breath. Then exhaled. "Gavin. Ella. You are my best friends. Can you please respect that I want to be left alone for now? Tell Cheyenne and James to let me be until morning. I can take care of myself."

They both stood.

"Please don't," Ella said. "We love you. We're trying to help."

"I know. And I agree what Gavin said. I just need time to think about it."

A tear glistened on Ella's face.

"None of this." I wiped her tear. "There are plenty of people who deserve your tears more than I do. I'm okay. It will be okay."

She sniffed, nodding as I tried to reassure everyone, including myself, that my future didn't look as dark as it seemed.

Everything would be okay.

It would be okay.

It would.

Right?

three

I sat at the window as the morning sun crackled through the branches that would soon be covered in shaky red and orange leaves. James and Cheyenne sat on a bench under a low arm of a crepe myrtle tree. Talking. He hung his head and clenched his fists. James expressed pain through frustration, not tears. Cheyenne touched his knee with one hand and pat his back with the other. His fists loosened. He placed his palms on his thighs, inches from her hand. They made eye contact, held it. Not an ounce of jealousy swam through my veins. I watched and waited. His hand inched toward hers. Their fingers desperately wanting to touch. Finally, he leaned toward her. She waited. Lips puckered just so. Slightly open in anticipation. Their fingertips touched and their lips met.

I woke up.

Stared at my ceiling. Turned over and looked at Cheyenne, sleeping in the bed across the room. I couldn't help but wonder why my dream didn't feel like a nightmare. I looked at the diamonds sparkling on my nightstand.

I guess I imagined everything to be different. Even my ring. I'm not prone to jealousy. Mostly, I lived a content life. Never wishing for unrealistic futures or anchoring myself to my past. Sometimes though—only sometimes—my best friend made me question my entire existence. Not because of her words or actions. Simply because of who she was made to be.

In public, guys always looked at me. Ella was simple. A classic beauty right out of the 1800's she so loved. She rarely wore makeup, never revealed her thighs or cleavage, and kept her flirtatious looks for the one she saw across a coffee shop. Her Gavin.

Meanwhile I wrapped myself in fashion and turned heads. It wasn't my intention and I didn't genuinely enjoy that kind of attention. In fact, I envied the girl beside me who men didn't devour with their eyes. Of course I never mentioned it to Ella, but it always bothered me a little that she was so oblivious to the lack of attention she received. The girl is downright beautiful, but she didn't carry herself in a way that demanded attention. She didn't care. She was so content in the man she saw at the coffee shop that she didn't even allow herself to glance at a guy with subtle interest. Meanwhile I turned few hearts and many heads. All the time. It was so normal to me that I didn't think about it. Until now.

Now, I wished for the simple beauty of my best friend. The kind of beauty that sacrifices for others constantly. The kind that ignores labor pains to comfort a friend. The sweet beauty of a woman who opened her arms and house to others when she was only a newlywed who hadn't had a chance to form a family with her husband. The kind of pure and gentle beauty that always thinks of others and never herself.

Then, there's her Gavin. I admit, the day he walked into my art class my heart skipped a few beats. The guy was practically flawless in appearance, had a great clean and stylish presence, and treated everyone with kindness and respect. He was every nice girl's romantic fantasy. Yet, he never acknowledged girls. No matter now beautiful and kind they were. They were not Ella. And though I didn't know it at the time ... all those nights I spent dreaming of him ... he was dreaming of his Ella, his love.

My best friend.

I FINISHED MY DREADFUL MORNING ROUTINE AND WALKED back to the bedroom.

Cheyenne jumped. "Oh, I didn't see you there." The diamonds shimmered as she set the ring back down. "I was just straightening up."

I held eye contact with her until her nervous eyes forfeited. Smiling, I sat on the edge of my bed and touched the ring. "You can keep it if you want."

She rolled her eyes. "Do you know how many girls out there are dreaming and longing for what you want to throw away?"

I nodded. "Yes. And I'm more than willing to trade with any of them."

"I'm serious, Sarah. You always were so beautiful. You always had guys after you. Don't you ever consider what it could be like for us average girls who don't have tons of potential spouses waiting in line?" She took a deep breath. "Don't you ever think about girls who may never be proposed to?"

I shrugged. "Look at me, Cheyenne." I stood. "Look at me."

She shook her head. "What?"

"I am not an average girl. I am below average. Kids giggle in the grocery store line and ask their parents if I'm a real monster or wearing a mask." I picked up the ring. Twirled it between my fingers. "This"—I held it up—"is not so important to me that I'm willing to subject others to misery and difficulty." I sat down. Out of breath. "I do think of girls who may never be proposed to, because while the door to 'happily ever after' is still open for them, still a hope within reach, it's closed for me. Forever."

"That's your choice. He has been by your side since the accident. He's waiting for you. That's true love. And you're spitting in its face."

"It's not true love and I'm not spitting in its face."

"Then what are you doing?"

"I found a dandelion. Held on for a while. But as much as I love the wonder of it I know it can't last in my pocket forever. So, I'm blowing it away so it can find new life."

"You're breaking its heart."

"No. I can't break what's already broken. I tried to fix it, but the yellow petals had already vanished. Now it's over. I can't be the one to bring him back to life."

"He loves you."

"And he will just as easily love another. Someone far better than me."

"You will regret this."

"I won't."

"How can you be so sure?"

"No man wants a wife like this. He will be happy and that's enough for me to never regret this choice."

She shook her head again and dropped her hands to her sides. "You're too stubborn for your own good."

Maybe she was right, but I wasn't interested in my own good. No one knew James like I did. His tough guy demeanor was only a facade. The real

James was a mess. He needed a wife who could breathe joy into his life. Maybe I could've been that person, but not anymore. He deserved a beautiful wife. Not a monster. And he deserved someone who didn't have to battle her own mind to force a smile. He needed someone better. Someone I could never be. And that's why I refused to slip his ring back on my finger.

Maybe it's hard to comprehend. I know most people thought I was rude and selfish. But for once I was doing something my best friend would do. Giving up my own desires for someone else. Yes, yes, I know. He wanted to be with me. He did. But sometimes what we want is the complete opposite of what we need, and in my opinion, those who truly love us will help us find what we need ... even at the expense of our desires.

James would fall in love again.

He would.

And I would help him.

CHEYENNE FOUND A JOB AT THE HOSPITAL IN LANCASTER City. When she left the next morning I found Ella downstairs nursing Adelaide on the couch. Another wave of jealousy crashed against my heart. I shook it off.

Ella smiled. "Hey, you."

I sat beside her, ignoring the suckling baby sounds. "I have come to enlist your services."

"Oh?"

"You are the ultimate Cupid. Can you please help me find someone for James? I need to set it up in a way that makes him feel like it's not set up."

"Are you kidding me?"

"I know, right?" I exhaled. "Sounds insane, but I'm dead serious."

She straightened her back. "You're kidding."

"Ella, I need your help. Seriously. I need to set him up. He needs to get over me. I've tried breaking up with him, but he doesn't let me. He feels so guilty about everything. It makes him want to stick it out, but it's not right. He needs someone else. Someone he won't wake up to every morning for the rest of his life and feel guilty for not putting the fire out when she asked." I let a few tears fall, wiped them, and continued, "Every day. He will wake up to guilt every day. Trust me, Ella. Please. I need him to fall in love and move on."

She wiped her face. "I love you."

"Does that mean you'll help me?"

"I'd die for you, Sarah."

I nodded. She reached toward me and pulled me into her. My head against her shoulder, her cheek against my forehead, I wept as Adelaide stared up at us. I couldn't hear over my own sniffling, but I didn't have to hear or see to know that Ella was crying along with me. Everything I felt, she felt. We were more than best friends. We were sisters.

She really would die for me, and because of that ... I trusted her with my life.

 *four*

E lla dropped me off in front of my physical therapist's office and said she'd be back in an hour. I smiled and walked away. The office was in a cute city house smashed between a row of similar houses. Two-and-a-half story houses embellished with shutters. Planters filled to the brim and overflowing with colorful plants. I loved the location. It reminded of that simpler time I longed for. Where people built houses with details and hands, instead of slapping stuff together with machines and watching it blow away during a storm.

I entered the office and signed in. The receptionist fidgeted with papers while trying to make eye contact with me. I thanked her and sat down.

When I was fifteen my parents took me to the State Fair in Baltimore with some old friends. They gave all the kids over fourteen some money and tickets and let us play for a few hours. I'll never forget the first thing we did. It completely ruined my night. I barely knew the kids I was with, so when they laughed their way to the back of a line, I sheepishly followed. I had no idea what we were in line for because I forgot my glasses and couldn't read the sign. We slipped a dollar into a box and entered a small room behind a big curtain.

I looked ahead as each person passed something on a platform. Some people giggled while others stared in bewilderment. My group finally reached the object. It was a woman. An adult woman about the size of my calf. She looked down, complacent and sad, as the kids in front of me laughed and spit in her face. I reached forward and wiped the spit with the sleeve of my shirt and apologized. She refused to look at me or thank me. She was too far gone.

I continued walking as the couple behind me covered their mouths and laughed into their hands. My heart split into fragments as I walked back outside. Fragments that I intended to use as a sword, but my group disappeared. Later I found out that they were embarrassed when I wiped the woman's face, so they abandoned me. I think the thing that bothered me the most wasn't the spitting or the sneering. It was that everyone called her "it."

I never thought I would also be referred to as an "it." Mostly by children, though adults averted their eyes from my own in public. The kids didn't look away. They stared. And inevitably they'd look up to their mom or dad and say, "What is it, Mommy?"

It.

"Ms. Jordan?" a young girl called from the front desk.

I stood, trying to smile.

"Right this way." She led me down the hall into a small room filled with various therapy equipment. A few minutes after she left, Vasili entered.

"Hey, Sarah. How's it going today?" His cheeriness was evident, but not overwhelming. Something soothing about it.

I nodded and shrugged.

"Care to talk before we begin?" He sat on an exercise ball and folded his hands. "I know I'm not a counselor, but I am a friend."

I almost laughed. "But you barely know me. This is, what, my fourth week here?"

"All of my patients are my friends. Otherwise I wouldn't do this for a living."

"What do you mean?"

"Just that I love what I do. I love people. My patients are people."

"Not all of them." I smoothed my skirt and pulled the hem of my shirt. "I'm not. I'm just another 'it.'"

"Says who?"

"Everyone."

He smiled. "Everyone?"

I looked up, almost to his eyes. Just short of the mark I rested my gaze on his neck. I saw burn scars again, creeping down his neck and under his shirt.

"Do you?" he said.

I looked down again. "Do I what?"

"Do you consider yourself a woman or an 'it?'"

I hesitated, then started again, "Why does it matter what I think if everyone else thinks something different?"

"I guess that's something you need to consider. If you care more about what others think than your own opinions." He stood. "Now, let's have fun with this appointment today. What do you say?"

"Fun is an afternoon with my toes dipped in the sand. Not this."

"You're doing great, Sarah. You'll be healed completely before you know it."

"You would know, huh?" I nodded toward his scars. "What happened?"

He shook his head. "That's not my story to tell."

"Who's story is it?"

"Anastasia's." He clapped his hands and steadied himself on a balance beam. "Come over here and we'll do a few stretches."

Sometimes I forgot that I was no longer pretty and misread friendliness for flirtation. Sometimes I felt like me again. I forgot I wasn't the same anymore. Who would ever flirt with me? Who am I kidding? I thought as I stood in front of Vasili with my hands at my sides.

He lifted my right arm and extended it in front of me. Then he moved behind me and gently held my left shoulder as he pulled my right arm toward my left side. "Stay straight and breathe in," he said. His palm warmed my back. I hadn't let James touch me since the accident and although my therapist obviously had no attraction to me, I somewhat enjoyed his touch. Not sensually. Not even romantically. I simply enjoyed the feeling of someone touching me like I was a normal person. I wasn't a monster.

After our session, I stalled at the door and turned back. "Who's Anastasia?"

He smiled. "My niece."

I nodded, hoping my internal relief didn't showcase itself on my face. Not that it mattered, I told myself. He'd never consider me.

"One more question," I said. "Do you know of any nice single women looking for love? I know a really sweet guy..."

"I'm not sure. I'll ask my fiancé and let you know. I'm sure we can find someone."

33

I ignored the pain in my chest as my mind lingered on the word. That word. Fiancé.

I stepped back into the room and closed the door a little. "You know, I was proposed to right before this happened."

He glanced at my bare left hand. "What happened?"

"He's waiting for me to put the ring back on."

"No, I mean, how'd you get burned?"

"Campfire. I asked him to put it out before we went to bed. I've feared fire since I was five. Always checked to make sure the fire alarms were working. Anyway, he fell asleep and the wind must've knocked gasoline over. Somehow the stream trailed to our tent and the fire followed after."

"Wow, Sarah. Sounds like a great gift you've been given."

I blinked, processing his response. "A gift? Most people apologize or nod their heads, unable to come up with the words to say." I smiled. "You are the first person who hasn't pitied me. Thank you for that."

"There's nothing to pity." He walked toward the door as I opened it again. "Are you doing anything this Friday?"

I hope I didn't blush. "Me?"

"My family is having an engagement party for me and Natalie. You could come. Meet little Anastasia."

I tried to smile. "Thank you so much for the invite. Maybe some other time. I don't want to crash the party."

"No. Not at all. My family isn't like that. Natalie would love you. And hey, bring your friend and we can try to find him a date."

I almost laughed. "Some other time."

I walked outside into the bright autumn day. Soon the leaves would be crunching beneath my feet, but for now they clung to their branches in various colors. Ella waved from her car. I held up my hand and crossed the street.

"Where's Adelaide?" I said, sitting down in her passenger's seat.

"She's napping at home with Gavin."

"Oh, I'm so sorry to hold you up. It's just th—"

"Listen dearie, no apologies needed." She waved her finger in my face as she reversed the car out of her parking space.

"My therapist invited me to his engagement party."

"Interesting. Why?"

"I'm still trying to figure that out. He doesn't feel sorry for me, so it can't be that."

"Are you going?"

I laughed. "Of course not."

"Just go."

"I'm not ready to be normal again yet."

Ella kept quiet until we got home. We parted ways once inside. I greeted Adelaide and Gavin, then meandered to my room. I couldn't wait to move into my own place. I felt like such a burden to everyone in so many ways.

Cheyenne sat up on her bed when I entered the room. "Hey. Looks like you're doing pretty well. I don't think you'll need me here much longer."

"You can take the full-time position if you want. I should be fine." I propped several pillows on my bed and reclined. The most venial tasks tuckered me out big time.

Cheyenne's face lit up.

James stood in the doorway.

She stood. "I can give you two some time."

"No," James said. "You can stay."

Cheyenne pretended to busy herself in her latest nursing textbook as James sat on the edge of my bed by my feet. He moved his hand toward my toes. I moved them away. His hand dropped to the bed. Cheyenne turned a page and looked down when I caught her staring. I closed my eyes. How could I convince him to move on? It was getting more and more difficult for me to hide my desire for him to hold me in his arms. I wanted his arms around me. I wanted to feel his lips on what was left of my face. But one touch from him and I'd lose it. And he'd never move on. Not if he saw how much I needed him.

When I opened my eyes he was staring at me. His eyes glistened. "I'm not going anywhere, Sarah. You can't push me away."

He tried to touch my hand. I pulled away, fighting back tears with everything inside of me. He brushed his fingers through his hair and sighed. I wanted his fingers tangled in my hair like the night he proposed. It wasn't supposed to be like this. *James*, I screamed inside as my chest tightened. *I still love you, sweet boy. I'm doing this because I want better for you.*

"We will never be together, James." I tried to look mean. "Look, I've done a lot of thinking and I realized we just aren't good for each other."

"We are so good for each other. You're the best thing that's ever happened to me. This terrible mess doesn't change that."

"You will find someone better."

"Please, Sarah." He covered his eyes with his hands and shook his head. "This is all my fault. My stupid idiot self. I've ruined everything."

And he'd feel that way every day for the rest of our lives if I didn't help him find someone else. I caught Cheyenne losing herself in him again. She looked away, embarrassed. As much as it pained me to let him go, I knew Cheyenne would be good to him. She deserved him. I trusted her with the heart I once held. My sweet James.

I reached for his hand and squeezed it. His eyes gained a little more color and life. He squeezed back.

"Could you do me a favor?" I said. "I'd love some ice cream from Bailey's shop."

"Caramel Brownie Dream?"

I nodded.

"Cheyenne," I said.

She pretended to look back to her book.

"Would you mind keeping him company? I need some time alone."

She practically somersaulted off the bed. James twisted the keys in his hand as he stood and waited for her. A few seconds later, they left the room. When the car doors shut and the engine started, I pulled a pillow to my face and cried into the fluff. I tried not to remember the pillows from his proposal as I pressed the cotton against my face. I tried not to imagine all the nights we were going to spend together, waking up to each other's smile. I tried, so unbelievably hard, not to cry myself to sleep as I blocked thoughts from growing seeds in my heart.

But I did. I cried myself right into a dream. A dream of life before the fire.

 *five*

Ella held Adelaide on Cheyenne's bed. I rubbed my eyes and looked at the clock. Three hours passed. I checked my nightstand. No ice cream. Did my plan work?

"James and Cheyenne brought you ice cream, but you were deep in sleep. It's in the freezer if you want it."

I shook my head. "You can have it."

"Are you trying to set James and Cheyenne up?"

"Why do you know me so well?"

She placed Adelaide on the bed beside her.

I prepared myself to sit up. Always hurt a lot to get up after sleeping. My poor muscles were so tense. Ella noticed my struggle and helped swing my legs over the bed while she kept her other hand on her baby's belly.

"Thank you," I said. "So, did it work?"

"I don't like this idea." Her phone rang. She silenced it and continued, "If you both love each other, why would you let an obstacle keep you apart?"

"This isn't an obstacle. If we stay together he will always blame himself. Life will never be normal for him."

"What about you?" She leaned back and rubbed Adelaide's face. "How are you?"

I stood and reached for the water bottle on my bed. "I'm fine. Everything will be fine."

"Sometimes everything isn't fine. And that's okay."

I needed to focus on others instead of myself, but how? I couldn't even drive myself anywhere. I longed for the day I'd be completely self-sufficient again. I dreamed of my own apartment from paint colors to bedspreads.

Funny, simply hanging a picture myself or opening a jar of jam would serve as a great accomplishment at this point.

Ella carried Adelaide to the door and smiled back at me. "I'll be downstairs if you need anything."

"Where's Cheyenne?"

"Exactly where you want her."

"James? Really?"

She sighed and disappeared down the hallway.

GAVIN HELD ADELAIDE AND WATCHED ELLA MAKE DINNER. Southwest stuffed butternut squash. I watched a rerun of *Home Improvement* while they enjoyed their family, trying to ignore the temptation to stare at them with envy. Ella always said I had it easy, but I felt the same about her. She was successful at everything she did. An amazing violinist and a brilliant entrepreneur. A sweet wife and a gentle mother. And we can't forget the cooking. Not only did she cook fantastic meals, but she presented them artfully, complete with song and dance.

She deserved it though.

I switched the channel to the local news. "Hey, guys. Isn't that your friend's husband? Mwenye?"

Ella and Gavin entered the living room and stood only feet from the television. Gavin wrapped his arm around Ella and pulled her into him. She pressed her lips against the back of her hand and inhaled deeply.

"Maybe someone should call Tylissa?" I said.

Without blinking or acknowledging me, Gavin watched the story unfold on the screen. I never understood why reporters seemed excited to release bad news. Didn't they have even a meager dose of empathy?

Ella wiped her face on a dish towel and picked up her phone from the fireplace mantle under the television. I motioned to Gavin to take the food out of the oven before it burned, if it hadn't already. He jogged to the kitchen as Ella paced the living room. "Tylissa, what's going on? I thought you got a lawyer?" She waited as Tylissa spoke. I couldn't hear the words. Only crying. "But he's innocent. You need to do something." More crying on the other end. "Yes, of course. Wait a week or so. We'll see you then. I love you."

Ella hung up and slapped her phone against her thigh. "I can't believe this."

"What happened?" I said.

"Mwenye is innocent and if they'd only run some DNA tests they'd see that."

"But he said he was guilty."

"He's saying it to protect someone."

"Who?"

"Not my story to tell."

"What's the deal with everyone saying that lately?"

"Who's everyone?"

"Well," I smiled. "You and Vasili. Is it because you don't want to gossip or what?"

"No. Just not my place to say. Sometimes we get so caught up in talking about everyone else's life story that we forget to live our own. I don't want to be one of those people who never hesitates to spout off the details of others lives."

"Well said." I laughed. "Kind of weird that I'm sitting here laughing when Tylissa's husband was just taken to death row."

Ella's face glowed. "Now you see. Life doesn't stop for anyone, no matter how much we feel bad for our best friends."

Someone knocked on the door. Ella opened it and welcomed James. My heart stopped beating for a few seconds, then started full force. He squeezed my shoulder from behind. "Can we talk?"

I nodded.

"Alone. Upstairs."

I followed him to my room and sat on the chair in the corner, so that he couldn't touch me. Kneeling before me, he took my left hand.

"Sarah," he said. "I want you. And no one else. Your body doesn't change who you are to me. Let me love you." He pulled something out of his pocket. My ring. "Will you please marry me? Please?"

I shook my head. Hold it together, I petitioned myself. Keep your emotions at bay.

I pushed his hand toward his chest. "You are one of the most endearing people I've ever known, James. It would be an honor to be your wife, but I ca—"

He pulled me into his arms. I pushed away, but he kept me there. Locked in his warmth. In his love. Without my consent, tears burned my eyes and fell to his shoulder.

"You can be my wife." He kissed my cheek and held my face inches from his. "And you will. We are meant for each other, honey." He slipped the ring onto my finger and exhaled in relief.

I held my breath. My chest ached. I wondered how long it had been since I last took a deep breath. A content and restful breath. James stood and pulled my hands until I stood before him. I searched his eyes and my own heart. I missed the simplicity of life before the fire. I went with the flow. Lived for the moment. Now, I no longer lived in the past, but I surely anchored myself to the future. Like waiting a long winter and imagining spring a month before it comes. Sometimes the only way I got through the day, especially in the hospital, was by imagining the future.

Only problem is my hopes seemed completely intangible at this point. All I wanted was a husband and a family. A normal life.

I missed being normal.

And, looking at James, the man I once vowed to marry, I wondered if I ever really loved him at all.

"Don't do that, Sarah," James interrupted my thoughts. "Don't go down into that place where you think too much. It's all going to be okay. I promise. I love you and I will do anything I can to make it up to you."

"There's nothing to make up. It's not your fault. Please stop saying that."

"It is my fault." Red washed over his face. "Without me you'd be my wife right now. Pregnant with our first child. Instead I'm standing here trying to convince you to marry me."

"James."

"No. Don't James me. I've bent over backwards for you all of these months. I've done everything possible. Have I ruined your life so bad that you can't even look at me?"

"It's not that." My eyes stung again. "It's not that at all."

"Then why can't you be happy when I walk in the room?"

I shook my head. No words came.

"This is ridiculous, Sarah. You know your choices for marriage are slim now. You let me go and what's going to happen? Are you going to end up a single old woman?" He stepped toward me with heavy eyes. "I'm sorry. I didn't mean to. I'm just u—"

"Stop." I walked to my bedroom door. "Please go."

"I didn't mean it. You're still beautiful to me."

"Who do you think is prettier? Me or Cheyenne?"

He stood beside me in the doorway. "You are."

"Don't patronize me. I may have been stuck to a hospital bed for a year, but I didn't lose my brain. I'm scary looking. Strange. Ugly. You name it. That's me. I'm not pretty. Cheyenne is way prettier. Please don't lie to make me feel better." I caught my breath. "I'm being honest here. At least treat me like an adult. I know I've lost my pretty face. I don't want someone to love what I used to be. If I marry someone I want them to love who I am now. And if I can't find someone, so be it."

He touched my face, the side without the burns. He always touched that side. Never my scars. I jerked away and stared at the ground.

He smiled and kissed my cheek. "I will never give you up."

six

Ella sat a plate of fried eggs and toast in front of me, then sat down across from me with Adelaide in her arms.

"So, do you think you'll come?" she said.

"I don't even know them." I picked up my fork. "Why on earth would I go to their wedding?"

"They invited you."

"I hardly know them and given my current situation, I'm not sure I feel up to it."

Ella and I emptied our plates in silence. She piled my plate on top of hers and placed them both in the sink. I stood as she turned back to me.

"Oh, now what?" I smiled. "Are you going to lecture me?"

"Really, Sarah. Eventually you need to face the world again."

"I do." I walked to the couch and put a pillow on my lap. "I go to the grocery store and physical therapy."

She raised her eyebrows.

"I'm not going to their wedding."

"You may not know them well, but Heidi and Patrick have become good friends to us. They're close with my brother too. And you know him. He's an usher."

"Forget the groom, I know the groom's usher. Yes, I should definitely go."

She set Adelaide down on the carpet and sat beside her. "Please. I want you to get out more. Live again. Are you going to hide away forever because you look different?"

"I just don't like the stares. It's overwhelming."

"You can't change what's happened to you. This is your life now. The only way you're going to find joy again is if you accept it and make the most of it. Otherwise I'm worried you will rot away in here, decaying in your own negativity."

"Easy for you to say." I stood. "Look at everything around you. Gorgeous husband, beautiful baby, amazing house, perfect job. There's nothing wrong with your life. You are pretty and sweet and your life is more beautiful than mine will ever be." I held the railing at the bottom of the steps. "My life sucks. It absolutely sucks right now. I am treated like a child by everyone. People lie and say, 'Oh, look at you. So beautiful.' James tells me I'm pretty. You are constantly trying to fix me. People talk to me with slow, loud voices now, like I'm a toddler that can't comprehend normal language. I'm sorry if I'm not living according to your standards, but you don't understand how horrible this has been. I'm living in a nightmare and no matter how many times I throw cold water on my face, I don't wake up."

Ella looked down and rubbed Adelaide's back. I turned and walked up the steps and flopped onto my bed. My phone rang.

Didn't recognize the number. Once the voicemail popped up, I listened.

"Sarah, uh, hey, it's Vasili. I told Anastasia about you. She really wants to meet you. I hope you don't mind, but I figured since you didn't want to come over that she could meet you at your next appointment. Just giving you a heads up before you get here tomorrow. She's nine years old. Sweetest kid ever. Okay, um, this is my cell. Thanks. Uh, okay, see ya tomorrow then."

He really wanted me to meet his niece. Wonder why.

Someone laughed. Sounded like James. I walked to the open window across my room and hid behind the curtains. James and Cheyenne sat on the bed of his truck. He didn't seem interested in her like she was with him. Her eyes were bright and her smile unmistakeable. He seemed distant, but he was laughing when she spoke. I couldn't remember the last time I heard him laugh.

My pulse quickened. I wanted him to be happy. To find someone who didn't make him feel like a failure. But a the tinge of jealousy fought to overcome my reason. And won.

Perhaps he would finally let go.

VASILI TOOK ME BACK TO HIS OFFICE AND A LITTLE GIRL WITH rich brown hair and big brown eyes sprung from his swivel chair and rushed toward us.

"You must be Sarah." She extended her hand. "I'm Anastasia. Most of my friends call me Ana, but I like my full name better. What about you?"

She didn't look at my scars. If she did I couldn't tell, but I looked at hers. They covered half of her face, just like mine. Her neck and left arm also had patches of burn scars as well.

"It's okay," she said. "You don't have to answer. I can tell you like Anastasia better anyway."

"Both names are lovely," I said. "But I think you're right. I like your full name better than the nickname."

She smiled and took my hand. Two scarred hands linked together. What happened to this poor girl? She led me to the mat in the middle of the room and sat down cross-legged. Confused, I looked at Vasili. He motioned for me to sit, then sat beside me.

"How did you get burned?" Anastasia said, so casually.

"Campfire accident. Lighter fluid leaked out and we forgot to put the fire out. The fluid made a trail to our tent and the fire must have crackled and somehow lit the trail."

"I was burned too," she said. "It happened right after I found out I have nueroblastoma. My Yia Yia was making dinner and had a big pot boiling on the stove. I tried to look inside and it started tipping. Vasili saw me and tried to stop it, but it was too late."

"Wow." I shook my head, wondering why he couldn't tell me the story himself.

"I was wearing a flannel shirt," she said. "So when I went to take it off it peeled my skin back right off my arm. It hurt pretty bad."

"Yeah. When I was burned the fire went right through my clothes and I could see to my bone on my left hand." I shuddered at the memory. "What's nueroblastoma?"

"A type of cancer. The doctors gave me less than a year to live last time I saw them. We'll see, I guess." She reached over and ran her hand down the scars on my face. "They feel just like mine."

"I had cancer too," I said. "Before the fire. It's gone now and hasn't come back since, but I definitely think about it. Honestly, after the fire I haven't cared much about getting cancer or not." I looked down. "It's just been really hard to live again."

"You mean all the stares? And the people pointing fingers?"

I nodded.

"It was the worst when I had to shave my head. My scars were even weirder. That's when I stopped going to school and Mama started schooling me at home. Uncle Vasili tried to tell me to face the bullies and keep going to school, but I got too tired to last all day anyway."

"Oh, sweetie. I'm sorry. Are you still going through treatments?"

She shook her head. "It made me so sick. I just want to try to feel as normal as I can until I die."

Until I die. The words were filled with certainty. A certainty that made me uncomfortable.

"It's okay," she said with hesitation.

"What makes you okay with it?"

"I guess I realized I don't have a choice."

Vasili laughed quietly. "She means she came to terms with her death and over time she's realized that all these years she's been fighting for her life would be pointless if she moped around during her last year with us. She decided a few months ago to stop treatments and enjoy the last months without a ton of hospital visits."

She smiled. "Ask Uncle Vasili. He knows everything."

I blinked away the tears gathering in my eyes. This child was dying. Nearing the end of her short life way before her first kiss. And yet I complained about my life every day.

Vasili touched my shoulder and Anastasia held my hand. "It's nice to have a friend who understands what it's like to be scarred. Now I know why Vasili wanted us to meet."

He nodded and smiled.

I wanted to help Anastasia. Somehow. Perhaps being a friend was the best thing I could do.

"I'm honored to be your friend," I said. "You've already taught me so much."

"Me?" She giggled. "I don't know about all that."

"Vasili," I said. "Is this how you got burned too?"

"Yes. Unfortunately Anastasia took the brunt of it, but I've got some scars down my arm and chest." He held eye contact. "I understand the pain. You're not alone."

I wanted to say, "But you still have your face," until I remembered the girl sitting before me. She lost part of her face too. She understood. I never thought I'd be so happy to have a nine-year-old friend.

"We're going to a wedding this weekend," Anastasia said. "Vasili and Natalie have two extra seats for me and a friend. Will you come with me?"

I so badly wanted to say no, but her courage loosened my worries. "Is it a family member?"

"No," Vasili said. "My buddy from school became a chiropractor. He's got a practice over in Philly. This is his second marriage actually. First one was a bit of a nightmare, but he found a nice woman now."

"You've gotta be kidding me," I said. "Is this the wedding for Patrick and Heidi Wheldon?"

"How'd you know?"

"Friends of friends. My best friend's husband is an usher."

"Oh, good," Anastasia said. "Then you can meet me there and we can sit together. I'll feel so much better with you there."

Oh, no. How could I get out of it now?

 *seven*

I stood in front of the mirror and wished I'd get sick and have a good reason to stay home.

"Wow, Sarah." Ella peeked her head through my door. "You look amazing."

I looked at her like she was crazy. "Stop."

"What? Since when is perfection a pre-requisite for looking nice?" She stepped inside. Her ankle length dress looked like a modern regency era design. Off-white with olive green accents, highlighting all of her features with simplicity. "You are never going to look like you did before the fire, but I'm not lying when I say you look nice. It's been a while since I've seen you out of those sweatpants and t-shirts."

"I'm embarrassed, Ella."

"Why?"

"Look at me. I've hidden the scars as best as I could. I did this loose pony tail look so I could somewhat cover this side of my face, but I feel ridiculous for hiding and ridiculous for exposing myself." I slumped into the chair by the window. "I can't get over it."

"One step at a time." She took my hand. "Let's go. Maybe, just maybe, you'll even have fun."

I stood and handed her a tube of sunscreen. "Could you help me put this on the top of my back?"

"But your back isn't exposed."

"Just being cautious."

"You didn't take your pressure garments off, did you?"

"Nope. That's why I'm wearing a dress that practically covers every inch of my body. I had to buy it from some online medieval costume shop."

Ella tried not to laugh. "Really?"

I smiled. "Yes."

We laughed as she gently rubbed lotion on my shoulders and back. Felt good to laugh again.

"Where's Cheyenne?" Ella set the sunscreen on my dresser. "She hasn't been around as much."

"I told her I'm okay. The physical issues I have are nothing compared to the emotional." I slipped into a pair of black flats. "She's working more at the hospital. I think she's looking for her own place now. I promise I will soon too."

"This is your home as long as you want it to be. It's been wonderful having you with me. Not a burden at all, Sarah. I know how your little brain thinks."

"Alright." I looked in the mirror one last time. "Ready?"

THANKFULLY THE CHAIRS WERE LINED UP UNDER THE SHADE of trees. I admit, when Ella told me that Heidi and Patrick decided to marry at the local skatepark, I thought it sounded strange. And, well, I suppose it is a bit unique, but they set it up so beautifully. The chairs were in neat rows leading up to a ramp with a platform at the top. The platform was covered in rose petals and the sides were decorated with fake ivy.

Ella and I sat down near the front with the baby. Others piled in behind us. I didn't want to look at them, so I stared ahead without moving. A few minutes passed and someone tapped me on the shoulder. Anastasia. I almost forgot. She sat beside me. We hugged as Vasili and a gorgeous brunette sat beside us. I held my breath.

"Hi, Sarah." The brunette reached her hand across Vasili and Anastasia. "I'm Natalie. Vasili has told me so much about you."

I shook her hand and smiled. "I didn't realize there was so much to say."

She was beautiful. I guess I shouldn't have expected any less. At first I wondered why she didn't mind her soon-to-be husband talking about me, but then I remembered.

Music began playing. We all straightened and everyone turned as the ushers walked up the mock aisle. I looked ahead. Waited until they appeared at the base of the ramp. Then everyone laughed. I couldn't help but turn. Patrick skateboarded up the aisle and right up the ramp, did some kind of trick thing, and landed on the platform as rose petals rustled and scattered beneath him.

I couldn't figure out the tune of the song. I nudged Ella as the bridesmaids walked to their spots. "What's the song?"

"*All of My Love* by Led Zeppelin." She was staring at Gavin the entire time. He did look rather handsome. Their outfits were cute. Untucked button down white shirts. Rolled up sleeves. Loose orange ties. Relaxed slacks. And sneakers. I kind of liked it. Derek, Ella's brother, stood beside Gavin. Other than that, I didn't recognize the other guys.

The only bridesmaid I recognized was Miranda, who seemed to be the maid-of-honor. Derek's girlfriend. They were grinning at each other too. All of this romance made me nauseous. I wondered what James was doing. If he still thought we'd be good together.

The music stopped. Heidi walked up the aisle wearing a silky white dress that hung off one shoulder. It draped and hugged all the right places. Her hair was pulled back, delicately, with wavy strands falling out. When she got closer I noticed several braids leading back to her messy bun. She looked so pretty. And for once I didn't think of my own lack of prettiness. I simply relished the joy of this new couple.

She walked up the steps of the ramp, holding her dress with her left hand so she wouldn't trip, and her flowers in the other. Patrick's face was absolutely priceless. He held one hand over his heart, like he couldn't breath when he saw her. It didn't seem like he was crying, but I couldn't tell from where I sat. The sun could've gone missing for a bit and no one would've noticed. Those two were plenty bright enough as they clasped hands and stared at each other with longing.

I caught myself tearing up and smiling as wide as the happy couple, completely lost in their love. So beautiful.

Anastasia linked her arm with mine. I turned to her smiling face and made eye contact with Vasili. He looked away and blushed.

Why would he blush?

I smiled at Anastasia and looked back to the happy couple as they exchanged their vows. At the end, they both grabbed a board and skated down the ramp and out of the park, hand-in-hand.

Fatigue crept up on me, but their reception was only a small gathering under the pavilion next to the skate park. Probably no more than twenty attendees. I wanted to struggle through the next hour or two for Anastasia.

Ella pat my knee. "I saw you."

"What?"

"You were happy. Really happy."

I shrugged her off.

She leaned over me. "Who is this young lady?"

"I'm Anastasia." She extended her hand. So cute and mature. "And this is my uncle." She pointed beside her without looking. "Vasili. And Natalie, my soon-to-be aunt."

"Nice meeting you all." She stood. "Would you like to sit at our table?"

Anastasia nodded. We waited for everyone to pile out so we could follow. I wondered why Anastasia wanted me to be with her. She seemed fine. Completely content with her scars. Me, on the other hand?

I wanted to go back to the car. I kept telling myself people weren't thinking about me as much as I was. In the past, when I saw someone with scars I noticed them, but didn't really linger on the thought.

Ella squeezed my hand, then let go when we reached Gavin by the picnic tables. She pulled his tie and kissed his cheek. He kissed her forehead and scooped Adelaide out of her arms. I still couldn't believe I missed my best friend's wedding. She wanted to get married at the chapel in the hospital, but there's no way I'd let her do that. They had a simple wedding in Gavin's grandfathers yard, which soon became their own yard.

I missed so much while I was confined to the hospital bed. It's amazing how life speeds on by with or without you. We're all just small parts in a big story. Life goes on. I analyzed the life around me as we all sat down. Heidi and Patrick stood together with their daughter, Riley, greeting everyone one table at a time. Vasili and Natalie sat so close to each other that I couldn't tell where his arm ended and hers began. Anastasia was already digging her fork into a plate of food. Ella and Gavin refused to stop touching each other. Classic newlywed syndrome. Derek and Miranda laughed hysterically a few tables down. He stopped to move a strand of hair from her face.

Other couples I didn't know talked and laughed. Smiles all over the place. Including me. I couldn't believe it. Ella was right. I discovered a morsel of happiness.

I caught Vasili looking at me again. He looked away when I saw him. Did my hair move? Were my scars even stranger in the sunlight?

I suppressed the thoughts and smiled at Anastasia. When I was her age Ella and I dressed up like brides and imagined Prince William whisking us away to England. I dreamed of one day being someone's bride.

But Anastasia took in the wedding around her with ease. She was dying. Never to walk down the aisle to a boy. Never to have a first kiss or learn to drive a car. No career or fostered talents.

I smiled at her when she looked up. She smiled back. Somehow that little girl knew more about true life than I did.

"What did you laugh at?" Natalie said.

"Me?" I said. "I laughed out loud?"

Vasili nodded.

"Nothing really. Just happy."

And, for the first time in a long while, content.

 *eight*

Anastasia and I both got tired pretty fast, so Vasili and Natalie offered to drive me home before taking their niece home. I agreed. Didn't want to inconvenience Ella and Gavin.

"My birthday is next Saturday," Anastasia said. "Can you come to the party?"

I wanted to, but....

"It may be my last party ever." She laughed and pouted.

"Anastasia!" Natalie twisted her body in the passengers seat to glare at the girl. "Why on earth would you say something so morbid?"

Anastasia slunk into her seat.

I opened the car door and swung my feet out. "Actually, I find her acceptance of death refreshing. She's helped me to accept my life." I stood outside of the car and mouthed, "Thank you," to Anastasia. She smiled and straightened her shoulders as I backed away.

Natalie popped out of the car and stood in front of me with her cell phone. "Let me get your number. Sarah Jordan, right?"

"717-555-1224."

"Okay. Now don't you want mine?"

"I, uh...."

"Oh, it's okay. I can just text you my number and name." She pointed to the compression garments around my left hand. "Does that hurt?"

I shook my head. "I'm fine. Thanks for asking. I better get g—"

"Yes. I'll talk to you later."

She sat in the car and Vasili waved as he backed away. I walked to the house feeling alive again. The wraparound porch invited me to stay a while, but I noticed James' truck parked around the side. I couldn't wait to see him. All the love from the day seeped into my heart and melted away the last of the cold. Well, maybe not the last. Still a lot of healing ahead of me. But I felt good. Ready to let James back into my life.

I opened the door as slow as possible, hoping to surprise him. No sign of life in the living room, so I crept up the stairs and down the hall. I stopped a few steps from my door when I heard Cheyenne's voice.

"Please," she said. "It's not like you're together anyway."

"She never said that," James said.

"Well it doesn't take a rocket scientist." She laughed. "Come on. Do I have to take off my clothes and beg you to do the same? It shouldn't be this hard."

He laughed too. "I've never been begged before."

"First time for everything." Her shirt landed by the open door, then her bra. "It's not like I have much competition with my cousin. I guess you could always marry her and use me for good sex."

I picked up her shirt and stood in the doorway. Too angry to cry.

"Oh my gosh." Cheyenne covered her chest with her arms. "Sarah, what are you doing back so early?"

James didn't turn around. He sat on Cheyenne's bed with his back to me.

Cheyenne tripped on her words.

"Stop." I tossed her shirt at them. "Get out, Cheyenne." She stared at me, blinking. "Get all of your stuff and get out of my life. Now." She blinked. "I said now!"

Scrambling, she stuffed all of her things in a few suitcases, then shot me an evil look. "It's not like you appreciated him anyway."

"You have no idea." My hands were shaking and hot.

"Actions speak louder than words."

"Not when you intentionally hide your love for someone to give them a better life." My body shook with anger and pain. "Turn around James."

He stood, but refused to look at me. Cheyenne stood beside me with her things.

"Thank you," I said. "For showing me what ugly really means."

She huffed and stormed out of the house. James dropped his hands to his sides. "Sarah, I'm sorry. I wasn't going to do anything."

"You certainly weren't stopping anything." I smiled. "But you know what? I can't blame you. I've been pushing you away for months, hoping you'd fall in love and let me go. I'm surprised you held on this long."

"So you're not mad?"

"I'm mad at Cheyenne, not you." I sat on my bed. "I've been wanting you the entire time, James. I love you. So much that I was willing to sacrifice my desires to make sure you lived a happy life. A life with a woman who didn't carry these horrible memories, causing you to say good morning to guilt every day." I sucked in air and held my breath, then exhaled loudly. "Today I really smiled again. I felt alive. I was just coming up to surprise you by putting my ring back on an—"

"Sarah, I s—"

"No. Let me finish. I heard your conversation. Silly me, I came back from this wedding inspired to give you a chance. To give us a chance. To maybe even plan my own wedding. I know most people think I'm hideous. I get that. But today I realized something. My life is too precious for this ridiculously immature stuff. I may be inspired right now, but I'm not inspired to let you back into my heart. I don't need you around to live a full and happy life. I don't need marriage. But if I ever get married it will be to a man who can look at me and truly see someone beautiful. That man is not you. I've said all I need to say. If you love me at all ... just go."

He hesitated, glanced at the engagement ring on the nightstand, and walked away.

He walked away.

Just like that.

THE NEXT MORNING I WOKE TO ELLA SETTING A DOZEN yellow roses on my dresser. I took off my burn mask and rubbed my eyes to be sure.

"Took all I had to bring these up here. I almost threw them in the trash when the delivery guy handed them to me."

"What time is it?"

"Almost eleven. I mean, does he seriously think you'll take him back after that?"

I willed myself to sit up, but it didn't work.

"You're not taking him back, right?"

I shook my head. "Ella, calm down."

"I'm just saying."

"I won't do anything stupid."

"And don't get me started on your cousin." She sat on the edge of my bed. "Are you sure you're okay?"

"I know I'm notorious for saying I'm okay when I'm not, but I actually am okay. Anastasia inspired me yesterday. Plus the wedding. Everything I experienced yesterday, including Cheyenne and James, has inspired me. I'm thankful. I really am."

"What did it inspire you to do?"

"Live."

 *nine*

I knocked on the door to Vasili's mother's house, trying my absolute hardest to remain calm. A short, older woman opened the door with an apron on and a spatula in one hand. "Ah, ti kenis? Nai?"

"Oh, um, I'm sorry. I don't speak Greek." I held up the gift. "I'm here for Anastasia's party."

"Nai, nai. I understand, honey." She tilted her head back. "Yanni, there's a pretty girl at my door for Anastasia. No Greek." She waved the spatula between us and smiled. "Sorry, honey. Little English for me. No greek for you."

A tall man who resembled Vasili stepped to the door. "Please come in." I entered as the woman shuffled back into the kitchen.

"I'm Ioannis, but my family and friends call me Yanni. You are?"

"Sarah. I'm a client of Vasili's."

"A client?" He laughed. "You're a friend if you're here."

He ushered me into the living room and a woman stood up. "Oh, hello. I'm Sophia. Anastasia's mom. Yanni is her dad. She has told us so much about you. She's napping until everyone arrives."

"Am I early?" I said, looking at the clock.

Yanni laughed. "Most of our family is Greek. As cliche as it is ... we are fashionably late."

"And by fashionably," Sophia added, "we mean at least forty five minutes."

"Are you Greek as well?" I said to Sophia.

"Hard to tell with my red hair, I know. My dad is Greek, but my mother is Ukrainian. I'm an interesting blend."

"Wow. It must be nice to know your heritage like that. Who knows what I am. A little bit of everything."

They laughed. I loved this family already. No one acknowledged my scars and it made me forget about them too. I felt normal again.

"Vasili, ella!" His mother yelled from the kitchen. We all jumped. Or maybe only I did.

"Did she just call Ella?" I said.

"No, no." Yanni laughed. "Ella is 'come' in Greek."

"Oh." I smiled. "Seems as though I have quite a bit of learning to do."

Vasili appeared in the living room as we all sat on the couches.

"Hey," he said. "So glad you made it. Anastasia is going to be so surprised. I see you met Yanni and Sophia." He looked around. "Where's Kyriakos and Eleni?"

"Not here yet," Sophia said.

I folded my hands on my lap and looked around. Vasili sat beside me and my heart thumped in my ears. I am not like Cheyenne. I would never display interest in a taken man, but every time he touched me or sat near me I felt like a fifth grader hoping her crush would sit closer so their arms would touch. I ignored the fluttery sensations.

"So," I said. "How many siblings are there in your family?"

Yanni cleared his throat. "There's me, Sophia, Vasili, Natalie, Kyriakos, and Eleni."

"That's nice how you consider Natalie part of the family even before the wedding."

Everyone looked down. Awkward moment. What did I say?

"Is she coming?" I tried to scatter the strange vibes.

Vasili shook his head. "She had to work."

"What does she do?"

"She's a cosmetologist."

"Oh, I should've known."

"Why do you say that?"

"She's just really pretty, that's all." I repositioned myself on the couch. A little closer to the arm of the chair and a little further from the man beside me.

"Looks aren't everything," Yanni interrupted. "That girl co—"

"Yanni," Vasili said. "Don't."

"My brother here sees gems in baby poop." Yanni laughed.

"That's what the elder says to do," Vasili said. "Our thoughts determine our lives, remember?"

The front door opened. A dark-haired couple walked in. Looked like movie stars. Everyone stood to hug them, so I followed and waited to be introduced. After a round of hugs and pats on the back, Sophia stood between me and the overly handsome man. "Sarah, this is the youngest brother of the family."

He took off his sunglasses and clipped them on his slightly unbuttoned shirt. "I'm Kyriakos." He shook my hand. "This is Eleni."

"Nice to meet you." She also shook my hand, but pulled away quick, then perched her sunglasses on top of her head.

"Oh, here she is now." Sophia bent down and hugged her daughter as though she hadn't seen her in years.

Anastasia came to me next. A huge grin donned her sweet face. I could no longer see the scars. My mind replaced them with young, unharmed skin. Perhaps that's how my friends saw me. If only I could look past my own flaws too.

After I hugged Anastasia she thanked me for coming and Vasili picked her up and put her on his shoulders. "Soon you're going to be too big for this."

"Probably not." She smiled.

"Ella, ella," their mother yelled from the kitchen.

"Time to eat," Kyriakos said.

We sat down at a large dining room table. Yanni stood and said a prayer while the rest of the family prayed in unison and made crosses over their chests. I felt uncomfortable, but everyone welcomed me with such warmth that I almost felt like part of their family. And I liked it. I enjoyed them.

During dinner I caught Vasili staring at me several times. Mainly when I laughed and smiled, which I did a lot. Kyriakos and Yanni bantered like five year olds and their mother, who they told me to call Mama, occasionally whacked them both with a dish towel. I'd end up laughing so hard I'd cry and every time I looked up Vasili looked away. I didn't understand. He stared at me the way a man stares at a woman he finds alluring. But he was engaged. And I was everything but alluring.

After dinner we sang *Happy Birthday* in English and something in Greek, then we settled on the couch and I checked my phone. Five missed calls and one text. James.

Please call me Sarah. I love you and I'm falling apart. Please.

"Everything okay?" Kyriakos sat beside me. "You look tired. If you need a ride ho—"

"I'm fine. Relationship problems."

Vasili glanced my way, but said nothing.

"Spill it," Eleni said as she scooted close to Kyriakos. "What's going on?"

"Eleni is getting her bachelors in psychology," Sophia said.

"It's a long story," I said.

Anastasia leaned into the arm of the couch next to me. "You are way too pretty to have relationship problems."

"Thank you, sweetie, but that's the last trait I'd use to describe myself at this point."

"Then maybe you should let us describe you," Vasili said.

I think I blushed so severely my cheeks nearly felt bruised. Everyone looked at Vasili, then me, then Vasili.

"Okay," Kyriakos jumped up and rubbed his palms together. "Anastasia insisted we play pin the tail on the donkey, but that's far too boring." He unfolded a large poster. "So I thought we could all play pin the tail on Vasili."

He taped the poster to the from door and we all laughed at the image of a donkey with Vasili's head morphed into its face.

"Very funny," Vasili said, snatching the blindfold from his brother.

I laughed so hard my stomach hurt. I'd pay for it later tonight and probably the next three days, but every second of pain would be worth the way I felt right now.

Mmm, I breathed in. Welcoming life back into my heart. "Life," I whispered to myself. "I love you."

Anastasia reached her arms around my neck and squeezed. "Life loves you, too."

Amazing how much more you appreciate the little things when all the big things are taken from you.

 *ten*

A fter a week of ignoring James, he showed up at Ella's house while I was taking a nap. Gavin wouldn't let him inside, so I woke to him screaming from the lawn for me to talk to him one last time.

I guess I felt bad.

I asked Ella and Gavin to let James come upstairs.

When he entered my room I didn't recognize him. Not with the disheveled hair, messy clothes, and droopy eyes.

He tripped over his shoelaces as he walked toward me, then slurred some kind of words together. Obviously he enjoyed one too many drinks. When he stood beside my bed I could smell the alcohol on his breath.

"Please, baby," he said. "I'm nothing without you."

"What happened to Cheyenne?"

He slammed his fist on the table beside my bed.

Gavin entered the room within seconds. "Sarah? Are you okay?"

I nodded.

"James." Gavin stepped toward him. "Maybe this isn't the best time to talk."

"There is no best time," James said, his tone rising with each shade of pink that covered his face. "My life is ... do you know what it's like to feel like a piece of crap who ruins everyone's life he touches?" He rolled his eyes. "No, of course not. Gavin the Great. Gavin the Wonderful. Gavin the nice guy who makes everyone smile."

"Man, you have no idea what I've done in my life. I'm not perfect. No better than you at all."

James laughed, then turned crimson. "Get out. I want to talk to my fiancé."

"This is my house," Gavin straightened his shoulders. "I'm staying right here."

James swung his fist at Gavin, but missed by a few inches.

"Would hitting me make things better for you, James? If so, have at it." He stepped closer and tilted his jaw. "Right here would hurt pretty good. Go ahead."

James turned to me. "You don't get it. My life is a living hell."

I sat up and held his hand. "James, I love you. A lot. But I am not the answer to your problems. You were like this when we met. It has everything to do with your brother and your guilt. Now the fire has only added to that." I kissed his hand and started to cry. "I am releasing you, James. You don't have to carry this guilt anymore. I love you, but not the way a wife should love her husband. When you truly care for a person, you let them go when you know it's for the best."

"This is not for the best."

"It is. If we got married we'd both be miserable. I can't change your life. I can't make you walk away from me today and start a clean slate with hope, but I can change myself. I'm already changing. I feel good. Please understand that. Please let me go." Tears continued to pour down my face. "I'm so sorry, James. As much as I want this, it kills me. It feels like a part of me is being ripped apart. Please trust me though."

"I have to make it up to you. I can't just leave you, Sarah."

"If you want to make it up to me, then do as I ask. I need you to accept that it's over." I wiped my cheeks. "I'm not trying to be mean. This isn't right. I don't know what right is, but this isn't it."

The blood vessels in his eyes turned the whites of his eyes pink. And the veins in his neck throbbed as he stood. "You're a bitch."

I shook my head and covered my face with my hands. Why did it hurt so much to hear those words?

"You will never find anyone to love you, Sarah." He hit his own chest with his hands. "You're missing the good stuff right here, baby. You'll regret this."

He turned around and spit in Gavin's face, then stormed out of the house.

I couldn't blink as Gavin and I stared at each other, trying to make sense of what happened. In the past, I saw James lose his temper a few times, but he never got this bad. This time he was straight up mean. Horribly mean.

I know it sounds crazy, but after everything ... I still felt sorry for the guy.

Whether he knew it or not ... I truly cared for him.

My phone beeped. I grabbed it off my nightstand before it vibrated off the edge.

A text from an unknown number.

Sarah... I hope you don't mind... I got your number from my brother... how are you?

I typed back. *Who is this?*

Oh, sorry. This is Sophia.

Me: *Hey, Sophia! I've been better. How are you guys?*

Sophia: *Same. Listen, Anastasia's doctor just told us that she probably has a month to live. We found her journal while she was sleeping and I read a few pages. There's a few things she wants to do before she dies. Could you help? Sorry to text this, but I'm trying to be quiet so it stays a secret.*

Me: *Of course. Just let me know what and when. Hang in there, Sophia. I'm starting to realize it's the difficult times in life that help us the most.*

Sophia: *Yes, yes .... you are right. This is the hardest thing I've ever done in my life. Could you meet me for lunch today? I can pick you up.*

Me: *Sure. Give me about 2 hours.*

SOPHIA AND I SAT DOWN AT A TABLE BY THE WINDOW AFTER ordering soup and salad. I admired the modern decor and spotted a familiar piece of art across the room. Could it be?

One of the girls at the cafe set our food in front of us and disappeared. Quaint little cafe on Prince Street. Right next to the Fulton Opera House. I sipped my soup and admired passing strangers. Life passing by as Sophia and I prepared to speak of her dying child.

"Do you like Lancaster?" Sophia said.

"I do." I dipped my spoon back into the bowl. "But I haven't been out much yet. This is only my second time in the city. It's definitely not Philly. Much smaller here. I like that about it."

"You and Ella lived in the city of Philadelphia?"

"Yes. We still lived together when the fire happened, but I was in a coma for months and pretty much glued to my hospital bed when she got married, so she put all of my stuff in her house for now. I think I'm finally ready to move on and find my own place again."

"Really? Let me know if you need help with that." She held back a smile, then pressed her palms on the table and leaned toward me. "I have a secret."

I couldn't help but laugh. "Oh?"

"My brother wants to ask you on a date." She wiggled her fingers. "He's worried it may not be the right time."

"But he's engaged." My soup almost came back up. "And I'm ... I'm ... this."

"Kyriakos isn't engaged. Not in the slightest."

Kyriakos? I didn't know whether to laugh or cry. "Is this some kind of joke? Why would he want to go out with me? And what about Eleni?"

"Eleni? She's their younger sister. Did you think they were together?"

I nodded.

She laughed. "They are close. Eleni was a surprise pregnancy. She was born only ten months after Kyriakos was born. As you can imagine, the two have always been inseparable."

"Aw. That's so sweet. I have one older sister, but she's eleven years older than me and we've probably spoken to each other less than you and I have." I lifted my broth-filled spoon. "If you guys are trying to get Kyriakos to go out with me to make me feel better ... it's not necessary. Besides, I'm still in recovery. I have surgeries planned. I'm nowhere near ready to date anyone."

"Vasili said something about you being engaged."

"Yes, and there's that. I mean, I'm not ... we're not together right now, but my heart isn't whole. I'm not ready to love someone else."

"When do you think you'll be ready?"

"When I love myself."

"I'll never forget when Anastasia was in the hospital recovering from her burns. She was eight. It was soon time to discharge her, but they wanted her to look in a mirror first. One of the child psychologists brought a mirror in and asked her if she wanted to see her new self. Anastasia held the mirror to her face and said, 'What's new about me? It's the same self I always was.' The woman tried to explain to her the scars on her face, but little Anastasia set the mirror in her lap and said, 'Oh, that's just my face, not my self.'"

"Wow. Such simplicity. If only we could always see life through the lens of a child."

"There's no reason we can't."

Sophia and I spent the next two hours talking and laughing as though we'd known each other for years. It was so lovely that I hardly noticed anyone looking at me.

We decided on a final list of things to do for Anastasia. Our main event would be a Christmas Eve family performance of *It's a Wonderful Life* at Anastasia's house. Her favorite movie.

Sophia and I placed our dishes in the bins above the trashcans and walked to the bathroom. I stood outside of the door while Sophia slipped inside. A few girls glanced at me with wide eyes when they thought I wasn't looking, then looked away. I tried to smile, but their eyes were already avoiding me.

I turned around and faced the wall.

I knew the photograph looked familiar. I took it three years ago when I visited an old friend in San Francisco. The way the squirrel perched himself so casually on the wire had been ingrained in my mind since. Hundreds of feet in the air with the city as a backdrop ... he sat there as though he were swaddled in his nest.

How did my photography get here? And why did it have a $200 price tag on it?

I checked my signature. Bottom right corner. Sure enough. Signed SJ. But how?

 *eleven*

S omehow, within the blink of an eye, the leaves swiveled from the trees, leaving them bare as they trembled in the cold. Thanksgiving Day Ella and Gavin invited Gavin's father over, since he had nowhere and no one else. The Koursaris family invited me over, so I made plans to head over there later.

For now, I helped Ella prepare their meal. She always loved my stuffing, so I chopped up celery and onions as she whipped up sweet potato casserole. We worked in silence. I really loved those moments with my best friend.

"You know," I said, using the back of the knife to scoot the celery into the pot. "I sometimes feel like the worst part of all of this is that I missed your wedding and the last few months of enjoying you before marriage. I came out of the hospital and our entire friendship was different."

"Oh, don't be silly." She smiled. "Nothing has changed. We're still close. And you even live with me."

"It's different. I'm happy for you, just wish I were standing beside you as you said your vows." Not sure why, but my eyes filled with tears as I said those words aloud.

Ella wrapped her arms around me and rubbed my head, like a mother soothing her child. I sniffed and composed myself, backing away from her embrace. "I don't know what came over me. Could be the onions."

"You're trying to adjust. It takes time. It's kind of like watching *Forrest Gump* then halfway through falling asleep and waking up to *Sweet Home Alabama*."

"Huh?"

"Just takes time to adjust."

"Oh, by the way, weirdest thing. I was in the cafe next to the theatre and saw my art for sale. I forgot about it until today. I was looking for my favorite photograph. I took it when I had the cancer scare and it symbolized hope. I wanted to give it to Anastasia, but I can't find it."

Ella beamed with joy. "Well, surprise!"

"What?"

"It was me. I did it."

"Did what?"

"While you've been recovering I've been selling your art. I've set aside the money for when you are ready to move out. I've got over ten thousan—"

"Please tell me you are selling copies and not originals." My heart rate accelerated.

"Copies? You had copies?"

"Ella!" My muscles tensed. "Those were all original photos taken with film. I didn't have copies."

"I'm sorry. I thought you would be ha—"

I shook my head. "Those were my favorites. They were all meaningful to me."

"I am so sorry. Sarah, please forgive me."

Before she finished her sentence I was already out the front door and heading to my car. Why? How did I lose everything I once valued all because of one stupid mistake?

This wasn't my life. Or my face. Or my heart. What happened to me? I wanted to wake up from the nightmare.

Perhaps most people would say, "It's just a photograph."

But they were more than that. They were reflections of my heart. Of who I once was. They were my visual diaries.

And now they were hanging in someone else's house.

AFTER DINNER MAMA KOURSARIS PREPARED THE TABLE WITH a vast array of desserts and teas while Kyriakos made everyone laugh with his commentary on Greeks celebrating an American holiday.

"Technically," Natalie said. "You are American. You're just a Greek one."

He ignored her dose of reality and continued his rant. I couldn't help wondering how or why this man wanted to date me. He never showed any hint of interest in me when I was around. Vasili, on the other hand, always held eye contact with me longer than normal. You know that feeling when someone looks into your eyes and you can tell they aren't searching or hiding ... they're just *being*? That's what he did. I don't believe he meant to. Otherwise he wouldn't have looked down so nervously when I caught him.

Anastasia left the room to take a brief nap after dinner while the rest of us sat around the table sipping tea and talking. Finally Sophia brought up the plans and everyone began to contribute their thoughts.

"Who are the actors for the play?" Natalie said as Eleni perked up.

"Actually, a few nights ago Anastasia wanted to decorate the Christmas tree and afterward we watched *It's a Wonderful Life*. I casually asked who, out of our family, she'd want to see in those roles."

Phew. Not me. Couldn't be me. I wasn't part of the family.

"She said she wanted Vasili and Sarah as the main couple."

My heart plummeted.

"Vasili? He's never acted a day in his life." Kyriakos picked up some kind of Greek pastry. "I'll do it."

"She wants Vasili and Sarah. We aren't going for an Oscar here, just a fun experience for our little one."

Everyone looked at me. I wanted to evaporate.

"I'm beyond honored that such a precious girl considers me family," I said. "Spending time with her the last few weeks has been life-changing for me. But I can't. I hardly have the stamina to endure a night like this, much less a lead role in a play."

"Please, Sarah." Sophia's eyes welled with the sorrow of a mother losing her baby.

How could I say no to that?

"You don't have to," Yanni said. "But it would mean so much to her."

I noticed Vasili and Kyriakos were no longer in the room.

"Okay," I said. "For Anastasia."

I excused myself to go to the bathroom and overheard Vasili's voice through a bedroom door to the right. I leaned in.

"Why do you care so much anyway?" Kyriakos said. "You're engaged."

"I'm not in love with her, but unlike you I care about her like a true sister in this family. That would crush her. I still can't believe you would consider doing something so horrible."

"It's not like I was going to tell her the truth. I would treat her like a princess and she'd never know the difference."

"What's the truth, huh? That you don't consider her worth actually dating?" Vasili's tone hardened. "She's more beautiful than you will ever be." Something slammed. "She won't fall for your scheme anyway. Even if she went on a few dates with you she'd never do the rest."

"She would if I made it seem like she was doing good for others."

"Get out of here before I do something I regret. And if you so much as look at her with false intrigue I will make sure you regret it."

I slipped into the bathroom and avoided the mirror. He wanted to use me. For what? I think I would have been more hurt had Vasili not defended me so much. And the fact that he didn't have romantic feelings for me lessened my apprehension with him. I could confide in him. Like the brother I always wanted.

God knew I could use a friend like him right now. Someone who didn't pity me. Someone who believed in me.

I know Ella did, but something about Vasili felt different. I needed a brother figure. He is a brother figure, I tried to convince myself. Only a brother.

twelve

I managed to avoid Ella for a few days. Not that I didn't forgive her. Honestly, I had a hard time asking forgiveness for my rudeness. She tried to do something to make me smile, and instead of smiling I ruined her day. I didn't like being that person. The one who gets upset for people when they accidentally step on my toes. I wished I could be more like her and overlook offenses, especially when they weren't intentional.

My dad once told me something that resonated with me now. "Pride has a lot of masks. One mask transforms you into someone better than you actually are. The other mask paints you into an ugly person. Both masks are just that ... masks. So if you catch yourself admiring yourself, feeling sorry for yourself, or hating yourself ... remember to take off the mask and be yourself. No human is worthy of too much praise and loathing. Don't be so full of yourself."

I missed him. And my mother. I wished they'd move back to Pennsylvania, but every few years they seemed to move further from the cold.

Dad was right. I needed to take off my pride masks. Right now, I was draped in insecurity and pity. Thinking too much of myself again.

I meandered downstairs. No sign of Ella, but most of my old photographs that were sold now sat on the couch, reflecting the dreary gray sky from the window.

"Oh, hey," Ella said as she popped up from the kitchen floor with a sponge in each hand. "I found all of your photographs and bought them back." She stood beside me and pointed with a sponge. "Except the one like that one. The other one with the city skyline ... couldn't find it. And I'm really sorry. I haven't given up, but the one you wanted to give Anastasia is still missing. The 11x17 one you named 'Out of Adversity' right?"

"How'd you know that's what I named it?"

"I'm your biggest fan."

"I'm so sorry, Ella. I know you've only meant to help. My reaction was immature."

"I completely understand. I didn't realize you did those in a dark room and didn't have copies, otherwise I would've made copies first. I just knew you sold your work back in Philly and thought I'd help so you had something to get back on your feet when you were better."

"I miss Philly."

Gavin appeared in the stairway with Adelaide.

"What are you doing here on a Friday morning?" I said. "Thought this was the day you taught art at that homeschooling group?"

He looked at Ella, then me. "Today's Saturday."

"Saturday?" I frantically pulled my phone out of my hoodie. "Shoot. I'm supposed to take Anastasia out today."

"Well, at least you're already dressed." Ella took Adelaide from Gavin. "What time do you need to be there?"

"Fifteen minutes ago."

I texted Sophia. *Running late. Be there in twenty.*

ANASTASIA WALKED TO MY CAR. SLOWER THAN NORMAL. Sophia said her body was weakening so much that she wasn't sure she'd make it to Christmas. *Hold on, sweet girl*, I said inside. *Just one more Christmas for your mama.*

I held my breath as I helped her frail body into my car. "You sure you're okay?"

She looked at my hands. "You sure you are? I remember how my skin tightened after the burns. I could barely move without hurting."

I smiled. "I take extra pain management medicine when I know I'm going to be more active. By the end of the day I'm beat though."

We drove a few minutes when she asked me to put on some music. As Adele chased pavements, we chased green lights until we arrived at our destination. I waved to Derek, Ella's brother, and got out of the car. He walked out the front door of the warehouse and smiled, then gave me a hug.

"Sarah, it's so good to see you getting back to life. I remember that feeling. Hiding and growing content in misery. You look happy now."

"Happier. I've not quite tipped the scale to happy yet."

"Happier is a start."

"Thanks for doing this, D. Anastasia doesn't want to tell her family."

"Very brave of her." He walked to the car and opened the door. "Anastasia, I've heard so many wonderful things about you." He bowed and kissed her hand. "I am honored to meet you." He helped her out of the car.

I escorted her to the door of the building and turned back to Derek. "Oh, my stuff is in the trunk. Can you get it please?"

Anastasia gasped when she walked inside. So did I.

Wow.

Derek entered and grinned as he set my equipment down. "Is it what you imagined?"

Anastasia tried to speak a few times, then finally said, "It's so much more. I can't believe it."

"Yes. Unbelievable," I said. "Just ... unbelievable."

"Hey, hey." Miranda appeared from around a wall. "Pretty snazzy, huh?" She put her arm around Anastasia. "Derek's pretty good at landscaping. I've even allowed him to landscape my heart with his love."

He rolled his eyes and we all laughed as I admired the scene. Anastasia told me she wanted to surprise her family with pictures of herself to show at her funeral. Except she wanted them to resemble *The Secret Garden*. In December. And I had the idea of making the ground of the garden look like ice. Symbolizing the hope that melts away the winters of our lives. She loved the idea.

I never imagined it to look so realistic. The huge windows of the warehouse beamed plenty of natural sunlight, even amidst the clouds. It was cold enough inside that Derek had a real sheet of ice on the floor with a light dusting of artificial snow. It must've had a hint of blue dye and sparkles in it, given the magical sheen. A realistic fake tree stood in the midst of the overwhelmingly beautiful display of flowers and a swing made of rope and boards hung from a branch. It looked magical.

"Did Ella make a dress?" Anastasia said, her face glowing like a pale winter moon.

"Of course." I knelt down and rummaged through my bags. "But ... she's a little fanatical about the regency era. So she went with a blend this time. Somewhat like the dress Rose was wearing when the *Titantic* went down."

"I've never seen that, but I'm sure the dress is pretty."

I pulled it out and held it against my chest. "What do you think?"

"Wow." Her eyes widened.

"My sister made that?" Derek said. "I don't believe it."

"You know she made her own wedding dress, right?" Miranda said.

"And every curtain and pillow in her house," I added. "Okay, girl. Let's get you dressed."

Miranda showed us where to change. "Derek has a heater set up so you don't get cold. Stay here until we're ready."

I helped Anastasia undress. Her burn scars were similar to mine. Covering her chest and erasing any resemblance of what could've been a growing woman. She wrapped her arms around her chest. I knew the feeling.

"I have my compression garments on," I said. "If I didn't though, I'd show you that mine looks the same."

"Really?" Her arms dropped to her sides. "Some of the kids at school used to call me The Crumbly Cancer Girl because my skin looked weird."

"What?" I held the dress as she balanced herself on my shoulders and stepped into the fabric. "That's horrible."

"Sometimes I felt that way too, but Vasili always reminded me of something one of our Greek elders said and it always helped."

"What was it?"

"Blessed are those who were born ugly and are hated on earth, because they will have the most beautiful place in Paradise, if they glorify God and do not grumble. Or something like that."

"I've done far too much grumbling."

"I did too. Until my uncle helped me see what's important and what's not."

"Vasili again?"

She nodded. "Who else?"

Certainly not Kyriakos, I thought as I buttoned the back of her dress. I had to use mainly my right hand since my left hand couldn't do buttons yet.

I brushed Anastasia's hair and braided two pieces back with baby's breath, then joined them to make a crown.

She touched the braids and thanked me, then said, "This is the dress I want to be buried in and I want my hair like this too."

"Anastasia, can I ask you something?"

She nodded.

"How did you come to accept your death like it's no big deal? You're so young and there's plenty of adults who panic at the thought of death. About two years ago I was told I had cancer. We got it cleared out, but before that I was on my living room floor in a ball."

"I did cry a little. Mostly when I heard my mom crying at night. Every night she comes into my room and and prays as she watches me sleep. Well"—she giggled—"at least she thinks I'm sleeping. Anyway, I used to cry after she left because early on she always asked God to help her become a better mother. She thought she wasn't a good mom to me because she had to go to work and cook and clean. I guess she felt bad for not spending more time with me." Her eyes held the maturity of a woman, not a little girl. "She's always been the best mom in the world though. You know, the other day she gave me a journal. She started writing letters to me when she found out I was pregnant. I mean"—she laughed again—"when she found out she was pregnant. I read almost two-hundred letters. She was meaning to keep going, but ... well, anyway, she's the best mom ever."

"That means you cried more about her sadness than your own."

"I guess you're right. I want to cry sometimes though."

I wanted to probe her for some kind of revelation on the acceptance of death, on her uncanny sense of joy, but I realized it wouldn't work. She didn't think like me. Somehow her innocence had been preserved. She counted her blessings and hardly noticed her trials. I wanted to be like her. I wanted to be simple. Joyful. Content. Like a child.

Like Anastasia.

Miranda called for us. We walked back into the marriage of winter and spring.

"If you get too cold"—I took the blanket from her shoulders—"let me know, okay? We can take breaks if needed."

Derek and Miranda set up most of my camera equipment, but I rearranged it and prepared myself while Derek carefully helped Anastasia to the swing.

"Real doves?" she said.

I looked up. Sure enough, Derek rented real doves. I laughed and peered through my lens. Been a while since Nikon and I spent time together. I missed it. Felt so good to wrap my hands around a camera again.

"Miranda, would you mind helping me with the light meter and other things?"

She smiled. "My pleasure. I'm so glad to be a part of this."

For the next twenty minutes I snapped photos of a beautiful girl so full of life you'd never be able to see death's grip on her. She smiled, spun, danced, and swung as high as she could on the swing. My favorite was the photo of her stooping down to let a dove out of it's cage, then smiling from below as it flew above her. The entire experience was one of those memories you want to encapsulate and save in a box of grand memories, then pass on to the generations to follow you.

And perhaps I would.

 *thirteen*

I walked back into Ella's house after a long Monday, wanting nothing more than to crash in my bed.

Ella handed me a stack of mail. "How did your doctor's appointment go?"

"Long." I walked to the steps. "I'm exhausted."

She stood at the bottom of the steps as I ascended. Adelaide slept against her chest, all snug in a baby wrap. "So what did the doctor say?"

"He said I'm healing well. Mobility should increase even more by spring. He wants to do some skin grafting again."

"When?"

"I asked him to wait until after Anastasia passes. I want to be there for her."

"How's she doing?"

"Okay. Sophia is worried that she won't make it to Christmas. I think she will though."

"Keep me posted. Oh, Tylissa is coming over this weekend. I'm a little nervous that I won't be able to console her. Will you be around?"

"I'll try to."

I walked to my room and reclined on my bed with a stack of letters in my hand. Bills. Hospital letters. Credit card offers.

"What's this?"

Written by a child. I opened the envelope and unfolded the construction paper. A drawing of me holding hands with a little girl. Large letters that read, *I miss you.* Signed, *Abby.*

So selfish of me. How could I forget Abby? At the same time, how could I maintain a relationship with James' daughter? After his last episode

I wanted nothing to do with him. Regardless of the pity I couldn't shake.

I suppose the kind thing to do would be to see her one last time and say goodbye.

I called James. His voicemail picked up. I was hoping for that.

"James, it's me. Hey, I'd like to see Abby again. I want to explain this to her so she doesn't think I'm abandoning her. I know it's hard enough for her, having lost both of her parents so young. I know you hate me right now, but consider Abby's feelings. Okay, um, thanks."

About ten minutes later he called back. I let it go to voicemail.

"Hey, got your message. Call me back."

I was hoping he wouldn't say that. I preferred voicemail conversations in this case. I dialed his number. We exchanged awkward greetings.

"I'm sorry for the way I acted," he blurted out. "Can I bring Abby and we can all meet for dinner tomorrow?"

"Can you be civil?"

"I said I'm sorry, Sarah. You're not the only one dealing with hard times. I never claimed to be perfect."

I felt sorry for him again, hearing that solemn tone in his words. "Where should we meet?"

"Since you're all into organic ... how about we try that new pizza place on Mulberry? I think it's called The Fridge."

"Okay."

"She gets out of school by three. Maybe I can pull her out early and we can get there by four."

I ENTERED THE FRIDGE AT FOUR AND ORDERED A VEGGIE smothered flatbread pizza for myself and a chicken, sweet potato, glazed onion pizza for James. I figured Abby would like both.

"Would you like wedges?" The kind cashier didn't look twice at my burns. She smiled at me like a normal person. "Ma'am?"

"Yes, please." I paid for it and thanked her.

"No problem. Should be out soon."

I sat down in the back where the windows lined the wall and laughed when I saw my art for sale again. This time I could tell it was a copy because of the large size. Well, if I wanted to count my blessings I sure could start with my best friend.

Abby charged through the door and into my arms within seconds. James sauntered behind. I kissed Abby's cheek and apologized.

She immediately rambled off every event I missed since last seeing her. From her school pet, Tippy the Toad, to her new haircut complete with bangs. James tried to reach across the table to hold my hand, but the cashier set trays of food down between us. Thankfully.

As we ate Abby filled the silence, then randomly said, "Are you guys still getting married?"

"Yes," James said.

I held her hand. "I don't think so, sweetheart."

"Why not?" Her big eyes wanted answers I'm not sure I had the strength to give.

"Sarah needs some time to heal, but she still wants to be your mommy." James held her other hand as I narrowed my eyes at him.

She looked back and forth from him to me. "Is that true?"

"Your daddy is having a hard time with this, honey, but we won't be together. There are lots of reasons."

"Like what?"

"Well, first of all, he doesn't think I'm beautiful anymore."

"That's bull, Sarah. And you know it."

Abby looked at me. "But ... but faces change and they die. Love doesn't, right?" She furrowed her brow. "What's a face have to do with love?"

"According to this world," I said. "A lot."

"But that has nothing to do with anything."

"It's more than that." I picked at a potato and looked at James. "I think you need to marry someone who makes your heart skip a beat. Someone who makes you feel more alive. Not someone who takes the very life from you."

Poor Abby searched us for answers. Took all I had not to cry, but I managed to keep it all inside. James controlled his anger as well. We finished eating in silence. Even Abby didn't know what to say.

I tried to relax my fists by picking at a napkin, but I ended up shredding it to pieces. Nausea crept up my throat, then settled back down with each deep breath.

Finally Abby finished. We cleaned up and headed for the door just as Natalie and Vasili walked in. James eyed Natalie up and down as she hugged me. I tried not to look at Vasili.

"Who's this?" Natalie asked as she smiled at James.

"I'm James," he said. "Sarah's fiancé."

"Oh?" she said. "Wow, Sarah. Why'd you keep this handsome fella a secret?"

He blushed. My face probably looked pink too. For an entirely different reason. Vasili and I made eye contact as Natalie and James blushed at each other.

"This is my fiancé." Natalie linked her arm with Vasili's. "We're getting married this spring."

The men nodded at each other.

"Well," I said. "We better get going."

I scooted by James and his captivated eyes. When I made it out of the door I turned to see if he followed, but he didn't.

Vasili turned and flashed his charming smile. Though it seemed weakened and forced. I smiled back and walked to my car.

James and Abby finally approached me. I gave Abby the warmest hug I possibly could and whispered in her ear, "I will always love you, Abby. Even if it doesn't seem like I do. Your daddy will find someone else. I hope she is as sweet as you."

"Maybe." She dried her cheeks with her hands. "I love you." She ran back to James and hid her face in his coat. He dropped his shoulders and wiped his own face.

Couldn't they see that it was better this way?

I sat in my car and turned the ignition. Neither of their sad faces moved. They watched me as I pulled out of the parking lot.

By the time I got to the red light and out of their view, I lost it.

Absolutely lost it.

 *fourteen*

Vasili wrapped his arm around my shoulders and pushed my arm in uncomfortable positions. "Ouch."

"Sorry," he said. "But if you don't do those stretches it's bad for your muscles and your skin. You have to muster through the pain for the end result."

I turned and faced him. "What is the end result? My doctor has a bunch of skin grafting plans for me. He's talking about plastic surgery every time I see him. I don't want that. I don't want to be fake." I sighed. "Everyone says I'm crazy. To just do it and get it over with. But what do I want the end result to be? I've been thinking a lot about this."

Vasili shrugged. "You lost me."

"Everything with Anastasia. Then James and Abby. I don't know."

"I have no idea what you're talking about."

I laughed. "I don't know. Do I want my end result to be fake perfection? Just another attempt to appear like the world wants me to? Do I want to feel safe and pretty and loved?" I turned and faced the mirror, taking in my new self. "Or do I want to embrace who I am now and tell the world to bug off?"

He laughed. "Bug off?"

I smirked. "What? You like that?"

"Sounds fierce." He touched my shoulder. "Let's finish up, okay?"

We did a few last stretches and he walked me to the door.

"Thank you for everything you're doing for my niece." He turned the doorknob. "It means a lot to me. She looks up to you a lot."

"I look up to her."

He smiled. We were close enough that I could smell his shampoo. I wondered if a man like him would ever love me, then shoved the thought away. I didn't need love. Or a man. I needed to find rest with myself. My new self.

I walked down the hallway and Vasili called out, "See ya tonight."

I waved and continued out the door. Yes, I forgot about tonight. Rehearsals for *It's a Wonderful Life*. I'd practiced my lines in bed for the last three weeks. I know it was something fun for a little girl, but I took it quite seriously. Even made Ella read lines with me. She was pretty good too.

Two weeks left until Christmas Eve.

WE ALL SAT AROUND IN THE LIVING ROOM OF MAMA KOURSA-ris' house again. Vasili stumbled over his lines as everyone laughed. I didn't buy it though. He wanted to make us laugh. Lighten the mood. Plus, I had a feeling he wanted to surprise us on opening night with a phenomenal performance. I could tell. He definitely knew how to act. The shy ones were always the best ones.

We finished the last of it when Natalie said, "So will Vasili and Sarah need to kiss in this?"

"No," he said. "I wouldn't do that."

I admired his faithfulness, but his quick response dampened my heart. Did he find me that unappealing? But he never seemed to push the plastic surgery thoughts. He was one of the only people who encouraged me to do whatever made me happiest, not prettiest.

"Sarah?" Sophia snapped her fingers in front of my face. "You in there?"

I nodded. "I'm just tired."

"I had to order her casket today."

"What?" I reached for her hand. "Oh, Sophia."

Her bottom lip trembled. "Yanni barely leaves her bedside. As hard as it is for me, somehow I think it's worse for him. He won't plan her funeral with me. I think he's in denial."

"I'm so sorry. I can't imagine."

"She's so happy, Sarah." She crossed her arms and touched her chin to her shoulder. "She doesn't need me. Every time I tell her, 'It's okay, dear.

Cry on my shoulder if you need to,' she tells me that she's okay and doesn't need to cry. I don't understand why someone so young and beautiful and full of life needs to die so young."

Vasili leaned into Sophia. "Death is only a stage of life. In fact, it marks the beginning of true life."

She sniffed and nodded, then fell into his arms. He pressed her head into his chest and held her as she wept. I rested my head against hers and cried with her. Within minutes, the entire family was crowded around. A tight, warm group hug. We stayed there for a while. Feeling the pain of a mother losing her baby. Until she finally lifted her head and inhaled. No one said a word after that. We didn't need to. It was understood.

As much as the pain seared the hidden recesses of my heart, I walked out of their house feeling alive. One step closer to being whole. It was then that I realized the joy of pain. The beauty in struggle. Sometimes the most human thing we can do is struggle. Together. Fighting for goodness and love through blood, sweat, and tears. Sometimes the moments we are most in tune with reality are not the fun times where we dance under street lights high on life, but the moments when we weep. For others. For ourselves. When we realize that the tears dripping from our eyes invisibly flow over the darkest parts of us, washing away the stains and revealing beauty we never knew we had. Real, strong beauty not shaken by even the cruelest of flames. Humble beauty. Like the earth anticipating the moistening of spring's tears, the heart, parched by its own selfishness, awaits these moments. These moments we so often push away and discard, not realizing that it's the tears which cleanse and enliven our hearts.

I sat in my car. And I didn't wipe my face this time. I let my tears soak into my cheeks. Dwelling there. Cleansing me. Renewing me. I smiled and drove away, knowing that for the first time in my life ... I felt a radiance the world and its cutting stares could not muddy.

I felt beautiful.

 *fifteen*

Anastasia mainly stayed in bed. She could still get up and walk if she wanted to, but her health had declined so severely that hospice nurses aided Sophia each day until sunset. Her favorite nurse, Laura, was a lovely woman from England who embraced the family with warm gentleness.

After a long day at her bedside, I kissed her sleeping forehead and whispered, "I love you," then hugged Yanni, Sophia, and even Laura. "I'll see you tomorrow. I promised Ella I'd come back early to greet Tylissa." My phone played *Canon in D*. "And there she is now."

"Thank you," Sophia said.

Yanni nodded in agreement.

"No need to thank me for loving someone so easy to love."

Laura walked me to the door.

"How long do you think she has?" I whispered.

"Honestly, it's difficult to say. Normally when they stop eating we see a steep curve, but right now she's hanging on and eating her veggies."

I tried to smile. "It's not painful, right?"

"Perhaps a bit, but not too much. She's on medication and it should see her through to the end."

I looked down. *The end.* More like the beginning of life outside the cocoon according to Vasili. "Thank you, Laura. You're a wonderful nurse."

"No need to thank me for loving someone so easy to love." She winked.

We both smiled as she closed the front door behind me.

The drive home was easy. Uneventful. I considered my own life, wondering how it would end. When it would end. Who would be at my bedside? Ella barely left my side at the burn unit. I'm sure she'd be there. Who else,

I had no idea.

I didn't see Tylissa's car when I parked. Phew. For some reason Ella insisted I get home before Tylissa. I never won any awards for being on time, but didn't like disappointing others either. Bad habit I always said I'd break, yet didn't.

I opened the front door and the darkness lit up like an electrical shock had zapped the house. I screamed as a flashback of the fire coursed my mind and dozens of smiling faces yelled, "Surprise!"

My mind caught up with my eyes. People. Faces. Ella. Tylissa. Vasili. Natalie. Kyriakos. Eleni. Dee. Derek. Miranda. Gavin. Matt. Lydia. Mom. Dad. Kelly. Nicole. And more. So many more. Why?

"You look shocked," Ella hugged me. "Happy birthday, sweet friend."

"Birthday?" I said. "Mine?"

"You've been so preoccupied with Anastasia that you forgot your own birthday. You made this easy."

The happy faces were yelling surprise for me? "Wow."

Everyone laughed.

"Oh, dear. I think I'm gonna cry. No one has ever—"

"We love you." My mother stepped up to me with tears in her eyes. "If anyone deserves this, it's you."

She embraced me as my father stood behind her, waiting. He never showed much emotion, but the way he hung his hands nervously at his sides showed me he cared. When Mom let go, Dad hugged me and kissed my forehead. "You're still my baby, Sarah. So glad to have you back."

"I miss you both so much." I looked around the room. "I don't know what to say guys. Thank you. All of you."

"Alright." Matt clapped his hands together. "Time to eat."

Everyone laughed, drawing the attention away from me. Perfect timing. I was beginning to feel a bit uncomfortable.

Each person waited in line to fill their plates with delicious food. Ella, as always, gave her speech about local animal products from humane sources. My parents sat down next to my grandmother, who I didn't notice until now. We smiled at each other and I sat beside her as I ate. She couldn't speak much after her stroke, but she nodded as though she were listening as I recalled childhood memories with her. Such a precious woman.

Bloom

I tossed my plate in the trash and leaned against the dining room entry-way, watching as my friends and family mingled in the living room.

Vasili nodded to me. I couldn't miss his eyes amidst a sea of people if I tried. Unusual for a Greek man to have such bright eyes. Especially bright considering his dark eyelashes. Like a mix of sky and land. What am I doing? I thought. He's taken. And I'm nowhere near as pretty as his fiancé. He's my brother, I reminded myself as he waved me over.

"Hey,", I said, suddenly dazed. All of this feeling normal stuff was starting to make me feel ... normal again.

"Happy birthday." He handed me a small bag. "Open it. It's from me and a special little girl who wished she could be here."

I unfolded the tissue paper and pulled out a frame. A picture of Anastasia and me. Framed by aqua matting shaped like a heart. A quote just below it read:

The best and most beautiful things in the
world cannot be seen or even touched.
They must be felt with the heart.
- Helen Keller

I stared at the photograph of our two scarred faces side-by-side, taking in the simple, yet profound, truth of the quote below it. Yes, I believed it to be true. I experienced it personally.

Helen Keller said it as a little girl with a dirty dress and windblown hair would say. Or a blind person who can only feel with the hands and heart would say. Or anyone without the tainted views of our society would say.

True beauty is not in the eye of the beholder. It cannot be held. By the eyes or the hands. It can only be experienced by those with a ripe, humble heart. And just when you think you've wrapped your hands around it ... it slips out of your hand like sand through a sieve.

"Thank you." I held the frame against my chest. "This means more to me than I can express."

He tapped the picture. "I didn't know you before. So I'm only speaking from what I know now, but the two girls in this picture are the most beautiful people I've ever known."

I tried to speak.

"I mean that." He walked away, brushing my shoulder. His subtle cologne lingered minutes after he passed.

I didn't know what to say or feel after that. All I know is the rest of the night people kept saying to me, "Your smile is brighter than usual."

Perhaps. Or perhaps they saw the effects of a woman who had finally found contentment, regardless of outward circumstances.

I enjoyed the evening, meandering from friend to family to friend. Laughing about the past and clinking glasses to the future. Then I thought of Anastasia. Leaving the world.

I hid away in the kitchen and texted Sophia. She eased my worries. Anastasia was awake and happy as usual.

"You okay?" Ella said.

"Just checking on Anastasia." I set my drink on the kitchen counter. "You know, I realized it doesn't matter how many people love us throughout our lives. I've spent my life trying to pretend to be perfect, thinking I was making people happy. It's all fake though. And it doesn't matter how many people show up at our funerals. Since I was a kid, I had this strange preoccupation with my funeral. Wondering how many people loved me enough to show up. How stupid of me, really. Take Anastasia, for example. I'm sure some people will show up who barely even know her, not because they loved her or even knew her. Maybe they're just a friend of the family. What really matters is not how many people kiss our cold hands as we lie in a casket, but how many hearts we've warmed while alive. And you know, the little imprints we leave on the hearts of others may go unnoticed sometimes, but not even death can erase them."

Ella raised her eyebrows. "Wow, Sarah." She wrapped her arms around me. "Welcome back."

 *sixteen*

I crashed after the party and slept like a bear in winter until an ear-split-ting sound woke me up. When I opened my eyes, I screamed almost as loud as the deafening beeps. The fire alarm.

I peeled off my burn mask and whipped my body out of bed so fast I pulled my calf muscle. Limping across the floor, I grabbed my robe and bent over to massage my leg.

My ribs hurt and my heartbeat resounded in my ears. Dizzy, I steadied myself on the dresser.

The door opened. Ella.

"Oh, Sarah," she said. "I'm so sorry. False alarm."

I closed my eyes and exhaled, slumping to the chair by the window.

"I am so, so sorry. I was baking some treats for breakfast and I fell asleep on the couch. No fire. Just black blueberry muffins."

I held my chest. "I have these nightmares still. I'm either burning or running through the smoky house, but can't escape. Each room turns into another room and they all collapse on me. I thought I was dreaming again until I stood up." I walked back to my bed. "What time is it?"

"Five in the morning." She helped me into bed. "I feel so bad."

"Don't." I almost laughed. "We'll be laughing about this for years."

She sighed in relief. "Tylissa will be leaving this evening. I figured we could have a nice breakfast with her tomorrow. I mean, today."

I nodded as I pulled the sheets to my neck. "I'll be down at seven."

"Okay." She closed my door and peeked through the crack. "Sorry again."

I couldn't sleep so I watched shadows flicker on the ceiling and thought about Ella. Our childhood memories, like when we dressed up as *The Wizard of Oz* characters and performed for our stuffed animals. When we nearly hit our heads on the ceiling as Jordan scored the winning shot for The Bulls, even though we couldn't stand sports. She was there for me when I had my heart broken for the first time and when I had my first real kiss. When I found out I had cancer and when I cleaned out our apartment and made her get rid of all of her chemical makeup.

Her, with her brown hair and petite body. Me, with my blonde hair and tall, curvy build. Her, with her *Downton Abbey* obsession. Me, with my Benedict as *Sherlock Holmes* giddiness. Her, idealist to the core. Me, scared to get my hopes up in fear of getting let down. Her, function over form. Me, window shopper to the core. Her, married with a baby. Me, single for life. Her, optimistic. Me, well, I guess I used to be that way too.

Opposites in so many ways, yet inseparable since we met. I loved her. And one day, I hoped to love people and life as much as she did.

7 a.m. came before sleep did. I pulled on some pajama pants and a t-shirt, then did my quick bathroom routine.

I came back into my room to find my slippers and saw blue and silver gift wrap glimmering on my bed. I opened the card on top of the gift:

Dearest Sarah,

Another year. Probably the most difficult year our friendship has ever endured. I'll never forget the day I got that call. And the first time I saw you after the accident. I held myself together while standing by you, but you were in a coma and couldn't hear me anyway. My hands were shaking as I stared at you ... I wanted so badly to take your place.

But I couldn't. I needed to go back home and live my life as normal as possible. It was so hard. I thought of you constantly. Sometimes I'd stare at Gavin and instead of being thankful for finding him, I'd get upset that I was here and you were in a coma. I almost felt guilty living, because you weren't.

Then, the worst part ... I got married without you. Before everyone arrived I set your picture on a bench under the tree where we said our vows. As I walked to Gavin I looked at your face and thought of your joy. You always had this joy that outshone everyone else's. You used to tell me your secret was that " a spoonful of sugar helps the medicine go down." I always joked that your sugar must've been crack. ;)

Seriously, though, your friendship has changed my life. Seeing you endure all of this and still keep going ... you've inspired me so much. I remember the first day you came back from the hospital just four months ago. You were exhausted and struggling with your new reality, but when I said goodnight to you ... you smiled and said, " It's not good yet, but I'm working on that."

For so many years you hid in your room when you experienced pain. Remember when Gordon broke up with you and you ran away, hiding behind that bush out front? Your parents even called the cops. You didn't want to show the world your tears and failures. That was the first time you admitted to life not being so good all the time. Since then, I've seen you grow and change so much.

The past few weeks you've smiled again. Really smiled. And it's been so beautiful to witness. You've stopped running for the first time in your life. As your best friend it's been amazing to watch. You still light up the room,

Sarah. You always say I have all the luck, but I don't see it that way at all. In you, I see so many qualities I lack. So many virtues I admire. You are the most loyal and faithful person I know. You're willing to give up everything you want for your friends and family. You see people in a positive light, even when it's hard for others to do so. You don't let many people into your heart, but when you do ... they never leave. You think I'm admirable? Pssh. It may sound cheesy, but you're the wind beneath my wings.

Just remember in the winter
Far beneath the bitter snow
Lies the seed that with the sun's love,
In the spring, becomes a rose.

You are more than my best friend ... you're my sister, my rose. And I love you. Joy is your middle name for a reason. Thank you for bringing joy to my life.
Happy birthday, dear friend.
Love,
Ella

I peeled back the wrapping paper and teared up at the painting. Gavin must've painted it. Exactly like I remembered.

Ella and I holding hands by the river. We were seven years old. The summer sun highlighted our hair as we dipped our toes in the murky water. We were both hesitant to get more than our feet wet. It was so cold. Then, she squeezed my hand and said, "Come on. Everything's easy when we do it together."

I squeezed back and we splashed into the shallow creek, laughing, exhilarated. We were a team. Some people go through their lives skipping friends like rocks on a creek. Picking them up only to toss them away and watch them sink out of sight. I never had a lot of friends growing up. But I didn't need them.

I walked downstairs and found Ella pulling another set of muffins out of the oven.

"Thank you," I said. "I'm so thankful to have a friend who understands me. Who can see me at my worst and still love me."

She gave me a quick hug, then pulled another tray of muffins out of the oven. "Thank you. For the same."

"Remember that time my family thought we were more than friends because we were so close? Because we cuddled when we watched movies?"

She laughed. "That was hilarious. I guess friendships like ours just aren't normal."

"No. I don't think they are."

Tylissa rubbed her eyes and greeted us. "I think I need some coffee."

Ella immediately put a kettle on the stove. "French press coming right up."

"Look at you, girl," Tylissa said. "Getting all gourmet on me."

Asylia toddled into the living room.

"I can't believe how big she's gotten," Ella said.

"Yeah. Time flies." She looked off into the distance. "Mwenye has barely been able to see her grow up. I've sent him letters, but never hear back. Sometimes we get to talk on the phone, but the stuff he's had to endure...."

"Ella wouldn't tell me what happened." I sat next to Tylissa at the bar that separated the dining room from the kitchen. "She said it's not her story to tell, but I just don't understand why Mwenye is taking the blame for something he didn't do. Especially something as terrible as this."

Tylissa rested her chin in her hand. "It's a long story. One that Mwenye doesn't want me to share. This is what he wants."

"So you haven't told Ella either?"

"I've only told her that he's not guilty. I have proof of that, and so does the court if they only wanted the evidence. They just want what they want. And that's exactly what Mwenye wants. I knew it when we got married. He told me there was a good chance something like this would happen. He's just had this guy on his back for years." She let out a deep breath. "Anyway, it will all make sense soon. I've learned a lot through this. Mwenye has taught me so much about life. I just hope"—she bit her lip—"that Asylia will understand when she gets older."

"I'm sure she will," Ella said. "I don't understand yet either, but when I do, I have no doubt that I'll admire what he's doing. I've always admired you guys for standing up for the truth even when it hurts."

"Thank you," Tylissa said. "So, Sarah, whatever happened with James? Did you guys break it off?"

"That's a long story too," I said. "Yes, we broke it off. Or at least I'm trying to. He's not so interested in dealing with reality though."

"Do you really think it's for the best?"

"The guy practically told me I don't deserve a husband because of the way I look now. Is that someone I want to grow old with?" I shook my head. "It's weird how someone can become a different person when hard times hit. I'm kind of glad for this, you know. I've seen a different side of him. Possessive and angry and hurtful. This is a time when he should be even more gentle and compassionate, but it turned him into a crazy person."

"That's sad." Ella handed us each a blueberry muffin, grilled with creamy butter melting into the tops. "I feel bad for him."

"I do too. Sometimes I stay up at night thinking I should just marry him and help him find happiness, but every time I let myself give into that idea ... I lose my own happiness. I'm not sure I'm strong enough to be a martyr. Some people can pull others up the ladder, but I'm afraid I'd just fall back down."

"It's for the best," Tylissa said. "It may not seem like it when you're tossing and turning. I know the feeling, trust me. It is for the best though. It'll be okay."

"I saw the way Vasili looked at you," Ella said. "He's engaged, isn't he? I saw a ring on Natalie's finger."

"Nothing gets by you, does it?" I laughed. "There's nothing between us. He considers me his sister. That's all. You saw Natalie. Do you really think he'd break up with her for me?"

"You give yourself less credit than you deserve," Ella said.

I shrugged. "I guess I'd rather err on that side."

"You always have." She laughed. "I'm leaping for the moon and you're still contemplating if it exists."

I smiled. "A little off subject here, but you know what? I realized this morning that I've looked in the mirror lately and haven't noticed my burns. I've stopped zeroing in on the negative all the time."

"That's great," Tylissa said. "I feel the same. I'm finally coming to terms with everything. I look at a picture of Mwenye and I'm proud of what he's doing, instead of getting all hysterical."

"Yes," I said. "We're coming to terms with reality while Ella still dances in the stardust."

"Hey," Ella said. "Someone's gotta do it."

 *seventeen*

James texted my phone as I pulled up to Sophia's house. Not a surprise. He texted me two hundred times in one day. Or close. It started with, "Christmas is coming, Sarah. We should be decorating a tree together. The three of us."

By the fifty-thousandth text he was cursing at me and calling me a slut. I didn't know what to do. I wished he would let go and make it easy. I tried to tell myself I was doing the right thing, but he made me feel guilty for moving on and attempting to rebuild my life without him and Abby.

So, for now, I blocked his number and hoped he would keep his distance. I actually started to fear him so much that I had nightmares of him lighting me on fire on purpose, just to keep me from dating anyone else. I kept waking up asking God to take away my bad dreams. I couldn't take it anymore.

I knocked on Sophia's door and Nurse Laura let me in.

"How is she?" I said.

"She's taking liquids, but she hasn't eaten in a few days." She held my hand in hers. "I think she'll make it to Christmas though. Only a week to go. Have you been practicing your lines?"

I tried to smile. "Barely. I think Vasili and I are going to win an award for most hilarious actors in a serious play."

"She will absolutely love it. I can't wait."

I tapped on Anastasia's bedroom door. Sophia waved for me to come inside. Yanni was asleep in the chair by his daughter, his hand atop hers.

Sophia whispered, "She's slipping away, Sarah."

"Not yet. She'll make it to Christmas."

Anastasia's eyes flickered. "Sarah?"

I sat beside her and ran my fingertips along her forehead. "I'm here, sweetie. How are you feeling?"

"I heard you had a nice birthday." Her voice weakened since the last time I saw her. "Did you like the gift we got you?"

"Of course." I continued to rub her head. "Thank you."

She closed her eyes and gulped for air. "I keep telling God I just want to see one more flower bloom, but it's not looking too good. I was hoping to die in the spring."

My chest hurt. "Maybe when you open your eyes again it will be your very own special spring. A whole new life filled with all kinds of wonderful things to explore."

"Do you believe in heaven?"

"Yes," I said. "I do."

"Me too." Her mouth seemed dry. Sophia noticed too and helped her sip water. Then she continued, "Father Thomas tells me that heaven is God's presence to everyone who loves him and hell is his presence to people who don't love him. I don't know why, but I keep thinking of people who don't believe in heaven and God and I keep asking him if there's anyone who doesn't go there, if maybe he'd let me take their place, but I don't know how to do that because I do love him and I don't know if I could pretend not to."

I smiled. "You're sweet, Anastasia. God will take care of the details. You just keep loving him and everyone around you."

"There are times when I wonder if when I die it will just be over and nothing will exist after that."

I admired her honesty. For such a young child, she always brought up interesting points.

Sophia pressed her finger over her daughter's lips. "Don't worry so much. Just rest, dear."

"But how do we know for sure?" she asked her mother.

Vasili entered the room. "Remember, the most beautiful things cannot be seen or even touched, they must be felt with the heart."

Her face lit up like a Ferris wheel glowing in the night. "Uncle Vasili!"

"Hey there, young lady," he said. "I thought I'd stop by before heading to work."

"Where's Natalie? I haven't seen her in a long time," Sophia said.

"She's busy with her cosmetology stuff. Beauty shows. Training."

Sophia nodded. "It would mean a lot to Anastasia if she'd come and visit."

Vasili avoided her eyes. "I'll see what I can do." He looked at me. "I gotta run. Your appointment is in an hour." He shoved my shoulder. "Don't be late."

He left and Anastasia drifted in and out of sleep for the next half hour. I kissed her cheek and said goodbye to her parents. Laura escorted me back to the door and handed me an envelope. "Don't open this until after Anastasia's funeral. She wrote this for you, but doesn't want you to read it until the spring. She said you can open it on her birthday."

"I thought her birthday passed?"

"They had a party for her, but her actual birthday isn't until spring. She doesn't think she'll make it until then, so they celebrated early."

"Why didn't she have Sophia give it to me?"

"She didn't want anyone else to read it."

"What is it?" I said, intrigued that a child would be so thoughtful.

"Don't look at me." She opened the front door. "I'm just the messenger."

VASILI FINISHED TORTURING ME WITH STRETCHES AND EXERcises, then stopped me when I headed for the door.

"Actually," he said. "I only scheduled you for today. Truth is, I need help with my lines."

I laughed. "Are you serious?"

He chewed the inside of his cheek.

I slapped his arm. "You're serious."

"I'm doing this for her. I've never acted before and I feel like a fool."

"Don't." I set my bag on the chair by the door. "Do you have the script?"

"Brought two." He handed me a rolled up stack of paper. "Thanks. I know it's just family, but I don't want to disappoint her."

"She's impossible to disappoint, it seems."

He finally relaxed a bit. I unrolled the papers and looked at him. He tensed up again, clenching his fists and jaw.

"Are you okay?" I said.

He paced back and forth and stopped in front of me with his hand on the door knob. "This probably isn't the best idea. I'm ... Natalie may not like this."

"You really think she'd be jealous of someone most little kids think of as a monster?"

"If she isn't ... she's not seeing what I see."

I rubbed the side of my neck and looked down. "We're like brother and sister. You said so yourself."

He nodded. "Right. You're right."

We stared at each other as a curious silence formed between us. His eyes were not as vivid today. I thought I noticed less life in his voice throughout my therapy session, but I figured it was Anastasia.

"Everything okay?" I said, fiddling with the papers. "You seem a bit ... off."

"What is love, Sarah? Can you answer that? Do you know?"

"Well, we all have our own answers to that, I guess. It's different for all of us."

"Is it?" He tapped his rolled up script against his leg. "Natalie wants me to move to Los Angeles with her. She was given this offer to work for a salon that does a ton of celebrity work right in the heart of LA. This is her dream."

I wasn't sure how to respond, so I didn't.

"I'm Greek."

I laughed. "Yes. You are. So what?"

"We're about family and tradition. Simplicity and ... well, okay, the truth is I don't want to leave Lancaster. This is my home. But if I'm not willing to make the slightest sacrifice for my wife, what kind of husband does that make me? I should be willing to do whatever makes her happy, right?"

"You're asking the wrong person."

"Why do you say that?"

"Because. If I did whatever made James happy right now, he wouldn't be happy later. Neither would I. What he wants won't make the right part

102

of him happy, and I'm not sure I want to please that part of him. So ... I've made him miserable and he's doing his best to return the favor. All in the name of love."

He smiled. "Are you saying moving out there would give Natalie a temporary happiness that isn't the right kind of happiness?"

"I don't know. Is there a right or wrong happiness?"

"I guess there's happiness ... then joy?"

I shrugged. "I guess the real question is not whether or not you're willing to sacrifice your every desire, because I think, knowing you, that you are, but maybe you need to ask yourself if the same things bring you both joy? We've all got tickets to the same destination in life. Every one of us. But we get to pick the flight we take and the stops on the way. Maybe she wants a different plane and that's what's bothering you."

He rubbed his chin. I spaced out, contemplating the words that came out of my mouth and wondering where they came from. Then I remembered. Fourth of July. I was sixteen and I wasn't as content in my singleness as my best friend. She was willing to wait for the right one while I wanted someone, anyone, to kiss under the fireworks.

My father noticed my downcast spirit as the fireworks adorned the sky with specks of color. He pulled me into his chest, kissed the top of my head, and said, "Life isn't always about fireworks. Your fireworks will come, Sarah. And they'll fizzle out just as fast. Life's an experience, not a destination. All of us have the same destination, but not one of us has an identical experience. You'll find someone who will be there when the fireworks fizzle out and the sky turns black and love you just the same. That's the one to hold onto."

I looked at Vasili. "Life isn't about romance. It's about love."

And with that, I left him to his thoughts. And me ... to mine.

 *eighteen*

The next morning I woke up to my phone beeping and a voicemail from Natalie.

Hey, Sarah. Could you come to Vasili's house today for lunch? It's really important. I've texted his address so you can GPS it. He lives in the city. East side by Shippen and Orange. Thanks.

I gulped. Did I have other plans? Could I make other plans? Could I pretend I never got the voicemail?

"Hello?" a voice came from the phone. "Sarah?"

Oh, no. I must've called her back without realizing it.

I hung up.

And felt highly mature and sophisticated. Wow. What on earth?

She called back. I answered.

"Sorry about that," I said. "What do you guys need?"

"Just need to talk about a few things. What time can you be here?"

"Noon?"

"Great. See ya then."

THE OUTSIDE OF HIS HOUSE WAS BEAUTIFUL. A NICE, OLD HIS-
toric city home with shutters. My favorite. Only his shutters were chipped and falling off. Kind of ruined the appeal, yet made it more charming at the same time.

I rang the doorbell and watched my breath move through the freezing cold air. Natalie opened and nearly toppled me over.

"Thank you." She squealed. "Thank you so much."

"What did I do?" I entered the foyer.

"Vasili has been analyzing the death out of my request to move to LA. He said he talked to you and whatever you said inspired him to sacrifice his own desires and move with me." She leaned toward me and whispered, "Can't thank you enough. I have a surprise, but I can't say yet. Do you want to eat here tonight? I'm begging Vasili to let me cook tonight. I can't handle one more Greek meal. Another lemony potato and spana ... spanacore ... spana—"

"Spanakopita?"

"Right. That wretched stuff. Not to mention the—"

"Hey, look who's here." Vasili motioned for us to come into the living room. "Welcome to my humble abode."

"Humble all right," Natalie said.

"Actually." I eyed the hallway, stairwell, and quickly glanced over the dining room and living room. "I think it's pretty amazing. How'd you afford something like this?"

Vasili laughed. "My dad owned a pizza shop and this is where I grew up. Kyriakos and I live here now. Mom couldn't stand living here once Dad died."

I looked around, taking it all in. Something so romantic about an old house. Well-lived. Well-loved. I entered the living room and stopped in my tracks. Above the mantel of the gorgeous fireplace a familiar photograph stretched across the wall. The original was a quarter of that size.

"You like that old thing?" Natalie said, her shoulder against mine. "Vasili kept looking at that every time we passed this dinky gallery on Queen Street. So on his last birthday I bought the depressing thing and had it blown up for him. Was one of the best gifts he's ever gotten. So he said. Right, babe?"

He ran his fingers along the petals. It took me five hours to set that picture up to be what I envisioned. I captured it perfectly.

"It doesn't look depressing to me," he said. "I think it symbolizes hope. I love the idea of a flower blooming from a crack in a graffiti-covered city wall. I think it's awesome. Caught my eye immediately."

"And he still hasn't pulled the hook out of his eye." Natalie sighed. "He's always in here staring at the thing like it speaks to him or something. What do you think, Sarah?"

"I ... I ... It's nice, I guess."

I hoped they kept the original. One day I'd ask for it. Not today though.

"Anyway," Natalie said. "We brought you over because we have a special question for you." She squeezed my arms. I didn't want to show her that it hurt, but it was getting hard not to.

"Let the girl go," Vasili said. "You're probably hurting her."

"Oh!" She jerked back, horrified. "Are you okay?"

Vasili walked away laughing.

"I'm okay." I hid my own laughter. "Just a little sensitive still."

"Just out of curiosity, have you considered plastic surgery?"

I looked at my feet. Should've expected the question from Ms. Cosmetologist.

"There's no shame in it, you know. Heck, I've even considered getting a few things done myself."

"The only surgeries I'll be having are skin grafts. I only wanted breasts to nurse a child and implants can't do that."

"But what about—"

"Girls, are you coming?" Vasili called from the dining room.

I hoped he didn't hear our conversation.

I sat own at the table. Vasili and Natalie sat down next to each other. He brushed her hair from her face and kissed her cheek. She wiped her cheek and fixed her hair, then scooted an away inch from him. I guess she didn't want her hair to get messed up and her makeup to smudge. Poor Vasili settled into his chair and stopped trying. I used to be that girl. The one who worried about her hair more than her boyfriend. Always trying to look good and checking my reflection in buildings and even the metal slats that held elevator buttons. Anything reflective. Now I spent the last few months avoiding such things at all costs. Only to find myself neutral. No longer obsessed with looking at myself or avoiding myself. Just trying to work on being myself.

"So, we want to ask you to be our wedding photographer." Natalie set a book on the table. "I know it's a big job, but it's not until April. That gives you a few more months to prepare for it."

I glanced back to my photo in the living room. The one she didn't care for. "But you've never seen my work."

"I saw a few things at Ella's house for your party. That last wedding you did before your ... um, well, that last one you did was gorgeous."

"You can talk about the fire. We all know it happened. No sense in treating it like it's the plague. In fact, it's changed me. I am better because of it."

"Really? That's a relief because I've been dying to ask you. Vasili was burned by water, which I'm sure is different from fire. How did it feel when your skin was melting off? Was it painful or did it shock you so mu—"

Vasili stood. "Enough, Natalie."

"What?" She smiled. "Don't be so serious."

"It hurt," I said. "Thank you for being so compassionate. I'll think about doing the wedding photography." I stood. "For now I need to get going. I want to stop by and see Anastasia before it gets too late."

"Oh, for crying out loud," Natalie said. "The girl doesn't need everyone sobbing at her bedside every second of the day. She needs to feel as normal as possible. We need to pretend that everything is okay."

"I'll be there soon," Vasili said, ignoring Natalie's comment.

"It's not like she's even awake most of the time," Natalie said.

"Exactly." Vasili walked me to the door as Natalie trailed behind. "You may think the actions that mean the most are the ones we get credit for, but I happen to believe they mean more when people aren't aware."

"Huh?" Natalie said.

I tried not to laugh as I walked out the door. When I got into my car I turned the heat on and wondered how many things I did while no one was watching. True altruistic acts of kindness birthed from love for others instead of love for praise. Did anyone fit that ideal?

Anastasia.

She did.

For the last few months she had been planning surprises for her family and friends to unveil after she died. It must've been love, because she wouldn't be around to hear the praises.

I longed for the joy and simplicity of a child. And yet, how does an adult with a history of pain, a present of bills, and a future of unknowns find that child-likeness again?

NO ONE ANSWERED THE FRONT DOOR, SO I LET MYSELF IN.
Sophia gave me an extra key for times like those. I peered into Anastasia's
bedroom. Yanni was in bed with her. His huge body all cramped on the
edge of the frilly little girl's bed.

No sign of Sophia and Laura.

I sat on the couch and texted Sophia.

She responded five minutes later. *Hey, I'll be back in a few.*

Ten minutes later she came in the door carrying a bunch of huge bags.
I helped her carry a few and noticed the fresh drops on her lashes. We set
the bags on the living room floor and she collapsed beside them, sobbing.
I knelt beside her and waited until she calmed down, then asked what happened.

"Yanni won't help me plan her funeral," she said. "He's in denial, so
Anastasia has been asking me to do all of these little things to plan for
it. She has quite a few requests for such a young person. I just want to be
beside her, but at the same time I want to get everything prepared exactly as
she wants." She sniffed. "My baby is dying and I've tried everything. There's
nothing I can do. We had to increase her morphine yesterday and it took
a little bit to kick in. I can't explain the torture I feel watching my little girl
suffer. I keep asking God to take me instead."

I waited to make sure she was finished, then said, "Let me handle some
of those things for you. I have nothing better to do. Just let me know what
and when."

"Are you sure?"

"Absolutely."

"She's been sleeping a lot more lately, but they told us to watch for
other symptoms to show that she might be close. So far nothing has happened. Laura said her pee may turn orange or brown as her liver fails, but
we haven't seen that yet either. Thankfully Christmas is only a few days
away. Have you and Vasili practiced lines? I think everyone else is good to
go."

"We'll be okay. Poor Vasili is nervous." I tried to smile. "Yesterday he
sent me a text asking why the movie was different from the script we had.
I told him we condensed it to make sure she could stay awake for it all. He
said it was his seventh time watching the movie."

She smiled. "He's been great. Those two have always been so close."

"I noticed. How'd that come about?

"He is her godparent. There's always a special bond there, but they'd be close anyway. Kindred spirits."

The front door opened.

"And there he is now," I said. A fluttery sensation began in my stomach.

"Sarah, glad you're still here." He sat on the couch across from Sophia and me. "I'm sorry for what happened with Natalie. She's had a rough week."

"Isn't that every week?" Sophia said.

He looked at her blankly.

"Not trying to be mean," she said. "But maybe you should stop trying to be so nice."

"You can't be too nice, Sophia." He leaned back into the chair. "Right, Sarah?"

"Umm...." I said. "In what sense?"

"Sarah inspired me the other day. To stop trying to hitch a ride on a different plane and instead to buy a ticket with Natalie, to take her plane." He tapped the chair and waited for us to respond. "Isn't that what I should do?"

Sophia looked him right in the eyes. "Are you happy?"

He switched positions in his chair.

"Yes? No?"

He stood. "Since when does it have to do with my happiness? That girl in there has shown me the complete opposite. You should see the gift she made me put together for her funeral. How can I concern myself with my own happiness when she has taught me to do the complete opposite?"

Sophia shook her head and touched my knee. "What do you think, Sarah?"

"Oh, no. Not me. I don't ha—"

"No. Let's hear it. What do you think? Should he marry someone who will make him miserable?"

"I don't know."

"What would you do?"

"Well, if I knew I was going to be miserable I wouldn't marry that person because I wouldn't really be able to love him fully. Then we'd both be miserable."

"I'm not going to be miserable," he said.

Sophia stood and walked toward Anastasia's room. "Suit yourself."

Him and I stared at each other, expressionless, for what seemed like seventy years. I don't know about him, but I barely realized he was there. He became the subject my eyes rested on as I mulled over my own decisions. When I realized we had been spaced out and staring at each other for so long, I laughed. Then he laughed. Then I laughed harder. Before we knew it we were both laughing so hard we were holding our stomachs. It didn't make sense and it didn't need to. We proved, in that instant, that beauty didn't need to wait until after the rain passed. It could flourish amidst the pelting droplets too, if only we stopped once in a while, ditched our umbrellas, and let the water drench our souls.

 *nineteen*

A nastasia illuminated the room like the sun she'd soon leave behind. Everyone gathered around in fold-up chairs as she rested her tiny body on the couch, tucked beneath a teal and white striped blanket. Vasili and I stood in front of everyone as Sophia introduced us and the purpose behind our play. Behind us, the patio doors revealed flurries glimmering in the moonlight as they landed on the already white landscape.

A white Christmas.

Her last.

She knew it and yet her face glowed like it was her first. *For you, sweet one,* I said inside.

And so we began.

AT THE END OF THE REAL STORY OF "IT'S A WONDERFUL LIFE," the town comes together and gifts George with money to pay his debt. That wasn't the best gift though. The best was the gift of friendship and the idea that his one life, albeit unknowingly, touched many others with a rippling effect. Like Clarence writes on a card at the end, "No man is a failure who has friends."

So, at the end, we all stood there doting over the fake money sprawled across the floor, then we turned toward Anastasia who was delighted beyond compare.

"My dear, dear Anastasia," Vasili said. "I remember holding your little baby self during your baptism. I was only twenty two years old and feared being your godfather. I wondered if I had what it takes to be there for you in that way, but you made it so easy. We always joked that you came into the

113

world smiling. And look at you know." His voice quivered as a tear fell from her eye. "You're still smiling. You've taught me more than I could've ever taught you. Thank you."

He sat beside her, kissed her forehead, and held her hand as one person after another expressed their gratitude for the stamp she inked into their lives.

Finally, it was my turn, with only Yanni and Sophia left. I knit my hands together and thumbed my compression garments, then focused on Anastasia.

"Anastasia, you and I have a lot in common, which is probably why Vasili wanted us to meet. We both suffered from terrible burns and have scars in the same places. We both endured mean stares and too many nights in hospitals. We both know the feeling of hearing the doctor say, 'I'm sorry, but the tumor is cancerous.' We both have a love for life and people. And people who know us would say we are filled with joy. But"—I swallowed hard—"there's one thing we don't have in common. I've smiled and made decisions not out of true love for life and people, but out of fear of what they might think of me if I didn't do what was expected of me. I wanted to die when I woke from a coma, but you've shown me how selfish that is. You've shown me so many reasons to live."

I looked down as everyone clapped and dabbed their eyes with tissues, then I moved aside, next to the Christmas tree, as Yanni and Sophia took center stage, gripping each other's hands so hard their knuckles turned pale.

"My sweet baby." Sophia tried to hold it together, but her entire body shook like a leaf on the verge of a storm. "I had four miscarriages before you and the doctor told me I'd never be able to carry a child to full term, but Father Thomas told me not to worry about it, that God had plans for the child we'd bring into the world. Eleven months later you were born at forty-two weeks. I remember relishing that time with you inside of me. It was just me and you. Your little feet in my ribs all night. Your life has brought joy to so many others, in such a short time. And now it's coming to an end, but the colors you've brought to our lives will never fade. Still, I can't help but feel like I did long ago, selfishly wanting to keep you in my womb so I could enjoy you. I don't want to say goodbye..." She trailed off as Yanni held her in his arms and closed his eyes.

Then, he began, "I'm not good with words, darling. I don't know how to say what I feel. You're my little girl. You've made my life sparkle and glitter, literally. Everyone keeps telling me to take a shower. Get out for a little bit. I can't. I can't leave your side. You are the sunshine in my life. You'll always be my little girl."

Anastasia wiped her glossy cheeks as her parents wrapped her in their arms.

Vasili and I escorted everyone except Eleni and Kyriakos to the door, then Eleni and I cleaned the house as everyone else helped Anastasia back to her room. An hour later, Vasili emerged. "You guys can go in if you want. She's sleeping now."

Eleni did. I didn't wanted to intrude.

Vasili stood by the patio doors and pressed his palm against the glass. He stood there a while. Not saying a word.

"Where's Natalie?" I said.

"In LA."

"For Christmas?"

"She had a winter beauty show she was invited to. Really good opportunity for her."

"But wh—"

"If we bundle you up really well, could you handle an adventure?"

I laughed. "What?"

"You. Me. Snow. Can you handle it or not?"

"I ... uh ... I gue—"

"Great. Be right back."

 *twenty*

We laughed as we stood in front if each other. He waddled to the back door in his brother's snow suit. His brother is two sizes taller and broader, so it was quite hilarious. I followed behind in Sophia's snow gear. Thankfully we were similar in size.

"What are we doing exactly?" I stepped into the cold winter night, thankful I had many layers to keep warm.

He helped me down the steps of the deck and grabbed an enormous plastic tube thing from a small shed. Looked better suited for white water rafting, if you ask me.

"This way," he said, tromping through almost two feet of snow.

I covered my face with my scarf so only my eyes were showing. "I'm gonna pay for this later."

"I never charge for fun." He gave me his hand. "Hold my hand and pull yourself up the hill with my help. It'll be easier."

We finally made it to the top of the hill. Finally. I didn't die.

"Whoa." I looked down the opposite side of the hill. "Um. We're going down the side we just walked up, right?"

He shook his head and pointed down an extremely steep hill. Two shakes from a cliff.

"But there's trees at the bottom," I said through my scarf.

"Do you trust me?" He slapped the raft thing against the snow and put his foot on it. "Come on. You've been saying you want to feel like a kid again. Most adults stay inside when it snows and make their kids shovel the sidewalks. So, let's be kids."

"What if—"

"None of that." He tapped the raft. "Sit."

"Well, I almost died once. What the heck."

He laughed, his breath swirling amidst snow flakes. I sat down and held the handles next to me, worrying my grip wouldn't be tight enough. He sat across from me and smiled like a mischievous four-year-old up to no good. I attempted to smile back.

He counted to three and pushed off the snow with his hand. We whirled into circles so fast I didn't have time to crawl back to safety. The world spun behind him as I held on for dear life. Then something happened.

My worry shifted to excitement and my adrenaline kicked in. Midway down the hill Vasili screamed, "Wahoo," and waved his hands in the air like a toddler would. I laughed so hard I forgot we were now twenty feet from a row of trees. I shrieked as he pulled the handles like a race horse and leaned back. We slid to a stop only a few feet from a tree trunk. Out of breath, he fell back into the snow and laughed.

I looked around. At him. At the snowflakes. At the wispy hills and snow-capped trees. He was right. I felt like a kid again. And I liked it.

"Let's do it again," I yelled.

He popped up. "Really?"

I smiled. "Yes."

"I've never seen you smile so big."

I touched my mouth and felt my scarf instead. "How can you tell?"

"Your eyes."

"After the accident my mom stayed by my side almost the entire time. She said she could tell when I needed more pain medication or rest or food or just about anything by the look in my eyes."

"Your eyes are deep. I've noticed that from the start."

"You're the only person besides her to say that." I looked down. "What about Natalie?"

"Follow me." He pointed toward a path that seemed to go around the hill. We began walking and he continued, "She's different. You're reflective. She's too busy looking out to look in."

"How'd you guys meet?"

"Freshman year of high school. I sat next to her in Algebra and swore I'd marry her."

"Wow. You've been together almost twenty years?"

"No. We were friends at first, then dated a little our senior year. She went to California for college and I stayed here for school." He drew in a breath, then another. "She came back and we ran into each other at the grocery store. We were both getting bananas. She calls it love at second sight."

"What do you love about her?"

"She has a good heart. I know my family doesn't agree and after what she's said to you, maybe you don't either. She is book smart. Her grades in school were incredible and she had a scholarship to every school she applied for. She's just not the smartest socially. She says things at the wrong time and it makes her seem a little out there, but I always loved that about her. Even if people hate her, she's not afraid to be herself." We finally reached the top of the hill. "I could give you a million reasons I love her. The better question to ask is ... what does she love about me?"

"Well ... what?"

He shrugged. "Beats me."

"Oh, come on."

"Ask her sometime." He helped me on to the raft. "And fill me in."

"You seem to really love her. I hope someday I find someone like you." Did I really just say that? "I mean, who loves me like that. I'm content now. After everything with James I'm content to be single for life, I think."

He sat across from me. "What happened with that?"

"With James?"

He nodded.

"I'll explain over some hot tea when we go inside." I leaned forward and squeezed the handles. "I'm ready."

He grinned and shoved us into a spinning adventure. Amazing how similar it felt to a roller coaster ride. I couldn't get enough. When we got to the bottom I begged to go again.

"I don't know," he said. "You sure? The snow is picking up."

"Maybe I am getting a tad ahead of myself." I pulled the scarf from my mouth and inhaled. "This just feels so good."

We admired the real life snow globe for a few more minutes, then forced our legs to carry us back.

We changed and warmed up inside. Eleni and Kyriakos were gone.

Yanni and Sophia were sleeping in Anastasia's room. I put on a kettle of water and Vasili set two mugs on the counter, then backed away.

"I still get uncomfortable with hot water around," he said.

"Yeah. I still flinch when people light a fireplace." I shuddered. "I don't think I'll ever be able to go camping again."

"I don't blame you." He leaned against the counter as I poured the water over the tea bags. "So, what happened with James? Is he still bothering you?"

"He's never bothered me." I opened the refrigerator. "Do you like milk in your tea?"

"Never tried it."

"Are you serious?"

"Is it that good?"

I grabbed the sugar canister. "What about sugar?"

"Yes to that." He smiled. "I thought you didn't eat sugar?"

"I concede for a good cup of delightful tea." I realized I was standing on my toes and pursing my lips.

"Are you advertising for tea now?"

"Are you buying?"

He laughed as I stirred the milk and sugar into both cups.

"Don't you love that sound?" I said, stirring once more. "Nothing like the clang of a spoon against a tea cup."

He laughed again. "You're quite the tea lady."

"I like that." I brought the steamy mug to my lips and inhaled the sweet aroma. "The tea lady."

I handed him his cup and we made our way to the couches. The soft glow from the Christmas tree lights blanketed the room with an amber hue. No other lights were on. I had never spent a Christmas Eve without my family, but at Sophia's I felt at home. These people really became family to me. I still missed my own, but Anastasia was worth being away for Christmas and my family agreed.

"I should get going soon," I said, realizing it was after midnight.

"After tea I'll drive you home. Weather looks pretty bad." He sipped his tea and raised his eyebrows. "Wow. That's the best tea I've ever had."

"Oh, stop." I waved his words away. "Don't make fun."

"I'm serious." He started gulping.

"Whoa, whoa. Tea is to be savored, not gulped."

He looked up, grinning from behind his mug. "So, will you get back with James?"

"Absolutely not."

"Why?"

"I'm not ready for that right now. Not with him. Not with anyone. Probably never."

"Never what?"

I cupped my hands around the warm mug and reclined on the love seat so that I was facing Vasili. He did the same on the couch.

"Never ... you know." Why did I suddenly feel shy with him?

"Never be in a relationship?"

I nodded without meeting his eyes.

"That's ridiculous. A girl like you—" He stopped himself. "There's no reason for you to rule out marriage."

"There are a lot of reasons, if you ask me."

"Like what?"

"Have you looked at me?"

"All the time."

I tried to ignore that. He meant nothing by it. He couldn't. He loved Natalie. The beautiful girl with a ring the size of my head on her finger.

"Well," I said. "Then you know I'm not exactly pretty."

"Would you quit doing that?" A subtle agitation rose in his voice.

"Doing what?"

"Thinking so negatively of yourself."

"I'm not. It is what it is. The mirror tells me so."

"Have you ever thought for once that when you look in the mirror you are hyper aware of your flaws? When the rest of us may see something different. Like a teenager with a pimple. She doesn't focus on her beautiful eyes and cute lips, she zeros in on the one tiny flaw and goes nuts over it." He put his hands behind his head and looked at the ceiling. "You need to stop obsessing over your scars. It's only a quarter of your face and I can't tell you the last time I noticed."

"It's not just that." My pulse quickened. "My chest. It's gone. Every bit."

He sat up and looked me right in the eyes. "And?"

"And ... I'm not ... It just wouldn't be kind of me to subject some poor man to a breastless wife with most of her body scarred."

"Kind of you?"

I tried not to cry, but I couldn't stop the single tear that escaped my walls. Neither of us said a word for minutes. Our empty tea cups cooled as we stared at the Christmas tree.

"I got you something," I said. "It's in my bag. There beside you."

He reached to the ground and pulled the silver-wrapped rectangle from my bag. I motioned for him to go on. After peeling all of the paper off, he surveyed the picture with serious eyes.

"Do you like it?" My words seemed to snap him out of a trance.

"I do. How did you know?"

"It's part of a series. The one in your living room is the first of three. The entire series is called 'Out of Adversity.'" I hoped he didn't realize it was me who photographed them. "That's the second of the three."

"How did you find it? It wasn't signed. I couldn't figure out who the photographer was."

"I'm a photographer, remember? I have my connections."

"Thank you." He held eye contact again. "Seriously, Sarah. Thank you."

I WOKE UP TO VASILI STARING AT THE PHOTOGRAPH I GAVE him. He looked tired, but not as tired as me.

"I fell asleep." I rolled to my side. "What time is it?"

"Three." He yawned. "Just sleep. It's too late and roads are bad. Do you have meds for tomorrow?"

I nodded. "Yes. Thanks to Ella the Organization Queen, I come prepared."

"Good. Sleep then."

SOPHIA WOKE ME UP, SHAKING MY SHOULDER AND SCREAM-ing. She coughed into her shirt. I couldn't move. Someone tied me to the couch. Panicking, I tugged at the ropes and wailed. The Christmas tree, on fire, engulfed the living room into flames. I couldn't see Vasili. Or anyone. Only Sophia as she ran out the front door and left me tied to the couch.

"IT'S JUST A DREAM. WAKE UP, SARAH." VASILI'S VOICE. I opened my eyes to a bright living room. Rays of sun catching everything in sight.

"What was it?" He was holding my hand and kneeling on the floor beside me. "You were flipping out."

"Did I wake anyone?"

"No. You didn't make sounds. Just started shaking your head like crazy."

"When will the nightmares end? They're terrible. So real." He helped me sit up.

Sophia entered the living room and jumped. "Oh. You guys scared me. What are you doing here so early?"

"We slept on the couches." Vasili stood and rubbed his eyes. "How is she?"

"I was just coming out to call you." Her hands were shaking. "Her breathing is labored. I called Laura and a few others. They think she has a few hours to a couple of days left."

"She made it to Christmas," Vasili said.

"And some Christmas it is." Sophia leaned into the back of the couch, hanging her head so her face was masked by her hair.

"She wouldn't want you to think like that, Sophia. Try to be strong. She's okay. She's not scared."

Sophia whipped her head back and breathed hard and fast, then paced behind the couch.

"Calm down. Please. For her." Vasili tried to reach toward her, but pulled back.

"This is my daughter." She paced in another tight circle. "My baby. Do you have any idea what it's like to hold my little girl knowing that in just a few days some guys are going to come and force me to put her dead body on a stretcher? Do you have any idea what that's like?" Hyperventilating, she tapped her chest as though her heart needed help beating, then fell to the floor.

Vasili and I knelt beside her. No words. Just our hands on her back as she wet the floor with her heartbreak and occasionally murmured, "My baby. No. Why my baby?"

I wanted to take it away. I wanted to sweep up the broken pieces of her heart and make them whole again. But I couldn't. Her baby would soon be gone. And the hole in her chest would never be fixed.

Could never be.

I rubbed her back, praying that somehow, together, we'd all have the strength to deal with the colossal wounds in our chests.

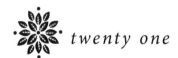 *twenty one*

S weeping strands of sunlight sat atop the mounds of snow as Anastasia's breathing slowed. Her eyes, closed ever so gently, may never see daylight again, I thought inside as I divided my gaze between her peaceful face to the peaceful face of the earth outside her window.

The curtains billowed from the flow of heat beneath them as squirrels skipped along the backyard. For a suburban house, their backyard seemed to have no end.

I watched Anastasia. Vasili, Sophia, and Yanni did too. Eleni and Kyriakos were on their way, but the messy streets would make it difficult. According to Laura, many of these children experience complications near the end of their battle, but thankfully Anastasia's last moments of life, so far, proved uneventful. As serene as her.

I think we all secretly hoped Anastasia would open her eyes and warm our hearts with her smile. One last time. But somehow I doubted.

I put on a kettle and started the coffee maker. Not sure anyone would want it at the moment, but I needed to busy myself. The melancholy look on Yanni and Sophia's faces pained me. With each tick of the clock we knew we were a step closer to holding a lifeless child. I listened to the coffee machine gurgle as I begged God to take me instead, knowing that my requests wouldn't be granted.

Vasili stepped beside me. "You okay?"

"Are you?"

He nodded. "I have peace about it."

"How?" A surge of frustration prickled my mind. "How can you have peace when everything is so messed up? I should be dead right now. Not like this." I sighed. "She should be alive. Not me."

"Maybe. Maybe we can spend our lives thinking of should's and should not's. Or maybe we can accept what actually is and believe that there's some kind of purpose in it."

"But it's not fair. I didn't want to live. I woke up in the hospital and begged to die. I dreamed of someone slipping me pills to end it all easily. And here I am. Alive. When other people who actually want to live shouldn't be dying."

"You don't want to live?"

I shook my head. "I'm okay with it now."

"That's not what I asked." He waited for me to respond, but I didn't. "I don't admire that. Death isn't some kind of escape from life. There's no such thing. Besides, a few scars on your body is not a big deal. There are others who have no limbs and manage to enjoy life."

"I know, I know." I pulled a few mugs from the cabinet. "Want tea?"

"Coffee. Thanks."

"I'm just saying ... it's hard to watch someone so full of life die."

He nodded. "I could say the same about you. Don't have to take your last breath to die, you know?"

We sipped our warm drinks in silence, then brought coffee to Yanni and Sophia.

Yanni held Anastasia's hand as he stroked her hair with the other, while Sophia curled up beside her daughter and kissed her head every few seconds.

Hours passed. My body ached from sledding and my skin felt tighter than usual. I sat in a comfy chair in the corner of the room and tried to process the scene before me.

At some point I woke up. Everything looked the same. Except I was covered in a blanket. Vasili sat on the floor beside me with headphones in his ears and an iPad on his lap. I glanced down to see what he was doing. Looked like reading. He yanked the headphones from his ears and mouthed, "Feeling okay?"

I nodded.

Sophia gasped and Yanni stood.

"Is that it?" Sophia cried, pulling her daughter into her chest and looking into her husband's eyes. "Is she gone?"

He nodded his head.

Vasili inched toward the bed and made a cross symbol over her body, then guided some kind of black rope through his fingers. I noticed he stopped on each knot and held it a few seconds, then moved to the next. Anastasia's arms fell limp beside her body as Sophia sobbed and drenched them both in tears. I felt wrong being there for such an intimate moment. Vasili must've sensed it, because he walked over to me and said, "She wanted you here. So do we."

I nodded, but kept my distance.

After an hour, Sophia calmed down and let Yanni hold Anastasia. Kyriakos and Eleni entered the room and immediately welled up. I retreated to the bathroom and cried where no one could see. Such a beautiful life ... over. Just like that.

Throughout my life I attended a total of four funerals, but never watched someone take their last breath.

Sobering.

I thought of the photographs we took and the slideshow she had me make. Reality seeped its way in. Only a few weeks ago her funeral was just a plan. Not a reality.

Now, the world was a little darker. A little less colorful.

TWO EXTREMELY KIND MEN FROM DANIELSON'S FUNERAL Home brought a stretcher into Anastasia's bedroom.

Yanni set his little one on the white sheets and held her face in his hands. "My little one." He kissed her forehead and her cheeks.

Sophia did the same, then we all took turns saying goodbye.

Yanni and Sophia walked beside the stretcher as the two men carried it outside. The rest of us watched from the front door as Yanni lifted the sheet over Anastasia's head and stepped back.

Her body disappeared into the back of their vehicle. They exchanged a few words and Yanni and Sophia walked back to the porch and stood, arms crossed, as the red taillights turned the corner.

It was official.

December 25th at 3:46pm Anastasia Sophia Koursaris left the world and took our hearts with her.

VASILI INSISTED ON DRIVING ME HOME, BUT I INSISTED I WAS
okay. He won the argument and took me back to Ella's. When we parked I
didn't see their cars, but I saw James standing on the porch with his hands
in his pockets. Of all days.

"Want me to stay until he leaves?" Vasili said. "He looks drunk."

"I'll be okay."

He nodded with apprehension as I opened the car door. James whistled
and waved as I walked up to him. I turned back and urged Vasili to go, but
he stayed there.

"Who's that?" James touched the hem of my coat.

"You're drunk. What are you doing here?"

"It's Christmas. All I want for Christmas is you."

I unlocked the door. "Come inside."

He swung his legs as though it took great effort, then fell into the
couch.

I stood at the bottom of the steps. "I need to change and do my burn
routine."

"Why? Where've you been?"

"Anastasia died. I was with her family."

"Who's Anas ... Anastia?"

"Wait here."

I sat on my bed and looked around, imagining Sophia probably in her
daughters bed. The funeral director said they could come to the church
the night before the funeral and hold Anastasia until morning. I couldn't
imagine.

I pulled my shirt up and over my head, then began taking my compression garments off. A few minutes later I stood in front of the mirror.

I ran my fingers across the scars. I no longer had any resemblance of
being a woman, or even a man, while looking at my chest. Scars upon scars.
My doctors kept telling me to see a plastic surgeon when my skin could
handle it, but I didn't see the point of adding two fake boobs to a chest full
of scars purely for aesthetics. I just wasn't sure if I'd ever be able to love my

new body. Fake boobs or not. Vasili didn't understand. I could never make love to a man like this. Not even with the lights off.

James appeared in the doorway, smirking. "Look at you."

I held my shirt against my chest. "I'm not finished."

He raised his eyebrows. "All I want for Christmas is you."

"You're not having me. Not now. Not ever." I stepped back as he came toward me. "You're drunk. Leave now or I'm calling the cops." He stepped again. "I'm serious."

He grabbed my arm and shoved me into the wall.

"Stop." I jerked away, but he forced me against the wall again. "James. Stop."

"I'm going to show you that I still think you're beautiful."

He squeezed my arms so hard I felt like my skin would rip apart. I kicked my feet, but he forced me over his shoulder and dropped me on the bed.

"Smile for the camera." He pointed his phone at me. "So sexy now. Come on, you can do better than that."

I wanted to scream and punch him in the face. Or give him a list of reasons why he was unattractive too. Instead, I pressed my face into the bed and mentally traced the lines on my quilt as I did when my sister and her boyfriends made fun of me years ago.

"Bug eyes."

"You're taller than a bean stalk."

"Your legs look like toothpicks."

"You're so pale. Are you sick?"

"Amazon lady."

"Your stomach isn't flat enough."

"That mousey hair. It washes you out."

"Is that what you call a dress?"

"Your teeth are yellow."

"Are those love handles?"

"Your shoe size is bigger than my head."

"You should wear your hair down. Those ears stick out too much."

"Your hair is too frizzy."

"Your nose is too big."

"Your lips aren't big enough."

Too much and not enough. All at the same time.

By my senior year my sister was away at college. She didn't get to see when I was voted prom queen and Most Beautiful in my class. She wouldn't have cared anyway. People always told me girls are mean to other girls when they're jealous. They don't feel beautiful within themselves, so they refuse to see beauty in everyone else. Their lives become one big game of tearing down others to feel good about themselves. Except they never feel good about themselves. They never feel good about anything. Whether they realize it or not, they paint everything ugly.

I refused to be like that. I told myself I'd always see beauty in everything. Even in an eel or a flower everyone despises. I became a photographer to capture beauty in things others missed or discarded. Every day I inspired others as I constantly preached to them about looking for beauty in all things.

And now, lying half-naked and humiliated, I found it difficult to see the beauty of my own imperfect body.

I drew in a breath and looked at the Edmund Blair Leighton painting on my wall. A young woman in a flowing white dress reached down from her balcony to give a grinning man a flower. The artist called it *A Favour*. How I longed to jump inside the painting and become a beautiful woman smiling down at a winsome fellow.

James continued taunting me, saying he wasn't much of a breast man anyway. I closed my eyes and tuned him out, imagining waves lapping against a shore. Camera in hand, I looked for hidden beauty to photograph. So easy to take a picture of the pastel sunrise. Instead, I waited for something unexpected.

My imagination wandered for minutes until James jerked me up and forced me to look at the pictures on his phone.

I came back to reality, away from the shores of my imagination, and pretended to smile. "Merry Christmas."

"Yeah," he said. "Now you'll marry me or I'll post these images all over the Internet."

I covered my chest with a pillow. "What have I got to lose?"

"Fine. You want me to do it? I will. Right now."

"Go ahead."

"You wanna play that game, huh?"

"I'm not playing any games. My life is already upside down. I'm not pretending to be pretty anymore, James. Just do whatever makes you happy."

"What makes me happy is you."

"Funny way of showing that."

He shoved his phone into his pocket. "Do I really have to blackmail you to marry me?"

"There's no blackmailing. Do what you want. I'm not marrying you."

He swung his arms and raked a hand through his hair. I clutched the pillow tighter and hoped Ella would be home soon. James tried to speak, but said nothing.

Our eyes met for a brief moment. Quick enough to mean nothing, but long enough for me to notice his bottom lip quivering.

"Please go," I said.

"Go where?" He slumped into the chair across from me and covered his eyes with his hand. "I have no one. Just Abby."

"Your parents."

"They hate me. Since my brother died, they hate me. They blame me for every problem and flaw they have, like I could possibly be to blame for milk they spilled when I don't even live there." He sighed and knelt down in front of me. "I'm sorry, Sarah." His eyes reddened around the edges. "I've been a complete jerk and I know it. I've been spending more time at the bar than with Abby." He squeezed the arm of the chair until his hand turned red. "For the entire year after the accident I tried to love you like before, but you didn't receive it. You've barely wanted me around since this happened. It's made me feel insane. I've been hurt and angry. Ripping old pictures of us, then scrambling to tape them back together. I thought maybe if I hurt you that it would wake you up. I don't know what to do." He hung his head. "Everything I love ... whatever I touch ... I mess it all up."

"I forgive you, James."

He looked up at me. "Really?"

I nodded.

"Do you love me?"

I hesitated, then whispered, "Yes."

"Do you love me, Sarah?"

"I said yes."

"Show me."

I closed my eyes. "James."

"No. If you love me, show me."

"I care about you. I love you the same way I love my other friends."

"How did we come to this?" He walked to the door. "If I would've put that fire out like you asked we'd be married right now."

"Maybe." I pulled my feet onto my bed. "Maybe we'd be happily married. Or maybe not. Maybe this happened to show us that eventually this would've happened in some way. If love can't survive flames, then maybe it wasn't love to begin with."

"Speak for yourself," he said, then slammed the door.

The wall next to it shook, tilting a picture of Ella and I when we were kids. I felt bad for James. Life dealt him a tough hand. His choices and lack of self-control throughout life seemed to backfire in his face all the time. Initially, I was attracted to him for that very reason. I saw a cute guy who needed a little sunshine in his life. Everyone always called me "Sunshine," so who better, right? We were happy at first. So long as I made him feel valued, even if it meant ignoring my true feelings.

Like one day when Ella and I wanted to go out to eat and James had a nervous breakdown when I told him we were traveling to Baltimore for the day. He tried to say he was worried because his brother died in a car crash, but really he didn't want me finding someone else. He threw such a fit about it that we never left. I told Ella I didn't feel good. She met up with Dee instead. I thought James would come over, but as soon as I told him I was staying home he decided to go to a bar with his friends.

I ignored his excessive gambling, visits to strip clubs, and depressive episodes where he threatened to kill himself if I went out with my friends. I ignored it all. I felt bad for him ... and Abby. I thought I could fix him. Give him a happy life.

I didn't realize in the process I'd lose my own.

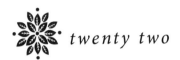 *twenty two*

Worried I'd forget something, I checked my bag over and over again. Anastasia had specific instructions and I didn't want to let her down. After verifying I had everything I needed—for the sixth time—I put on a pair of black flats. Anastasia requested we all wear teal at her funeral instead of black, but I didn't own anything teal and forgot to buy something, so I asked Ella if I could borrow something of hers. I preferred loose fitting shirts for now. With that in mind, she gave me a teal shirt dress that buttoned down and fell to my knees. I wore black leggings underneath. With my coat, scarf, and intentional hair swooping down the side of my face, I appeared somewhat like the old me.

Part of me didn't like it though. I wanted to stop hiding. Completely.

I hung the bag over my shoulder and walked downstairs. Ella stood in the kitchen, hunched over the counter crying.

"What's wrong?" I set the bag down on a barstool and touched her back. "Ella?"

She laughed. "Just these darn onions."

"Onions?"

"They're making my eyes water so bad. I can barely cut them without closing my eyes." She tossed a handful of diced onion and red pepper into a large pot. "Whew. Never had that happen before."

I walked back to my bag. "I was rather alarmed. I thought maybe you were more normal than it seems."

She wiped her hands on her apron. "What's that supposed to mean?"

"Your life seems so perfect sometimes that I want to throw up."

"Wow. Thanks."

I laughed. "It just seems like you and Gavin never argue. Everything is golden. Beautiful girl. Gorgeous husband. Sweet baby. Successful business. Dream house."

"Gavin and I argue."

"I've been here almost five months and haven't heard a peep."

"Well, we don't scream across the house, but we argue."

"About what?"

"Little things, big things. I don't know. Sometimes I get annoyed at silly things. I'll get on him for loading the dishwasher wrong, making the mattress sink, kissing me while I'm drinking something and making it spill down my shirt. Things like that. Or he gets upset with me for pushing my standards on everyone around me and getting mad at people when they make—what I consider—the wrong decisions. We had a disagreement because I wanted to keep Adelaide in the bedroom with us until she turns one, but he said six month max."

Gavin walked into the room with Adelaide in his arms. "What are you guys talking about?"

"How you guys are more normal than it seems," I said. "Sometimes it feels like you set an impossible bar for romance and marriage."

He laughed. "No way. We love each other, but it's not like we stare into each other's eyes every night."

Ella smirked. "Last time we had sex was ... what?"

"Seven months ago," he said.

"What?" I said. "Why?"

"Ella was uncomfortable the last two months of her pregnancy and we haven't had a chance since Adelaide."

"Haven't had a chance." I smiled. "Well, you are more real than I thought. Thanks for sharing."

"Yes," Gavin said. "Always willing to discuss my failings if it helps another dear soul find meaning and joy in this—"

"Alright, smarty pants," Ella said. "We'll see you later, Sarah. I hope everything goes well. Give the family our love."

I nodded, said goodbye, and closed the front door. It took me a few minutes to walk to my car. The cool air felt so good and I needed to prepare myself for what I was about to endure. Never in my life had I seen a child in a casket and I'm not sure I wanted to.

But I couldn't let her down.

I STOOD AT THE BACK OF THE CHURCH FEELING QUITE OUT of place. Everything whirled by in one huge blur of confusion and strangeness. Eventually I mustered up the nerve to walk inside the sanctuary.

Sophia, Yanni, Mama Koursaris, Kyriakos, Eleni, Vasili, and Natalie sat in the front row of the church, to the right of the open casket. Surprisingly, they weren't crying.

I sat in the back and watched the service unfold. Most of it seemed incomprehensible to me. I'd never been to an Orthodox service before and most of it was in Greek.

One section stood out to me though. In English the priest said some things about being made beautiful by God, but the word "scars" struck me when he said something like, "Though I bear the scars of my stumblings, have compassion on me."

After that I tuned out again, dreading the talk Anastasia wanted me to give during her slideshow. Hopefully at a distance no one would be able to see my face. I tried to cover the scars as much as I could.

Together the church sang, "May her memory be eternal," what seemed like a thousand times until finally everyone left the pews to greet the family in the first row and pay their respects to Anastasia.

I didn't want to.

I wanted to skirt around her casket and avoid seeing her. It made me nervous. Especially being up there on the altar in front of everyone.

I greeted the family, stopping at Sophia to give her a hug and a kiss on the cheek. She tried her best to remain calm, but her wet cheeks betrayed her.

I turned toward the casket where another person stood, holding Anastasia's little hand and kissing her forehead. I swallowed and walked up the steps. Hands clasped in front of me, I waited.

The woman in front of me sniffed and stepped away.

There she lay. Flowers in her hands. Picture frames and letters tucked into the edges of her beautifully adorned casket. She wore the dress from our photography session and a cross necklace sparkled on top of her chest.

So peaceful.

I cupped my hand over hers and willed the tears away, then kissed her cheek and stepped aside. Surreal. Only a few days ago she reclined on the couch, beaming at our rendition of her favorite movie.

I imagined plenty of adorable memories as I stood at the back of the church.

After everyone said their goodbyes, the family stood one-by-one. Kyriakos and Eleni went first. Then Natalie and Vasili. They all managed to maintain a serene composure.

Finally, Sophia and Yanni stood. Yanni pulled his wife into his chest and helped her up the steps. For a few seconds, they stared at their daughter. The entire church remained so silent I could hear the person in front of me breathe. Sophia held a tissue to her face and leaned forward, resting her head on Anastasia's chest as she filled the silence with high-pitched sobs. Yanni placed one hand on his daughters head and the other on his wife's back.

They stayed like that for minutes as many faces in the room watched, blinking, a fresh dew of heartache covering their faces. And mine.

Sophia quieted, then placed her cheek against Anastasia's. I covered my mouth and closed my eyes, biting back my own tears.

Yanni kissed Anastasia's forehead, then backed away and pulled Sophia with him. Two men placed their hands on the couple's back, then, with Yanni's assistance, they closed the casket. A soft, yet profound thud echoed through the room, stilling everyone with its glaring closure.

"Goodbye, sweet one," I whispered.

AFTER THE BURIAL WE ALL LEFT THE CEMETERY. MY STOMACH twisted in knots as I drove back to the church. The slideshow didn't bother me. Standing in front of hundreds of people did. Thankfully Anastasia gave me a letter to read to everyone, although I promised not to open it until it was time to read it. So at least I didn't have to prepare my own words to stumble over.

People arrived in the church hall a little at a time. When it seemed like almost everyone found a seat and began eating, Vasili walked up to me.

"I've got something Anastasia wanted me to show everyone," he said. "She said for you to do yours right before."

I nodded.

He stood on a small stage, microphone in hand, and pointed toward a screen.

"Attention, everyone. As many of you know, Anastasia spent the last few months preparing her own memorial service. During that time I saw her writing a lot of letters and asking others to help her plan surprises. I knew she'd eventually ask me for help and sure enough, she did. On December 22 her health severely declined. We hoped she'd make it to the surprise we had for her on Christmas Eve, and she did, barely. On December 23rd she asked me to record a video of her saying goodbye. I'm going to show that video today, but first a dear friend of ours, Sarah Jordan, has something to share."

The letter in my hands, still sealed, shook terribly as I walked up to Vasili and took the mic. I stood somewhat sideways and positioned myself so my scars were less visible, then handed Vasili a disc. "She wanted this to play."

He walked away and within a few seconds the slideshow started.

"The pictures taken on this slideshow were shot only weeks before today." I tapped my foot, hoping to dispel my anxiety. "She wanted me to read a letter while these images were shown. I haven't read it yet." I opened it and unfolded the paper. "So here goes."

Dear family and friends,

A lot of you think of me as happy. It's true, we have happy memories together, but today I want to admit something.

Daddy always told me to think good thoughts. He said bad thoughts make bad people. I've been trying to have good thoughts since they told me I have cancer and when kids at school made fun of me when I got burned. For lots of days I've been trying to be happy because I hoped maybe my happy thoughts would keep me alive.

It wasn't working but I learned something anyway and that's why I had these pictures taken.

I may be young but I'm not stupid. I knew I was dying for a while and even when people tried to hide the bad news from me I saw it on Mom's face. I had a lot of bad dreams and thought a lot of bad thoughts until one day it clicked.

I thought I could stay strong for my parents so my last days were happy for all of us, but still write everyone to say the truth.

My truth is that I've been sad and angry sometimes. I saw stories of kids who smile until they die of some disease and end up on the news and I secretly wanted to end up on the news too, but that's not for me.

Because my truth is I haven't been smiling inside all this time, just outside.

I want to live to be sixteen and drive a car. I want to see my cousins who aren't born yet. I want to eat Dad's famous brownies on my birthday next year. I want to have four babies of my own and a cute husband who looks like my dad. I want to travel to Greece and see where my grandparents lived. I want to do a lot of things and I can't. That's made me sad a lot, but I smiled for my mom. She couldn't handle it any other way.

The reason I'm saying this now is because I don't want to be another story of how dying is easy and happy, because it's not. I'm excited to meet God and the angels, but I'm sad to leave all of you.

So for my last words I don't want to pretend anymore and I wish for everyone in the world to stop pretending and hiding all the time. Sometimes there's bad news and sometimes there's good news. Sometimes we have pain and sometimes we have smiles.

I died knowing I'd miss all of you and it hurt me to the very last minute. I may not have told you and it's because I love you. All of you. I didn't want you to be more upset because of my tears, so I smiled for you, but trust me, I was sad to say goodbye.

Think of me, okay? Think of me as you live another year, and maybe another, and when you feel like giving up or hiding ... think of me.

Love always,
Anastasia

I LOOKED INTO THE CROWD. THEIR FACES WORE A MIXTURE of astonishment and pain. Vasili stood beside me and reached for the mic.

"I just have something to add," I wanted to say, but couldn't.

My legs turned to rubber as I walked off the stage, arguing with myself.

Turn back and say something. Show them who you really are.

No. It's embarrassing. This isn't about you anyway. Be quiet. Stand in the background.

Show them how Anastasia inspired you.

I'm not inspired.

People clapped and stood as the last of Anastasia's pictures stayed on the screen. Her swinging in the garden, ice shining beneath her, and a huge, genuine smile dimpling her face.

I stood to the side of the stage as Vasili pressed play on the video and waited for it to begin.

Anastasia's face lit the screen.

"Is it on?" she said. "Oh, the red dot? Okay, it's on." She straightened her posture. "Hi Mom, Dad, everyone. By now you've already read my letter that I gave to Sarah. If you're wondering why I chose her, you'll find out soon enough. I just want to say that since writing that I have come to terms with my death and it's mostly because Vasili has taught me what life is all about and that it doesn't matter what I get to experience or not. He told me what really matters is what I leave behind.

"My mom has a special gift she helped me make everyone. We couldn't make too many because of the time, but we made a hundred. Please take one today and if you don't get one, you can make one yourself.

"I signed up to do Make-A-Wish. I really wanted to see Greece, but I didn't get picked. So my wish is changed and now it's pretty simple. I just wish for everyone else to do something nice for someone every day. Don't let one day be missed, okay?

"Mom, I love you very much. I was awake all those times you cried and watched me sleep. I remember so many times you would hold me and say you're sorry for not being a good mom, then you'd pray that God would help you be a better one. I know you feel like you were too busy and didn't have time for me, but Mom, no mom ever loved a daughter like you love me. Thank you for being the best mom ever.

"Daddy, I'm still your girl. I'll always be your little girl. My best memory with you is all those times you put me on your shoulders and the one time I had ice cream. You kept telling me to be careful and sure enough my ice cream dripped on your face. A huge glob. I thought you were going to yell and put me down, but instead you said, 'Thanks,' wiped it onto your finger, and ate it. Thank you for always making me feel like I was loved and not a burden like some of my other friends dad's do. I spilled cereal all over the floor once and you said, 'Well, now. That's an interesting way to eat cereal.' You taught me to be patient and kind and never let mistakes mess up my day. Thank you, Daddy, for being the kind of prince I wanted to find one day.

"To everyone else, don't forget to be nice to each other. I love you all. Sagapo."

She stared off camera and waved.

"Just hit that button," she said, and that was it.

Gone. With only her footprints left behind.

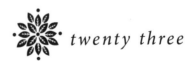 *twenty three*

The weather following Anastasia's funeral described my mood. Cloudy, dreary, but no precipitation. The opaque grey sky stood on the verge of a few drops, but never tossed them to the earth.

I watched crows fly overhead from my bedroom window and thought of Anastasia's desire to make it to spring to see the flowers bloom one more time. Such a simple desire compared to my own.

Perhaps a funeral like that is supposed to change a person, make them want to live and love better. Seeing a child stiffened by death, lying there in a box, alone, no warmth to her touch, no blink of her eyes, affected me, but not the way it should've.

I wished I stood up there after her slideshow, confident and inspired, and gave everyone a speech to remember. I wished I did everything differently.

I should've said what I wanted to say. I replayed it in my mind the way I thought it would go if I had the nerve to speak.

"MY NAME IS SARAH JORDAN," I'D SAY. "I WAS BURNED IN A campfire accident last year." I'd swoop my hair behind my ear to show my scars. "Just today, before coming here, I stopped at the gas station. The pump didn't accept my credit card, so I went inside. The guy in line beside me was gorgeous and he was standing to my left, so he couldn't see my scars. I saw him smile at me out of the corner of my eye, but instead of looking at him and showing him my entire face, I paid for my gas and turned so that he never saw me for who I really am. I liked feeling pretty again. I liked someone not seeing my scars. But Anastasia's right. I'm not

143

pretending anymore. This is me." I'd wipe my face. "This entire day I've been so consumed by my own flaws that I worried more about standing up here and showing everyone my scars, then I worried about Anastasia's grieving parents. I'm so wrapped up in myself and my own issues that I haven't fully loved others.

"The photoshoot with Anastasia was beautiful. One of my favorites. She proved that life isn't about perfection and happiness. She showed me that life is about love. It's about finding beauty in unexpected places. It's about taking the cards we're given and playing them wholeheartedly, not to win, just to play.

"This little girl and her amazingly loving and accepting family have changed my life. I can only hope that when I die, I inspire others as she has inspired me." I'd pause and hold eye contact with Vasili, then say, "Thank you."

I WAS SO MUCH HAPPIER AND INSPIRING IN MY IMAGINATION. So real and brave. I replayed the imaginary speech in my mind many times, but it only caused me to feel more depressed.

My entire life seemed like one big mess of post-it notes with the words "What If" printed on each one.

Anastasia didn't want to die. She wanted to make more memories and see more of the world.

Yet, I woke up each morning with air in my lungs and a beat to my heart, wishing I wouldn't. Wishing she would instead.

Ella kept bugging me to get out of the house all week, so I loosened my grip on the curtains and walked away.

Vasili and Natalie wanted to go over their wedding photography again. Natalie had new ideas. I thought it was a tad too soon to be diving into wedding stuff again, but it was only a few months away and she was excited. Handsome, sweet guy like that. I couldn't blame her if I tried.

I parked outside of a pretty old building on the west side of town. Home of *Rachel's Creperie*. Natalie's choice.

I saw her waving at a table by the window before I even entered. I admired her spunk and energy. Vasili deserved someone who lived so excitedly and passionately.

The bells jingled as I walked in and subconsciously let my hair fall in front of my face. When the hostess approached me I realized my absurdity and pulled my hair back into a low pony tail, revealing every last scar. "I'm meeting a friend. She's right there."

The tattooed girl didn't flinch at my scars. She didn't seem to notice at all actually. Somewhat relieved, I sat across from Natalie and attempted to smile.

"So, I have a surprise." She leaned across the table with wide eyes. "Don't tell him. Okay?"

"Vasili?"

"Yeah. I'm going to surprise him." She sat back in her seat like a normal person. "I don't know how much he's told you, but last year I was offered this incredible opportunity at a salon in LA. Money, celebrities, status, you name it. Obviously I got really excited about it and wanted to take it, but I could tell Vasili didn't want to leave his family. So, all this time I've been pretending to want to live there and I've been taking trips to LA a lot, so he believed it."

"Wait ... why were you going there then? You missed Christmas Eve with Anastasia."

"Well." She wiggled her fingers before resting her palms on the table between us. "It was for Vasili. I'm bringing it up because I need your help with something, but don't want to tell him yet."

"Hey, girls." A waitress stood at our table, pen and paper ready for our orders. "What can I get you today?"

"Oh, I'm sorry." Natalie said. "We haven't looked at the menus yet."

"No problem. Take your time."

I slipped my coat off and hung it on the back of my chair. "So you aren't moving to LA?"

"No." She smiled. "Of course not. I love him too much to see him leave everything he loves. So, here's the—oh, oh, he's here." She twirled the diamonds on her finger with her thumb and stood. "I'll tell you later."

Vasili touched my shoulder and smiled, then gave his future bride a kiss. I looked away, wondering why I felt a sudden urge to hide in the bathroom.

They sat down in front of me. Natalie opened a magazine with beautiful wedding photos. I found myself staring at Vasili's hands, picturing them intertwined with my own.

I berated myself inside, while smiling on the outside.

"Something wrong?" Vasili said, interrupting Natalie.

I shook my head and watched Natalie as she spoke. She was petite and cute, the complete opposite of me. Perfect nose, somewhat full lips, dark eyes that changed color depending on her shirt. Not to mention her fashion-sense. She didn't look uppity, but she looked nice. Put together. Like I used to.

I remembered she was speaking and tried to listen again.

"Do you think we could pull that off?" she said. "I know it's a lot, but I think it will be so beautiful."

I touched the magazine with my fingertips and pulled it toward me. "Yes. We can do this, but we need more equipment than what I have and probably at least three helpers to assist me with lighting."

She looked at Vasili. "What do you think, babe?"

"Whatever you want," he said.

My phone buzzed in my pocket. I peeked under the table as the love bugs ordered lunch.

A text from James:

If I can't be with you, then I'm better off dead. I've written you a goodbye letter and in my will I've given you guardianship of Abigail. It's better this way. For her to have you instead of me.

"And for you?" The waitress said.

"Oh, um, whatever she's having." I glanced at my phone again. The last thing I wanted was to be responsible for someone's death.

Vasili wouldn't stop staring at me. He knew me well enough to know something wasn't right and now I hated that he knew. I hated that I knew him. Hated.

Mom always told me not to say "hate." She used to say, "Not even the devils of the world deserve such a strong emotion directed from us. The only people using that word should be the devils themselves."

But no other word seemed appropriate for the moment. I hated the cards I plucked from the deck and it made me hate the game. Yes, hate.

Somehow my friendship with Vasili planted a false hope in me that I didn't realize existed until now. Naively, I thought a guy like him might like a girl like me, scars and all. So stupid of me. Of course he loved her. She wasn't perfect, but neither was he. How could I possibly be so ridiculous?

Natalie excused herself for a bathroom break.

Vasili thanked the waitress for his iced tea, then looked at me. "What's up, Sarah? You seem preoccupied with something."

I sipped my water and shook my head. "Don't you find it a little strange to go on living when she's gone? It doesn't seem fair."

"Life isn't fair when you play by life's rules. When you play by your own, on the other hand…"

I laughed. "What?"

James walked by the window. With a girl. Cheyenne. Vasili looked over his shoulder when he saw my gaze follow them, them he turned back to me, tapped the table, and turned back again.

I couldn't believe it. He sent me lies about killing himself with my cousin wrapped around his arm? The nerve!

"I gotta go." I stood and tossed a twenty on the table. "I'll talk to you soon."

"You're not running after him, are you?"

"What do you care?" My face flushed with warmth.

"What's going on?" Natalie said. "Sarah? What happened?"

I left without answering her, got into my car, and texted James back. *I saw you with my cousin. You are such an unbelievably psychotic jerk. Stop toying with my life. Leave me alone.*

I had already left the city when he responded. *I saw you with that guy. Smiling and laughing. Wait till I tell his fiancé you two are having an affair.*

Me: *We're not. She was in the bathroom. We were meeting about wedding photography.*

James: *Riiiiight.*

Me: *Unlike you, I don't lie.*

James: *Is that why you hide your scars behind your hair?*

Me: *Leave me alone, James. Just go away now.*

James: *Just because I'm with Cheyenne doesn't mean I wasn't serious about what I said. Do you expect me to sit around single while you help engaged guys have affairs?*

Me: *I'm not even having this conversation. You said it yourself … who would want me?*

I turned my phone off and blasted the radio. Dixie Chick's *I'm Not Ready to Make Nice* came on and I belted it out as though I wrote the lyrics myself.

The nerve! I thought again, slamming my car door and stomping up Ella's front steps. And when would I stop calling my home "Ella's House?" I wanted my own house. I wanted my own life. I wanted a reason to wake up again.

I wanted to take the cards of my life and shuffle them back into the deck, then start over. But I couldn't and I was frustrated beyond reason.

I walked back down the front steps and stood in the front yard, staring at the evening sky. Then, with my fists clenched by my sides, I screamed as loud as possible until my lungs begged me to stop.

The front door whipped open. I turned. Gavin stared at me, his eyes wide as the moon. He put his hands on his hips and squinted.

I laughed.

I laughed so hard, hunched over in the winter landscape, that I cried.

And they were good tears.

Needed ones.

Hydrating ones.

Ella peeked around Gavin's shoulder.

"I'm okay." I waved. "Just telling life I'm not playing by her rules anymore."

They looked at each other and I laughed again. Oh, dear, now I was the crazy one.

THE NEXT MORNING I WOKE UP REFRESHED WITH AN ODD determination to photoshop my life a new brand of blue. Away with the desaturated melancholic hues and in with some funky cerulean tones.

I considered my new color as I showered. Which was fast. Still dreaded showers.

If I got really daring I could ditch blues altogether and opt for scarlet or electric lime.

Maybe.

Maybe I'd even go shopping for new clothes. That would shock everyone.

I finished my morning routine and sent everyone a mass text. Everyone except James and Cheyenne. It said:

In honor of simpler times, I'm about to toss my cell phone into the Susquehanna. Or maybe just donate it. Either way, if you want to contact me I'm only accepting in-person visits or letters. Yes, remember those? The kind you stuff in an envelope and put a stamp on. If it's something important I suggest you stop by or send the letter far in advance. I will no longer be communicating via telephones. And no ... you can't call Ella to relay messages. Letters and faces. Signing off now, so don't bother texting if you want to know why I'm doing this. Over. And out.

I turned the phone off and smiled.

Ella tapped on the door frame and walked in.

"What's the deal with the phone thing?" she said as she rubbed Adelaide's head.

"I thought you, Miss Jane Austen, would understand."

"Well, I like the romance of that time, but I appreciate the technology of today."

"I'm just tired of being so easy to get in touch with. One text at the wrong time has the power to ruin your entire day if you let it. Information at the touch of a screen, whenever we want it. Google in our pockets. Social media while we're driving. Nothing takes time and work anymore. How many contacts do I have in my phone? And how many of those people will keep in touch with me now that the relationship takes a little effort?"

"What about email?"

"Nope."

"Wow. I mean, you know how I love simplicity, but isn't this actually making things more difficult for you?"

"Depends how you look at it." I grabbed my purse. "Some see a tattoo as a permanent scar of regret and some see it as art."

"Are you getting a tattoo?"

I laughed. "Not yet."

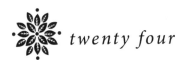 *twenty four*

March was never my favorite month of the year. Not in Pennsylvania at least. You've waited all winter for the first glimmer of spring and it arrives. That lovely sixty-degree day when everyone rolls their sleeves up and their car windows down.

Then, it snows. The next day. You whine inside and wait for it to melt, hoping by next Monday you'll never need your jacket again. But you always do.

Today was a pleasant fifty-nine degree day, but I didn't get my hopes up. In fact, the day reminded me to soak up the moment and stop living in tomorrow's shoes before I've put today's on.

Since giving up phone and email communication, the last days of winter skated by with more peace and stillness than I think I'd ever experienced in my life.

Ella made fun of me for constantly sitting by the window, staring out like an old woman as I scribbled in my journal. I'm sure it seemed like I was sitting there doing nothing, but I was planning for the spring.

For change.

Today, nice as it was outside, I left my perch and decided to go for a walk.

"Where ya going?" Ella said as I slid the back door open.

"A walk to the creek."

"Oh. Let me leave a note for Gavin. He took Adelaide to the store to give me some time to clean, but I just finished and a walk sounds fun today."

"Kay. I'll be out here."

"I REMEMBER THE FIRST TIME I CAME DOWN HERE," ELLA SAID as she sat on a large rock at the edge of the creek. "You and Gavin are so much alike. We always joke that I married the male version of my best friend."

"He's so much girlier though." I laughed as I skipped rocks into the shallow water.

"He's sensitive." She tried to defend him.

"I know, I know. It's a good quality. I'm just kidding."

We sat together without speaking. The water rolled over rocks creating a soothing sound. If I closed my eyes it felt like spring, but the buds on the trees were barely visible yet. So I kept them closed.

"You got two letters today," Ella said. "One from Natalie and one from Sophia."

"Natalie wants me to shoot some pictures for her new salon. She's surprising Vasili. He thinks she wants to move to LA and he was willing to do it finally, but them she told me she's just been messing with him. The salon in LA is starting an east coast branch and asked her to be the head cosmetologist. It's some upscale place in New York. She plans to commute from Lancaster."

"How's that gonna work?"

"Don't know. She's pretty excited though."

"What will he think?"

"I don't think he'll care that much, but he loves her so I'm sure he'll be supportive."

"You're just like my husband."

"What now?"

"You guys never say how you really feel. It's like drawing blood from a corpse."

I laughed. "Is it that bad?"

"Sometimes. For someone like me it's one of the most irritating qualities imaginable and the two closest people to me both excel in it."

"I'm not in love with Vasili, if that's what you're implying."

"Then what are you?"

"We're like brother and sister. Their family has become so dear to me."

"When will you read the letter Anastasia wrote you? The one taunting me on your dresser. I can't believe you haven't read it yet."

"She said to wait until her birthday."

"When's that?"

"Next month. Two days after Vasili's wedding."

"We should head back." Ella stood. "I feel weird without the baby. Oh, don't tell Gavin yet. I haven't said anything to anyone, but I took a pregnancy test this morning an—"

"Get out!"

She glowed and nodded.

"What? How? Adelaide is, what, seven months?"

She nodded again. A huge smile on her face.

"Wow. If I ever have kids it will be when your kids are ready to babysit."

"That's the first time you've said that like it's a possibility."

"What? Me having kids?"

"You've really been more positive lately. "

We walked back toward the house, over sticks and through barren trees, their branches resembling the veins of their own leaves, which would be budding soon. For a minute, it felt like we were kids again. All those days we spent in the woods at my grandma's house, making mud pies and decorating them with wild berries, climbing trees, trying to catch bunnies. We came home dirty. Every time. So dirty our clothes were permanently stained. Eventually our parents gave us a special set of "mud clothes," as they called them.

Then middle school changed us forever. Well, Ella not so much. She looked down and pretended not to hear when people made fun of her. I wasn't so strong. I needed to do something.

"Do you remember that time in middle school when the popular kids made fun of us?"

She squinted and thought for a few minutes.

"When Carrie and Emma told us that Mark and Josh wanted to French kiss us in the stairwell after school?"

"Oh my goodness." She laughed. "That was hilarious."

"I wish I was still like that." I touched the trees as we passed them. "I wish I still had that kind of nerve."

"I'll never forget their faces. They waited with those little disposable cameras. Who knows what they would've done, but you showed up dressed like Wednesday Adams with a fake tongue hanging to your belly button."

I laughed. "Oh, man."

We reached the last of the trees and began walking toward the hill. Their house sat at the top surrounded by a few trees, like something out of a nineteenth century movie.

"I wish I were still like that," I said. "Once high school came around people actually thought I was pretty. Maybe if they didn't I'd never have these problems. I've just gotten so used to trying to please people."

"You would've had some kind of problem with yourself. We're practically trained to hate ourselves in this world."

"Why do you say that?"

"Well, if everyone loved their faces, then who would buy cosmetics? It's a batrillion dollar business. Every commercial for that stuff is a big lie whispered to every woman, 'You aren't good enough like that. So buy this!' Haven't you seen all those magazines flaunting images of celebrities without makeup? I can't stand that stuff."

"But you wear makeup."

"I never said I didn't believe the lies myself." She sighed. "Hard not to."

We sat down at the top of the hill, out of breath, and looked back at the woods. Sometimes I longed to melt right into the earth. To become an integral part of a landscape. But even nature had it's blemishes and scars—it's power lines and blinking towers. What would the earth be like, what would we be like, if we never believed that we needed more than we were given?

"We're all racing to our deaths," I said, still looking ahead. "We always want more, more, more and it's killing us."

She nodded as she picked apart blades of grass. I gave her the look. She only picked at things when she was nervous or contemplative. I could tell it was the latter.

Eventually she blew the pieces of brown and green from her hand and reclined in the grass, looking up at the sky.

"There was a time," she said, "when I wouldn't sit in the grass like this because I was afraid my clothes would get dirty and my hair would get leaves in it."

I leaned back and rested my head beside hers. I knew the feeling. A

Bloom

favorite dress was cared for with more vigilance than the heart and soul of the very person wearing it.

"It's not just looks either," I said. "It's like Danny Gates. Remember him? He grew up in a roach-infested one bedroom house with six siblings. Now he lives in a ten bedroom house with one child. He says he can't afford more. Growing up he didn't have space or money or a nice house, so he values those things now. Probably the same way we value our hair and clothes."

"Like I said, we're trained to hate ourselves."

"Maybe." I thought for a few seconds. "Or maybe we're trained to hate contentment."

"True. Who's doing the training?"

"The Grinch?"

We laughed as the sun brightened our faces and, perhaps, our lives.

"I may never get married, Ella. And I'm okay with that. Really, I am." I sat up and looked at her. "I'm just thankful I have you. Not many people have a friendship like this. We're opposites in so many ways, but when we strip down all these outer things and talk about life, the deep stuff, we're the same." I stood and didn't brush off my jeans, or my hair. "Living with you for my recovery was exactly what I needed, because you're one of the only people I know who actually lives."

She stood and smirked.

"What?" I said.

"Vasili lives."

"Vasili is engaged."

"Are you really going to let him get married and never tell him how you really feel?"

"I'm not like that. He's engaged. Their wedding is next month. I'm not telling him."

"So ... you do love him, then?"

I shook my head. "You're so annoying."

"That's what friends are for."

155

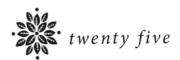 *twenty five*

I stared at the note from Anastasia. Sealed. By her own hands. How does life slip by so fast? In my hospital bed I imagined my funeral many times. Lying there like a mummy, it was hard not to.

Today was the first day since then that I actually woke up and thanked God for another morning.

I grabbed my keys and purse and headed downstairs, then stopped and watched Ella mess up her hair and toss books on to the floor. I cleared my throat and she jumped. A messy stack of baby books sat at her feet.

"What are you doing?" I said.

"Um." She looked around like I caught her doing something wrong. "I was just making it look messy in here."

"Do I want to know why?"

"I have guests coming. Are you coming tonight?"

"I thought people clean up for guests? You seem to be making a mess."

She nodded. "Last time Heidi was here she made a comment about me and my house always looking so clean and put together, like it was so easy. I could tell she felt a little down on herself, so I just wanted to make it look a little haphazard this time."

"But you love cleaning. It's your favorite hobby."

"Very funny." She tossed a blanket to the floor. "I do love cleaning and it comes natural to me, but I can't stand the idea of making someone else feel horrible because of me."

"Ella." I picked the blanket up. "You're lying when you do this." I set the blanket on the couch. "I can't even believe you're serious."

"I just don't want her to get upset and feel bad."

"That's noble." I tried not to laugh. "But I don't think it's our job to make sure everyone feels comfortable. If you stroked my ego constantly and walked on egg shells doing everything to make me happy, I wouldn't be smiling right now. I'd still be wallowing in my own misery. I don't think it's our job to prevent everyone from pain or insecurity. We can't anyway. Just give her a hug and tell her we're all different. Each with our own strengths and differences."

"Don't you do the same thing, Ms. People Pleaser?"

Gavin stepped into the room. "Oh, no. Not this again."

I smiled. "I think I talked her into being normal. Don't worry so much, Ella. If you're clean, that's fine. If not, so be it. Just be who you are."

Gavin sighed. "And you know ... few people have the humility to succeed in hiding their virtues." He squeezed her shoulders. "You're not that humble."

"Thanks." She leaned her head back and kissed his jaw. "Fine, fine. I'll clean it back up and brush my hair."

I said my goodbyes and laughed myself to the car.

Only Ella....

NATALIE WALKED INTO THE CAFE, SMILING AS THOUGH SHE won the lottery. She sat across from me, tapped the table, and leaned in.

I waited, thinking she'd speak, but she stared at me without speaking. I asked her to meet me today because I wanted to tell her how I felt about Vasili. I couldn't tell him behind her back. And I certainly couldn't tell them at the same time. So I chose this path. Ella was right and it grated on me. I needed to be honest. With others. With myself. With everything. Even if I got hurt in the process.

"Yes?" I finally said.

"Oh my gosh." She flapped her hands. "I think I'm gonna have a heart attack from all of this good news."

"Okay...."

"Oh. My. Gosh." She fanned herself. "Am I dreaming?"

"You look like something out of one of my nightmares, but no ... we're awake. I think."

She laughed. "Funny. Okay. First, what did you want to tell me?"

"You go first." Please go first.

"Vasili booked our honeymoon. He just showed me the tickets today."

I swallowed. "Oh. Where to?"

"Paris!" She nearly jumped out of her seat. "I've always wanted to go there. We're staying for two whole weeks."

"That's ... great." I thought of what I said to Ella earlier. "I thought Vasili always wanted to go to Greece for his honeymoon. Swim in the Aegean."

"What? Really? Did he say that?"

"No. I just figured since he dreams about it so much."

"Oh." She looked down. "He's always doing that for me. Sometimes I forget to even ask what he wants."

"You don't have to ask. Just listen."

She nodded. "Maybe I should surprise him and change the trip so the last week is in Greece instead?"

Two young boys pointed at me through the window. I tried to ignore it, but they kept looking at a paper in their hands, then back to me, revolted.

Natalie was still talking, but I stopped listening. I excused myself and went to the bathroom.

That's when I saw it.

I ripped it off the cork board and went into the bathroom, locking the door behind me.

The paper had a lot of words, but I couldn't stop looking at the pictures of myself. One, before the fire. The other, me on my bed, topless, as James snapped pictures of my scarred chest.

I paced in the bathroom, feeling like a seventh grader all over again. My hands and legs shook. I couldn't tell if I was angry or hurt. Or scared. Scared to death that the entire world was seeing the one part of me I never wanted anyone to see.

Especially Vasili.

Right, I thought. So stupid of me. I didn't want him to see my body under these clothes, but I entertained the idea of actually marrying him.

So stupid.

I leaned against the sink and closed my eyes.

Back in middle school my dad found me crying in the bathroom after school. Some girls were picking on me for the size of my boobs and the boys went to snap my bra, but realized I didn't have one. Humiliated, I ran home and prayed that God would give me bigger boobs. I stood in front of the mirror, stretching the skin on my chest and wishing for puberty to kick in.

My dad knocked on the door. I slipped my shirt back on and unlocked it. He pulled me into his arms and let me cry, but never said a word.

That night we had root beer floats and watched *Free Willy* together. At the end of the night he tucked me in, kissed my forehead, and said, "The only person who should be able to make you cry like that is yourself. People can betray you all they want and you'll survive. Even if it hurts and a few tears come, it will be over soon. Betray yourself and everything inside of you will die. That's something worth crying about. Do you understand me?"

I nodded, but had no clue what he meant.

Until now.

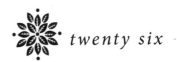

twenty six

The pictures were everywhere. Stapled to poles. Pinned to cork boards. And even worse ... on the Internet. By the time I got home that day Ella already knew. She came into my room with darkened eyes.

"What are you going to do?" she said. "Was it James?"

"I guess so."

"I'm sorry, Sarah. This is horrible. I can't believe he did this to you."

"I've decided not to think like that."

She tilted her head and set the baby on the floor. "Like what?"

"So everyone knows my body is no longer what it once was. If some people want to make fun of me, that's their problem."

"But—"

"I'm not playing these games anymore. This is my life. I may not have the power to make other people nice, but I do have the ability to not pay attention to them." I sighed, hoping my words would seep from my mind to my heart and maybe I'd eventually believe them. "I'm so tired of negativity. Criticism. Picking apart meals at restaurants. Nitpicking books. Judging people by their appearances and music tastes. I'm so tired of it all, Ella. I want to enjoy life again. People and their ridiculous negative spins on life. They get pleasure from making fun of anything that doesn't resemble them and their preferences. I can't stand it anymore. I'm not going to allow James to ruin my life just because people know who I really am. I'm done pretending and hiding. This is me. And life is about more than my stupid skin."

Ella smiled a little, then a little more.

"What? Are you inspired by my rant?"

"I am. However, I hope you stick to it once you look out the window."

"Oh, please. Now what?"

A reporter stood at the edge of the road with a camera a few feet from her. Close enough to get the house in the background, but far enough to be off the property.

My pulse quickened as every ounce of tranquility vanished. I gripped the window frame and clenched my teeth, suddenly wishing I had a phone to scream at James until he went deaf. Another joy of the slower paced life, I guess. A lot more difficult to say something you regret.

"Remember what you said." Ella stood beside me and peered across the street. "Don't let people and their opinions bother you."

"You're right," I said. "Be right back."

I walked outside saying to myself, "Don't be angry. Don't be angry," over and over again, but let's face it ... I was fuming.

Vile, revengeful thoughts poked and prodded my mind as I stood behind the news anchor while she spoke. I tried to smile, but I wasn't happy.

The camera man pointed at me and the woman turned around. Her eyes lit up when she saw me. I stared. Blankly.

She waved me over and said to the camera, "This must be her now."

I tried not to notice the fifteen layers of makeup slathered on her skin, and the fake voice she used while the camera rolled.

I wanted to be bold. I wanted to tell the truth and actually inspire people. This was my chance to do something. But I couldn't.

I couldn't open my mouth, so I turned to walk away. Then I saw Anastasia's face. Her sweet smile. Her last words to everyone. So simple. Be nice and be real.

I turned back and leaned into the mic.

"Wait a second," the anchor said. "You can't be—"

"My ex-fiancé got upset because I refused to put my ring on, and he did this."

She looked at the cameraman, then me, dumbfounded.

"I didn't make the flyers. My ex, James, and I ... we never had true love. I dated him because I felt sorry for him and I made myself believe I loved him. Maybe because my best friend is in love with love and it rubbed off on me. Maybe I wanted to be married so much that I glossed over the red flags. I don't know why I did what I did, but I was never in love with James.

I don't think I've ever truly loved a man, flaws and everything, until these last few months and it's not James. Yes, yes, he stayed by my hospital bed for months and months. But love is more than that, you know. It's not so much the actions as it is the motivations behind them. A guy can bring a girl flowers every day just to get her to have sex with him, while a real lover may never buy his wife flowers, but he knows how she twirls her spoon when she eats ice cream. With James, his motivations were always selfish and so were mine. I wanted to help him because it made me feel needed, and he wanted to cling to me because he didn't have anyone else to ease his guilt."

The woman kept nodding as though I were speaking, but I wasn't. I looked at the camera, then back to her. "Are you still recording?"

She nodded and scrambled for words.

"I'm sorry if this isn't what you expected, but my story isn't as inspirational as you think. I didn't post these flyers. Someone else did to humiliate me, but it's not working. I'm not pretending anymore. This is who I am. I've struggled with depression, thoughts of suicide, and many days found it difficult just to wake up. I'm not secure and confident with my new body. I worry about myself too much. I'm a mess. I'm doing better now, but it's not easy to lose everything you once were. It's like my favorite Edward Sharpe song says, 'Life is hard, come celebrate.' That's how I feel right now. It's not easy, but that's life. May as well celebrate it, instead of spending our lives complaining about it."

I nodded to the camera and the news anchor.

"I ... okay ... and your name is?" she asked.

"I'm Sarah. Sarah Jordan. Weren't you looking for me?"

"We're here because of Spencer Parks," she said.

"Who?"

"Is he here tonight?"

I hope my face didn't look as embarrassed as I felt. Oh, what the heck, I thought. I had no idea if the camera was still rolling or not, but I looked right into it and smiled. Then I laughed under my breath as I walked away. When I reached the porch I saw Ella standing there, hair parted down the middle, pale white makeup on, and a fake tongue hanging down to her chest.

That's what friends are for, I thought, then laughed my head off as the

Marilyn Grey

jitters from my on-camera experience faded.

"Got any champagne for this party tonight?" I said. "I want to make a toast to life and celebrate all of its beautiful disasters."

THERE'S A TIME AND PLACE FOR HONESTY. WHILE WE WERE all in the living room talking and sipping our champagne, a stop-you-in-your-tracks beautiful woman walked in with an extremely attractive man holding her hand. I wasn't about to show my true feelings, so I hid every ounce of jealousy inside.

"Nora!" Ella said, running to her and giving her a warm hug. "So glad you made it. Congrats on your movie. I can't wait to see it." Ella turned to everyone. "For those of you who don't know, this is Nora Maddison. Friend of Heidi and Patrick, and us. She just completed her first movie. Yes"—she tapped the man's shoulder—"this is *thee* Spencer Parks."

Everyone pretended to act normal as they asked them a bunch of questions.

"What's it like to work with Brad Pitt?"

"Is Kate Winslet really as down-to-earth as she seems?"

"So, how much money did you make?"

"What's your next project?"

"What was it like to fall in love on set?"

I observed everyone from the corner of the room. Heidi rarely spoke and watched Patrick out of the corner of her eye. I guess I'd be pretty jealous too if my husband were talking to a woman who looked like that. I didn't know this Spencer Parks guy though. Handsome, for sure. But the way he snapped his fingers when he wanted Nora to get him a drink irritated me. Thankfully they didn't notice me. I managed to slip by everyone unnoticed.

Then, as though she popped out of thin air, Nora gently touched my arm and whispered, "Thank you."

I tried to scoot by her.

"I admire you." She stood in front of me so I couldn't pass. "I know you don't know me very well, but I'm close with Pat and Heidi. Over the last year Ella and I have gotten closer as well, but I don't have many girl

164

friends. Not many who understand me, anyway." She waved her hands up and down her flawless figure. "All of this, it's not who I am. Anyway, let's talk later. Here's my number." She slipped a card into my hand. "Keep in touch."

I went back to my room, closed the door, and set the card down on my dresser. Nora and I would never be close friends, but something about her intrigued me.

I found my ear phones, and decided to read and respond to a few letters while listening to some chill music, as I called it.

Most letters were normal day-to-day keeping in touch kind of messages. I responded the same until I reached Vasili.

I decided to write how I really felt, but not send it. If anything, just to be honest with myself and spill my heart for once.

Dearest Vasili,

For the first year after my accident I felt like the worst representation of a woman. In fact, I haven't felt like a woman at all. Women are supposed to be soft and beautiful. Their faces bright and welcoming and their bodies soft and curvy. I never believed a woman needed to be "perfect" to be feminine, but now that I've lost my chest and half of my face, I've had a tough time believing that I'm worth the love of a man. What man would even want me? That's what James told me as he snapped those pictures of me. I'm sure you've seen them by now.

I'm not an idealist like my best friend. I didn't spend my life waiting for Mr. Right to come and sweep me off my feet. As Ella drew hearts on her notebooks in drivers ed, I flirted with the guy next to me. She waited for Mr. Right while I dated a bunch of Mr. Wrong's. The reason I

did that is because somewhere inside I didn't
believe in true love. I came to believe marriage
was a sacrifice of your own desires. Period.
It could never be this beautiful friendship that
melts into a passionate relationship where my
own desires became "our desires." That was
far-fetched to me.

Then I met you. I'm not the type of girl to
obsess over a guy. So it's not like I've been
sitting here thinking about you all day every day.
I think I got that butterflies in the stomach
feeling once when you walked in the room, but
when I'm with you I don't need all that fancy
stuff. There's a comfort I feel with you that
I've never felt in my life, much less at this
point.

I've watched you for the last few months.
I've listened. I can tell you that your favorite
color changes weekly, depending on your mood.
Last week it was orange. This week, it's gray
again. I know that you prefer to eat soup with
a fork instead of a spoon. I know that your
eyes twitch when you're holding back tears.
You dream of swimming in the Aegean and visiting
ancient churches in Greece. Your mother means
the world to you and you take your faith seriously. I've seen you live for others, constantly
giving up your own desires for them without
even realizing it. And you've helped me breathe
again. I feel like I've been holding my breath
since the fire.

You've always looked beyond my scars. I can't even recall a time where you treated me any different than a normal woman. You saw Sarah. You saw my heart even when I couldn't.

I saw yours too. I've been suppressing my feelings this entire time. Telling myself you'd never want me. Natalie is gorgeous and sweet, albeit a little absent-minded. She tries to be a good girlfriend and she's come to me several times asking for advice. Like what to get you as a gift or what you'd like to do for fun Saturday night. I've felt like your sister a lot lately, but then these pictures came out and I realized I didn't want you to see them. The entire world could make fun of me ... but not you. It would kill any part of me that's still alive.

I love you. I don't know how it happened or how to stop it. I've had the worst luck imaginable and I'm afraid to love you. I'm afraid to hear you say you love me too. Could I really ask the man I love to give up a beautiful wife for me? Could I really imagine making love and not giving him the full pleasure of enjoying every part of a woman's body? Could I really be that vulnerable with the one I love the most?

I don't think that's love, dear Vasili. It wouldn't be fair to you, which is why I'll never send this letter. I will photograph your wedding next month. And as I look at you through my lens I'll whisper these words to you in silence. I'll love you from a distance and wish you the best.

I truly wish you the best, my love. You've changed my life and made me feel beautiful again. You've made me feel alive.

Thank you.

Thank you so much.

Yours truly,
Sarah

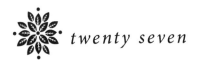

Gavin smiled from the bottom of the stairs as I skipped down them. He switched Adelaide to his left hip. "You're in good spirits today."

"Why, yes," I said. "I am."

"And to what—or to whom?—do we owe this pleasure?"

"There's no *to whom*. Where's Ella?"

"Grocery store."

"At six-thirty in the morning?"

He nodded. "She likes to go early. Where are you off to at the break of dawn?"

"Trying to catch the fog today." I stepped out the front door. "I want to snap a few pictures of it."

"Sounds good. Have fun." He closed the door behind me.

Hard to imagine that only a few years back I had an immense crush on him. He became a brother to me. A true brother, unlike Vasili. Those old fluttery feelings seemed so distant. Of course, most of my life before the fire seemed like a completely different life.

THE FOG SAILED ACROSS THE OPEN FIELDS LIKE A LOW SLUNG river of mist. Newly adorned branches poked their tops into the fresh spring air as the morning light pushed it's golden fingers through the white and grey mass. Soft and wonderful. I watched for a few minutes before looking through my lens. It almost seemed like you could walk on top of the thick fog without falling to the ground. There's something so magical about nature. Standing there with my camera in my hands, my feet remained on the earth, but my heart traveled somewhere else. Nature, to me, felt like a gateway to another world. Far from the noise and clutter of our culture. When I took pictures of nature's finest gifts, I never wanted to stop, but sure enough, within minutes the sun would climb higher in the sky and the scene would change. So I clicked and clicked, smiling as I caught stills of something that never stood still.

After refreshing myself with a cool drink of photography, I headed to my early morning physical therapy appointment with Vasili, hoping my unsealed letter to him would stay sealed inside my heart. For some reason, writing the truth made me feel more uncomfortable seeing him, even if I didn't tell him.

I hoped he would bring up the pictures instead of pretending like he didn't see them. I didn't want to pretend anymore. It was less embarrassing to admit it and get over it.

His office was quiet. Only one other person waiting.

"Sarah," a young woman said. "Come with me."

I smiled at her and asked her name, realizing I had never done so before.

"Jennifer, but most call me Jenny." She led me to a different office. "Dr. Maloney will be with you in a few minutes. Vasili isn't available at the moment."

"Oh, thanks." I sat down, hoping I didn't seem disappointed.

Dr. Maloney, a young woman about my age, came in a few minutes later. She was kind and helpful and we went through all of my exercises with ease. She made small talk, but I couldn't stop thinking about Vasili. Why would he refuse to see me today?

When she finished I left the room and went across the hall to the bathroom. After that, I made sure no one was around and pressed my ear against Vasili's door.

Natalie's voice. It had to be her. I couldn't make out the words, but it didn't sound good.

Then I heard his voice cut through the muffled sounds. "I would never cheat on you, Natalie. I'm not like that."

"If you want to end the engagement just tell me." I finally understood her words. "I want you to be happy."

"I'm not ending anything. Stop talking like this."

"Then will you stop talking to Sarah?"

"Why? What does she have to do with this?"

"I don't want her to do our wedding photography. I don't want to see her anymore. Can you do that?"

A long stretch of silence, then, "Yes. I can do that for you."

The door opened. Natalie stared at me as Vasili hung his head and covered his eyes with his hand. I tried to speak, but couldn't. I was prepared to watch him marry someone else, but to never see him again felt like death itself had woven its claws around my heart.

Natalie looked at me, blinking. We stared at each other for a few minutes, then a single tear fell from her eye. I tried to apologize, but my mouth wouldn't cooperate.

I didn't know what I did, but I felt bad. So I walked away without saying a word. For his sake, I'd never come back again.

And the tiny fragment of joy I experienced earlier, standing amidst the smoky river, evaporated as I drove away.

AFTER SPILLING MY HEART TO ELLA, SHE SAT ON THE EDGE OF my bed and cleared her throat.

"Don't hate me," she said. "I didn't know this would happen."

I snapped my head up. "What did you do?"

"Please don't be mad."

"Ella."

"Promise not to be upset?"

"Ella!"

"Okay, okay." She fiddled with her hands. "Um, well, I saw the letter you wrote."

"You were snooping in my room?"

"I was grabbing your laundry and saw it. I know it's horrible of me. I don't know what came over me, but I read it."

I sighed. "Then what?"

"Don't be mad."

"I'm already mad." I stood. "What did you do?"

"I mailed it to him." She cringed and dropped her shoulders. "I thought I was helping."

I crossed my arms and walked to the window.

"I thought you said you didn't need a man to be happy?" she said. "Don't let it get you down. At least he knows the truth now. It would've eaten y—"

"Easy for you to say." I turned toward her. "Mrs Perfect with Mr Perfect in their perfect house with their perfect love story with their perfect child, and another one coming. Your life is all roses with no thorns, and here I am." I slammed my hand on my dresser and looked in the mirror above it. "Look at me. Just look at me." My face reddened. "Every glimmer of joy I find is turned upside down. I'm trying the best I can and what happens? Life screws me over at every turn. Every thorn missing from your life is right here in mine. I'm all thorns with no roses."

She tried to speak.

"No. No. No more. Just let me be."

"I'm sorry," she cried. "Please forgive me, Sarah. I didn't mean—"

"Let me be. Please."

She closed my door. I waited until I could no longer hear her sniffles, then I turned back to the mirror. I pulled my hair back and analyzed my scars. Then I placed my hand over them and looked at the normal side of my face, as though the scars didn't exist.

Shaking, I dropped my hand and looked at the entire picture. "I hate you," I said to my reflection. "I hate this. All of it. It's not fair."

Anastasia's smile came to mind.

"None of this is fair," I said, then I drove my fist into the mirror. And again. And again. Until my reflection no longer tormented me and only shards on my dresser remained.

THE NEXT MORNING I WOKE UP TO FLOWERS AND A LETTER by my bedside. Assuming they were from Ella, I turned away from them and looked across the room. The picture of us caught my eye. Ella and me. Young and happy. I thought of our walk in the woods. My words to her. "I may never get married ... thankful I have you ... not many people have a friendship like this."

I turned back to the flowers. The handwriting on the envelope wasn't Ella's.

I sat up in bed and rubbed my eyes, then opened the letter and scanned to the name at the bottom. Natalie.

Dearest Sarah,

I never meant to hurt you. I saw your letter in Vasili's mail and I guess I was just curious, so I opened it and your love for him didn't surprise me. I saw it from the start. I've been a little jealous too because you have seen things in him that I didn't, but because of you I've realized what a gift I have in him and I don't want to let him go. I haven't shown Vasili the letter because I'm afraid to. I'm afraid to lose him. I keep staring at the ring on my finger, imagining it gone, and it hurts so bad. I know if I showed him the letter that I'd lose him, even though you tried to convince him to marry me.

You may not see it in yourself, and I think if you did it would ruin it, but you are one of the most beautiful people I've ever known. My face may be pretty, but I'll never be as beautiful as you.

Since you came around, I admit ... I've been jealous. I was even jealous around Anastasia. Mainly because I know Vasili is attracted to that kind of beauty that I don't have. I don't even know how to find it inside myself. Meeting you has changed me for the better. You've helped me more than you know and the way you praised me in your letter brought tears to my eyes.

You were wrong about something though. I don't deserve him, not even his last name. But please know that I will do the best I can. I appreciate your honesty so much, Sarah.

I won't show him the letter. Let's keep it as our little secret, okay? After the wedding we'll be in touch again. I trust you. I know you would never do anything to hurt me. That's one of your shining qualities.

Thank you for everything.

Your friend,
Natalie

I reread the letter fourteen times. A mixture of disbelief and longing battling inside of me. The fact that she believed he would actually be tempted to leave her for me, even after seeing those pictures of me, made me anxious. Half of me wanted to jump up and down like a girl who just saw her crush's name on the caller ID, but the other half of me knew she was right. She could trust me. I despised hurting people. I wouldn't say a thing.

They'd marry next week. And I'd keep our little secret.

All that aside, I wasn't as beautiful as she thought. If I were, I wouldn't have blown up last night. I wouldn't have made my best friend cry. And really, do people with that kind of beauty shatter mirrors and hate themselves?

I folded her letter and set it by the flowers, then picked a yellow rose from the vase. Turning it in my hands, I thought of my life. From beginning to end. Good mixed with bad.

Anastasia's letter came to mind. The one I read at her funeral. "Sometimes there's bad news and sometimes there's good news. Sometimes we have pain and sometimes we have smiles." Yes. That would be life in a nutshell.

I smiled as I pictured her on that swing, the shimmery ice reflecting her happiness. That moment when time stopped as we compared our scars. That was true beauty. A moment of truth. Two people connecting and smiling amidst their struggles.

I set the rose back in the vase and stood. "Okay, life. You've knocked me down, but I'm getting back up again."

Not for myself either, I thought. For the millions of others who feel like they can't find the strength to go another day. I knew it when Anastasia showed me her chest. We all have different shapes and colors to our scars that make us feel alone, but we're only alone when we hide.

It was time.

I plucked a rose petal and inhaled its sweet scent.

Time for me to bloom.

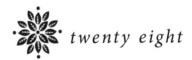 *twenty eight*

On a rainy April morning I visited the burn clinic to go over a few things about my scars. Instead of treading through puddles with my woe is me attitude, I wore colorful rain boots and brought bags of gifts for the doctors and other patients.

My visit went well enough, I suppose. They said my scar color was great. Nice and pink. My range of motion had improved a ton. I could even open jars myself and my showers were no longer the most dreadful experience of my life. I was less tired and my pain was under control. I showed them how I could write letters and twist pen caps off.

We scheduled my surgery for skin grafting. Four days after Vasili's wedding. They would take skin from my back and graft it into my neck to help with movement. I'd be home within a few days.

I wasn't looking forward to the surgery, but I knew it was for the best. For months I wallowed in self-pity, missing the old Sarah. Now, I genuinely looked forward to the new Sarah.

The old Sarah was nice and all, but she concealed her true feelings and, well, she was a people pleaser. Not because she cared about them, because she cared about her own reputation.

I no longer cared about that. The world could say what they wanted about me. It didn't matter anymore.

I spent the rest of the week as the new Sarah. I invited people into my life and made eye contact with strangers. I still refused to use my phone, so when I sat in waiting rooms with a bunch of people staring at screens, I made it a point to bother them and force a real life conversation. By the end, they thanked me for it. And it felt good for me too. It felt like living. Really living.

By the end of the week I was exhausted when Ella handed me the mail. I carried the letters to my room, plopped onto my bed, and read the return addresses. One from James. One from Vasili.

This should be interesting, I thought. I saved the best for last and opened the letter from James first.

Dear Sarah,

I just wanted to let you know that I'm sorry. I saw the pictures and I heard about the news thing. It wasn't me. It was Cheyenne. We got into a fight over you and she got mad. I would never do that to you. I'm sorry I even took the pics. I know you're better off without me. I can see that now. Maybe when everything calms down you can visit Abby and me. She'd like that. Let's try to be friends. I won't bother you anymore.

James

I hated that I always felt sorry for people who hurt me. Sometimes I wished I were one of those people who held grudges for ten months and stopped talking to people who hurt me. That's something old Sarah and new Sarah had in common. We both wanted to take the blame for our enemies. I guess I didn't see them as enemies. I saw them as fellow hurting people, just as broken and in need of love as I was. My bitterness would only hurt them even more. And me.

So I snapped my pen and wrote James a quick note.

Dear James,

I forgive you and I love you as a friend. I always will. Looking back, I feel like this was meant to be. We would've gotten married if it weren't for the fire and I know part of you still thinks we should, but I hope one day you see what I see. For me, marriage is only worth it if both people become better people simply through their love for each other. I don't think we did that for each other and I'm sorry for my part in it. We didn't inspire each other to live. Slowly, we stole the air from each other's lungs. We were suffocating.

I do love you, James. Enough to tell you the truth. It was never meant to be.

Find yourself someone who gives you a reason to wake up every morning. Be kind and stop blaming yourself for your brothers death. And for my scars. My dad once told me, "Why are you so arrogant that you think the world's problems are your fault?" It's true, James. We're only hurting ourselves when we hold onto guilt. Even when we hurt people on purpose, it's up to them to accept our apology and move on. We can't dwell in our issues. It's selfish and it will ruin you. So please move on. There's nothing I want more for you than to see you smile, really smile.

We'll keep in touch soon.

Always,
Sarah

I addressed and sealed the envelope, then turned Vasili's in my hand. I feared opening it. The closure that it would bring made my chest ache.

I couldn't do it.

I glanced at the calendar on my wall. Three days until his wedding.

Someone knocked on my door.

"Come in," I said.

Ella entered my room and sat beside me. "Everything okay? I saw who wrote the letters."

"James was nice. He didn't post those pictures. My very kind and loving cousin did."

"I wasn't talking about James."

"I haven't opened it yet."

"What if you regret it?"

"I won't."

"You might."

"I can't ruin his life. He has a beautiful girl who wants to do whatever it takes to be the perfect wife. I'm not going to ask him to give that up for me."

"I'm tempted to tell him myself, but I won't."

"Thank you."

"You could always do what they do in movies."

"What's that?"

"Show up while he's at the altar and scream, 'No. I love you. Don't do it.'"

"Right." I laughed. "I'm okay. I know I'm doing the right thing. If I'm meant to get married, someone else will come along. I'll be better by then. Less insecure. It will work out."

She sighed. "I hope so."

"What's that supposed to mean?"

"I waited ten years to see Gavin again. One glance is all it took. I wanted him and I wasn't willing to let my dream of him go. When I got set up with Matt and thought it was Gavin, it crushed me. In that moment I let go of my fantasies. I realized love doesn't need to be magical to be true. Then he came. And you know, I was expecting fireworks when we finally saw each other again. It wasn't like that. We sat in my cafe until the sun came up. Sometimes talking, sometimes not. The best part about it was that in place of fireworks, we had contentment. It was like walking through a desert for years and finally finding your home." She walked back to the door, then peeked back in. "There's no place like home. Once you find it, no matter how many houses you move in and out of, there will never be another home."

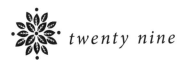

twenty nine

Mom and Dad wrote me quite a few letters, most of them ending with, "Can we come and see you?" And I always responded the same by saying, "Soon."

They thought I lost my mind when I gave up the phone. I wanted peace and simplicity. And I got it in abundance. Immersing myself in technology again didn't have the slightest appeal.

I wrote Dad again and asked them to come for my surgery next week. Without Cheyenne poor Ella would end up taking care of me and she had enough on her own plate.

After mailing a few letters I drove to Philadelphia. Something I hadn't done since the fire. I couldn't bear it.

As I drove into the busy city, I was reminded of the reason I spent so long avoiding the streets of Philadelphia. Every turn and stop light, every house and tree, every single detail of every single street reminded me of my life before.

I stopped in front of my old apartment building. The one I shared with Ella when I found out I had cervical cancer. She moved out while I was in a coma. I still hadn't opened the boxes of clothes she packed from my closet. I didn't want to see them. Or smell them. And remember the memories I created in them. I didn't want to bury the girl I used to be.

I parked my car near my favorite diner and stepped outside. The cool spring air felt good as I inhaled and caught the fragrance of a blossoming tree.

Walking down the city sidewalks, I swept every last detail into my mind. From the sidewalk chalk stick figures to the colorful tulips sprinkled amidst weathered bricks and strips of pavement. Kids laughed and chased each other from one set of steps to another, while parents chatted on their porches.

I came to Philadelphia to look for an apartment. To surprise Ella after my surgery with plans to find my own place and let her growing family be together without me. But the more I walked those familiar paths, the more I felt that I had moved on.

I stopped and leaned my back against a shop window. Looking out at the place I once called home, I missed my new home.

The quaint city of Lancaster, a hidden gem surrounded by cities too large for their own good. It's tiny shops and local markets. The humor of hearing rap music disappear down the street, followed by the clippity clap of an Amish buggy. And the look you give your friend when you say, "Only in Lancaster."

I walked back to my car and smiled. Without hesitation, I could bury the old Sarah and walk away, because somewhere along my recovery I had already moved on. I already changed.

And I didn't mind it.

In fact, I quite liked it.

I ARRIVED BACK IN LANCASTER BY SUNSET. INSTEAD OF GOING home, I parked on King Street in the center of town and meandered from shop to shop, buying little gifts for my friends as I discovered them.

In a thrift store on Prince Street, I spotted Vasili near the entrance. I ducked behind a rack of clothes and pretended to sift through them, hoping he'd leave without seeing me.

"Ready for the big day?" the guy behind the counter said.

"I'm as ready as I'll ever be." Vasili leaned on the counter and pointed to something in the glass case. "Looking for a gift for her. She wanted to exchange something after the rehearsal dinner."

"Then off to Paris with a hot mama you go." The guy smirked.

I sunk further into the clothes and something fell.

"Everything okay back there, miss?"

"Uh-huh," I said, in a more high-pitch voice.

Vasili walked toward the clothing rack. I panicked and wedged my body inside the clothes. As he came around the back I slipped through the front of the rack, but something caught my shirt.

I tugged on it, but it wouldn't even rip. The guy at the front raised his eyebrows at me and grinned. Then Vasili came around the rack and stopped.

We stared at each other for a few seconds without speaking, but he didn't look too happy to see me. His brow lowered toward his nose and his mouth didn't have the slightest hint of a smile. I yanked my shirt and apologized, then jogged out the front door.

He didn't follow, thankfully.

I stopped at the corner of King and Prince and decided to get my nails done. He'd never expect me to go in there, which meant he'd never find me.

I sat down in front of an old woman who smelled of Marlboro Lights and burnt hair, like my great grandmother. Her hands shook as she gave me a French manicure. I laughed inside as the nail polish dripped down my fingers more than my nails. She tried to avoid my face and pretended not to notice the compression garments around my wrists, but people always seemed more obvious when they pretended not to look.

"I was burned in a campfire accident," I said casually. "I was in a coma for months and it still hurts when I wake up to this day."

She fumbled over the nail polish container as she said something under her breath, still refusing to look me in the face. The other people in the room, however, were staring right at both of us.

"You can look at me," I said. "I'm still a person like any other." I looked at the other women. "Actually I'm a better person now. Less afraid to get hurt and more willing to do what's right, no matter what it costs me. Nearly dying and then waking up looking like this can really change the way you see life."

No one said a word. Eyes blinked at me to the sound of cars whooshing by outside. The woman still wouldn't look at me.

"Am I that ugly that you can't even say hello to my face? Why is this world so bent on looks, looks, looks?" I stood. "I'm still a normal woman."

The woman finally peered up at me, her eyes heavy and sagging into puffy circles. "It's not you." She shook her head and looked away again. "My husband was a fire fighter. His crew saved a family, but the kids screamed and cried for their dog. He ran back inside to save that damn dog and the roof collapsed. He burned over 97% of his body and when his crew found him he said, 'Tell Penny to let me die. I don't want to live like this. I love her too much to put her through this.'"

At first, my mind retreated to thinking, *Yes, poor me. I don't deserve to be a wife when I can barely open a jar of almond butter on my own.* But I didn't allow myself to go there. Instead, I put my arm around the woman and squeezed.

She pat my hand. "I'm sorry, honey."

"I'm sorry you lost your husband," I said. "Sometimes I wished to die too, but I'm okay now. One day at a time. It's a very difficult and painful thing to endure. In a sense, I'm glad your husband was spared."

"He died anyway. On the way to the hospital his heart stopped and they couldn't get him back." She stood in front of me, held my hands, and looked right into my eyes. "He didn't fight to live. He fought for all of those other people, but not for me. Not for us."

I held onto her hands, speechless. She stopped speaking as well, but her eyes locked into my own as though she needed to tell me something, or hear me say something, but neither of us had anything to give.

I forced a smile into the awkward scene, then placed my hand on her cheek. "I needed to find a reason to live too. I think I'm still trying to figure that out. Honestly, I don't think love is everything. It's not enough motivation to fight such a painful battle. Your husband knew that. I don't know what that is yet, but if I figure it out I'll let you know."

I laughed a little as I left all of the women to get back to their nails. When I turned to look back, they were all staring at me. Disbelief still widening their eyes. I waved and crossed the street.

As I passed strangers I smiled at them. Even better, I noticed them. The world didn't revolve around Sarah Jordan and it would keep spinning without this tiny little life.

So I noticed each passing face. I smiled and asked God to brighten their lives in some small way. Then I saw him.

Leaning against my car with his arms crossed, he refused to break eye contact. So I did.

"I didn't mean to hurt you," he said without moving a single body part except his lips. I wanted to uncross his arms and put them at his sides. Carefree like the time we played in the snow. I didn't like seeing him so serious and stern.

"How could you, Sarah?" He stepped onto the curb and stood beside me. "You, of all people. I can't believe it."

My pulse raced to the panic attack finish line. I hated conflict. Especially when it was somehow because of me.

"Do you have anything to say?" he said.

"I'm not sure what you mean."

"The letter you sent. You could've at least told me to my face." He paced the sidewalk with his hand on his chin, then stood inches from me. "How am I supposed to break the news to her this close to our wedding?"

A wild assortment of conflicting emotions wrestled for the front row seat in my heart. I let confusion win. "I don't know what to say. I can't help the way I feel. It just happened."

"Who else am I supposed to find now?" He finally stood still and looked at me. "I'm sorry. This wedding is way bigger than I ever wanted and it's turning me into Groomrilla."

I held back a laugh. "You mean Groomzilla?"

"Isn't it a guerrilla?" He threw his hands into his pockets. "If I talk her into letting you do the photography, are you still up for that?"

I had no idea what he was talking about, then it hit me. We were talking about different letters. My friend was going to do the wedding with me and when I backed out she took over, but she got nervous and said she didn't feel comfortable, so I wrote them to explain.

"I have another friend," I said. "Didn't you finish the letter? He'll be there and he knows the plan."

He stepped closer to me. That smell of his playing games with my heart.

"I want you there." He took my hand.

I jerked away and clasped my hands behind my back. "Please don't."

"Don't what? I'll talk to her. Even if you don't take pictures, I need you there."

"Need? You can't poss—"

"Need."

I shook my head and unlocked my car. When I stepped down from the curb, he did.

"Please, Sarah. Your friendship means so much to me."

"I can't. Please stop. You have no idea what you're asking me to do."

I moved to sit in my car, but he stood in the way. "But you get me. I thought we were close."

I couldn't tell him the truth. Natalie trusted me. If I ruined their wedding I'd never forgive myself. He deserves better, I kept saying inside, but when I brushed against his shoulder to sit in my car I couldn't help it anymore. I said loud enough for everyone around to hear, "I love you, Vasili." People turned. I sat in my car and looked up at him before closing it. "I fell in love with you. I can't watch you get married, okay? It's too much. Please. Let me go now. Be happy. Enjoy your life. Just try to let me be. It's hard enough."

He stepped back to the curb as I turned the car on and shifted into drive.

That's it? I thought as he stood there watching me drive away.

He let me have the last words. And I didn't want them.

THE NEXT DAY I STOPPED BY SOPHIA'S HOUSE WHEN I KNEW Vasili was at work. I drove by his office to make sure.

Sophia made my favorite tea and a pot of coffee for herself. We sat at the dining room table and talked about little things for a while, then I pulled a gift from my bag and set it in front of her.

"Could you give this to Vasili?" I said. "It's my wedding gift for him."

"You aren't going? What about the photography? What happened?"

"Ask your brother." I sipped my tea. "So, you said you were going to clear Anastasia's room. Did you finish?"

She focused on the fake tulips on the table. "I can't. Not yet."

We finished our drinks in silence, placed our cups in the sink, and she led me to Anastasia's room. I stood quietly as she searched through a drawer of papers.

The bed, unmade, almost showed the imprint of where her body once rested. Her IV no longer stood beside her bed. Her chest, rising and falling beside her parents, fell for good and lay alone under the ground.

I wiped my face, but couldn't look away from her bed. I could so easily see her waking up and trying to smile for her mother.

Sophia held a paper. It crinkled as it trembled in her hands.

"The worst part," she said, "is that she never told me the truth. She pretended to be strong for my sake, but that entire time she slept there in that bed I'd cry and cry. Not because I was afraid to lose her, although that was part of it. I just wanted to be needed. She was always so strong growing up. When she got sick she would take care of herself. Whenever she fell and skinned her knee she'd have a bandage on before I knew it happened. Selfishly, I wanted my little girl to need me." She smoothed her palm along the sheets and smelled the pillow. "The thing that bothers me the most is that she feared hurting me, so she didn't tell me how much she really needed me. She felt like a burden or like it was her fault we were upset. But if I had just been honest with her, if I had just said, 'Sweetie, I want to hold you and make the pain go away,' then everything would've been different. I feel like my baby died alone because I couldn't be the bigger person and open up to her." She sat on the bed. "I didn't want to admit it though. Yanni and me. Neither of us wanted to believe it."

She handed me a drawing. Anastasia signed the bottom in blue. The picture made me smile. She drew Sophia and Yanni holding her as a baby. The sun shined to the left, birds flew to the right, and an owl sat in a tree beneath the birds.

"Look at the back," Sophia said.

I turned it over.

Vasili and Sarah, my Nono and Nona with my cousin.
(They better not name her after me.)

I flipped it over, looked at the picture, then read the words again. Sophia smiled at me, but I couldn't smile back. For some reason, it frustrated me.

"I'm not going to say anything else," Sophia said. "Either way, you are always going to be part of our family."

"How did everyone know?"

"How did we not?"

I shrugged. "Well, I told him yesterday. He didn't say anything and the wedding is tomorrow. This isn't a Hollywood rom-com where I ruin a bride's day by stealing the groom and then ride off into the sunset as she stands humiliated in front of her family and friends. I can't do that." I shook my head. "He knows the truth and the truth is...."

"Go on."

"The truth is life isn't about love and romance. It's not even about tallying up good works and feeding the poor. Life is about everything ... everything except nothing. I know I'm not the most religious, but—"

"Sure you are."

"No, I'm really not."

"We're all religious about something. It's devotion, that's all. Devoted to God, to music, our careers, ourselves. We're all religious. Every last one of us."

"Well, either way, I realized through all of this that the secret to everything isn't in love and relationships, or charity and virtue. It's inside of us. We can choose to see the world and all of its sorrows and scars as something beautiful, or we can dwell in criticism and pick apart things until we see ugliness in beauty. Life ... for me, I love your brother, I do, but even if I married him I could lose him tomorrow. Do you see what I'm saying? It hurts so bad to let him go, but it's not the end of me. It's all for the best. You'll see."

You'll see, I said to myself again and again. You'll see.

 *thirty*

I slept in the morning of their wedding, then got cleaned up, dressed, and curled back into my bed. Ella and Gavin visited Philly for the day, so I had the house to myself, but I chose to stay in my room anyway.

I imagined scenarios. Crazy things like me trying to look nice for once and showing up just as they said their vows. Or Vasili discovering his love for me and showing up at my door.

Nothing like that happened. I wanted to erase every romantic movie from my memory and stop entertaining such impossibilities.

I decided to turn my phone back on. Kind of torturous, but I asked Sophia to text me pictures. I couldn't bear taking pictures or being in the pews, but I loved him and missing it altogether felt wrong.

She hadn't sent anything yet. I passed time by replaying memories, trying to figure out exactly how and when I fell for him. It's not like me to fall for someone so easily, but maybe it wasn't easy. I couldn't pinpoint an exact moment. Like a natural progression, I grew to love him.

The comfort his presence brought. The way he cared for Anastasia. The gentle kisses he gave his mother. Every time I caught him looking at me as though I didn't have any scars. His inspiring view of life and love. The way he'd give up anything, including his own happiness, for the one he loved.

How could I not do the same?

A text finally came in. Sure enough, from Sophia.

About to go into the sanctuary.

Then a picture came through. Handsome Vasili all dressed up sitting by a window. I zoomed in and traced his jaw with my finger, then I realized he was holding my gift to him. He looked down at it with a slight smile. A photograph of Anastasia in her garden. On the card I wrote:

Third and last photo in the "Out of Adversity" series. I thought this completed it well. The artist sends her love and wishes you the best.

Once again, I imagined him calling it all off and running to me, but I didn't hear back from Sophia and no one knocked on the door.

A few hours later the sun disappeared. I managed to go downstairs and force myself to eat, then Sophia finally texted me. As soon as I read it, I dropped my apple and opened the floodgates.

All she said was: *I'm home now. Are you okay?*

I couldn't respond. I gripped the edge of the kitchen counter and gained control of my emotions.

"All for the best," I whispered aloud. "You'll see."

I kept whispering to myself and within a few minutes the pain subsided. Then, under my breath, I laughed. A soft, quiet laugh. How did the girl who never gave anyone the keys to her heart slip them into the hands of someone who couldn't keep them?

Sometimes life is like a movie. And there are times when the actors go off script and the camera breaks and the lights go down and all we can do is sit back on the set, take a look around, and laugh.

Vasili taught me that.

THERE'S AN EMPTINESS YOU FEEL WHEN YOU WAKE UP ALONE after a breakup, whether you loved the person or not. A part of your life is over. For good. A chapter has ended and the next page is blank, ready for new love. Then, there's the emptiness you feel when you wake up knowing the one you love is flying to Paris to make love to his gorgeous bride as the Eiffel Tower sparkles in the moonlight. You finish the chapter, turn the page, read the first few lines of the next chapter, then roll over in bed and hope someone throws the book out the window before you open your eyes again.

I can't say I wanted to wake up, but I did. Ella didn't ask. She knew me well enough to know I'd open up when I was ready. I showered, got dressed, and picked up the letter from Anastasia. Months ago she made me promise to read it on her birthday and not a day sooner.

The day had come.

I managed to slip out of the house unnoticed. Before heading to the cemetery, I stopped into the local florist and picked up my order. Two dozen teal blue roses—Anastasia's favorite color—complete with thorns.

"Thank you." I smiled at the cashier and slipped a hundred dollar bill into her tip jar when she turned away. "Have a wonderful day."

I used Pandora on my phone to listen to music on the way to the grave. When I parked Bruce Springteen's *Secret Garden* song came on. I unplugged my phone, but kept the song playing as I walked through rows of headstones, until I finally stood before the freshly engraved "Anastasia Sophia Koursaris - Papa's Little Girl." Thinking of her sweet face, I knelt down beside the teddy bears and flowers and opened her letter.

Dearest Nona,

I knew you would marry my Nono before I even met you. The way he talked about you, I could just tell. I'm sad that I won't be alive to see it. I love Natalie, but they don't look at each other like you two.

I considered you my Nona from the start, even though you aren't part of our church. Maybe one day you will be? Well, I guess if you marry my uncle hehehe :)

Thank you for everything. You're probably looking at my grave right now. It's weird to be writing this while I'm alive. I'm picturing my body all the way under the ground while people come up to my gravestone and kiss it like it's my face.

Don't cry. I'm not dead. I'm more alive than I've ever been. You will be too one day. And you and me will look at each other and we won't have any scars. I can't wait for that.

Oh, and my last wish, I know this is weird but ... don't name your baby after me. Tell Vasili to do it the proper Greek way. He loves you. He'll listen. It will make Yia Yia happy.

I love you. Make new memories and remember me. I love all of you so much.

Love,
Anastasia

I folded up the letter and stared at a picture of her that someone else must've put beside the stone.

"She wanted us to get married," a voice said behind me.

I jumped.

Vasili looked down at me, a grin hugging his cheeks.

"What the heck?" I said, almost falling into the flowers.

He laughed. "I got your picture. The gift."

"Where's Natalie?"

"She insisted on taking pictures before the wedding so she wouldn't ruin her makeup if she cried. She told me she couldn't marry me without telling me about it. Then, we talked about life for a while and she told me she didn't want to marry me."

"What? Why?"

"She didn't want to feel like she needed to live up to the way you loved me. She said she wanted to find a man she can love the way you love"—he cleared his throat—"me."

I stood in front of him. "Vasili, I—"

"Shhhh...."

"No, but I—"

"Later." He knelt in front of her grave. "Let's focus on her for now."

WE STOOD AT OUR CARS IN THE MIDDLE OF THE CEMETERY, staring at each other. He tapped the hood of his car as I jingled my keys. He tapped again. I jingled more.

We never had an awkward moment before. It was always comfortable air between us, even if the air lacked words. But this was flat-out strange.

"So ... now what?" I said.

He looked around. "Want to go to Paris?"

"No." I laughed. "I can't. Not like this. Did you see the pictures of—"

"I saw them."

"And you—"

"Don't care."

I nodded. He tapped. I jingled.

"Oh, come on." He swung his arms and clapped his hands. "This feels like the most bizarre blind date ever. It's you and me here."

"You said we were like brother and sister."

"I said what I needed to at the time." He pointed to my car. "Let's go get ice cream and fudge or something. Meet me at Central Market?"

WE WALKED AROUND THE MARKET, LOOKING AT KNICK-knacks and breathing in the freshly baked breads. He bought us five pounds of fudge, a little bit of every flavor. We decided to skip the ice cream. I didn't like to eat a lot of sugar. Not since the cancer scare.

We sat outside on a bench, sampling fudge and listening to an old man play guitar. We smiled at him as he strummed away, then suddenly began playing a crazy guitar solo. His long beard shook as he played. Vasili and I exchanged glances as we ate. For a second, it almost seemed like old times. Except I couldn't toss the idea of who he was intending to be with right now and where.

"Can I ask a question?" I dabbed my face with a napkin.

He put the fudge in his lap and nodded.

"You really loved Natalie, right?"

He nodded while shrugging.

"Is that a yes? I'm just wondering because you were about to commit to spending the rest of your life with her, and she decided to end it at the last minute. You didn't put up a fight. Then, you're sitting with me the next day, eating fudge like you never experienced any of that. Did she tell you about the salon? She never really wanted LA more than you."

"Can I ask you a question?"

I looked down. "Sure."

"Why did you write the man you love, finally telling him how you really feel, only to convince him to marry someone else?"

"I thought it was the right thing to do."

"What is right and what is wrong in this situation?"

"Depends, I guess."

"For you, the right thing to do is to have me marry Natalie. For Natalie, the right thing to do is have me marry you. For me, I don't know. At first I thought the right thing to do was stick to my word. Commit to Natalie and give her my best, even though our time together lacked any sort of substance since she became obsessed with celebrities. I'm a man of my word, but was I wrong? Should I be a man of my heart, even if it betrays my word? What if it betrays another person? I don't know. How far does a person go before their right becomes a wrong? How do we ever know if we're right?"

People walked by as I processed his words. He looked deep in thought as well, occasionally bringing a slice of fudge to his lips. I tried not to notice.

"Want to know what really did it for me?" he said, staring off into the distance. "Those photographs. All this time you knew that my favorite piece of art was your own work. I spent nights looking at that thing for hours. Natalie never understood what I saw in it." He paused, then looked at me. "You know what really gets me?"

"That we both understand the beauty in something she couldn't see?"

"No," he said. "Well, that too." He set the fudge on the bench between us. "I could seriously eat that entire box."

I smiled. "It's really good. It has a milky creaminess to it without that gritty texture a lot of fudge has."

"Man, I know. It melts in your mouth."

I laughed. "I liked the mint chocolate chip one."

"So, what amazed me the most is that you knew about it all that time and you kept it a secret. You didn't want to hurt Natalie or cause problems." He snuck another chunk of fudge and we both smiled. "And that really made me think, because Natalie hid your letter for the complete opposite reason. She was only looking out for herself."

"She's a good person. She just doesn't think the same. I was always on the receiving end of inconsiderateness, so for me thinking of others is almost like a habit. It always annoys me when people in the city have multiple vehicles and they park them all out front, not even considering the family next door who has to lug five kids and groceries two blocks because they had to park their one vehicle super far away. But other people, like Natalie, always had people serving them life on a silver platter. Even you did it to her by always giving her what she wanted. It's not her fault that she naturally considers herself first. She's practically been forced into thinking that way, but she's a sweet girl and she really wanted to try to be more considerate of your feelings."

He rubbed his jaw. "Interesting."

"I'm not completely selfless either, you know. Yes, I didn't want to hurt anyone or become the source of problems, but also it scared the living daylights out of me."

"What did?"

"The possibility of being with a man like you." I let my hair fall from behind my ear, creating a shield from his eyes. "Now that I'm like this."

"I have scars too, Sarah. You haven't seen me naked yet."

I blushed and tried to hide my laugh.

"I didn't mean to say yet." He laughed, stumbling over his words. "I mean, well, I have scars all the way down my chest to my ... stuff."

I cracked up laughing and leaned back into the bench, holding my stomach and basking in the odd relationship we now had.

"Oh, Vasili." I couldn't stop laughing. "Your ... stuff?"

"I know, I know. Sounds very manly." He stood. "On that note, I promised Mom I'd stop by today and explain everything. Should I tell her about you?"

"What about me?"

"That we're, you know…"

"Dating?" I stood beside him and we began walking toward the parking lot. "No. Not yet. I don't know how to do this."

He nodded as he walked, then stopped by his car door. "I'll pick you up at seven."

"For?"
"Our date."

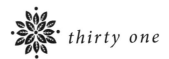 *thirty one*

Ella and Gavin invited Matt and Lydia over. Gavin's best friend and his wife, and their little one. I didn't expect to see them when I walked in and I noticeably sighed.

They looked up from their couch conversations and waited for me to say something. I stood there, like an immovable statue. Could this really be happening to me?

"What's wrong?" Ella said. "You look worried."

"Try again."

"Sad?"

"Again."

"Angry!" Matt chimed in.

"Confused out of my mind." I walked to the steps. "Ella, I need to talk."

"Oh, you can tell us," Matt said.

I looked at Ella.

She shrugged. "Sarah is kind of private." She stood. "I'll be back."

"Oh, fine." I motioned for Ella to sit back down. "I blame this all on you anyway. You and your addiction to romance."

"Did you show up during the wedding and scream for them to stop?" she said.

Everyone stared at me, even the babies.

"Worse," I said. "Natalie refused to go through with it and I was visiting Anastasia's grave today for her birthday when he shows up. We went to market and now he is picking me up at seven for our date."

"What?" Ella squealed and jumped up.

"That's great." Lydia smiled.

"No, it's not really," I said.

"You're sad for Natalie?" Gavin said.

"Yes," I said. "I feel terrible about that. Absolutely horrible. He wants to take me on a date the day after his canceled wedding? That doesn't seem right at all. Or romantic. It's kind of weird."

Lydia laughed.

"Well," Matt said. "It is a little weird when you put it that way, but you only live once."

"Can't hurt to go out on a date," Ella said. Was that a tear on her cheek? "It is romantic, if you ask me."

"It's dreadful," I said. "When I fantasized about this day it was amazing, but now that it's real I'm freaked out. I'm worried about Natalie's broken heart and my own too. I don't think I can let him love me like this." I sucked in my bottom lip to keep from crying. "In my dreams I could, but this is real life. I don't think I want to be that close to a man whose opinion I care so deeply about."

"You need to stop," Gavin said. "You and I are really similar, Sarah. As someone who can relate, you just need to get your mind out of hell or your life will turn into a living hell. If you want to call that living."

"What's that supposed to mean?"

"Don't be so pessimistic. Don't think so much. You have no idea what could happen if you let it. You're fixated on keeping yourself in your safe little bubble. Well, I did the same thing. Always suppressing hopes so I'd never get let down or hurt. I can't speak for your life, but I wrapped my bubble so tight that I started to suffocate in my own prison. All that to have a slight wind pop the bubble." He rubbed his hands on his jeans and looked around the room. "What?"

"What about us?" Ella said.

He laughed. "I meant before us." Looking back at me, he sighed and gave me a crooked smile. "I'm not trying to upset you, although I can also relate to that feeling too. The second someone tells you to stop moping you want to throw the nearest object at them and tell them they don't understand you. I'm saying this to help you. Let go, Sarah. Let go of it all and live. Just live already."

"I don't think that's fair," I said. "I've been doing really well. I don't see how dating a guy constitutes a full life."

Matt stood as though a lightbulb turned on in his head. He held up his index finger. "I get it!" All eyes on him, he continued. "It's the one thing you want more than anything and the thing you fear the most. By giving up, you'll live forever with regrets. But"—he held his finger up again—"if you try and you get hurt, at least you didn't let the fear stop you from trying."

"That's good, man," Gavin said. "Pretty deep for you. I was just going to say something cheesy like—"

"Spare us," Matt said, sitting back down.

I think I actually laughed.

"So," I said. "Life is simply about trying then? Taking the training wheels off and getting back on the bike when you fall? I still don't see how that makes life so amazing."

"It's not the trying that matters," Ella said. "It's just that it means you don't live based off of fears. For you, it's the fear of getting hurt, not being perfect, not being a people pleaser."

"Gee, thanks." I smiled. "Got anymore?"

"For me," Gavin said, "it's always been the fear of losing something or someone I love. Also dealing with my own failures and guilt. Being a people pleaser too."

"My issues have always been commitment-related," Matt said. "Fear of staying the same too long. Of getting bored."

"Which really stems from a fear of being quiet and looking in the mirror," Gavin said.

"Yeah. Thanks oh mighty counselor." Matt laughed.

Everyone else did too.

Lydia folded her hands in her lap and shifted in her seat. "Mine ... I'm kind of uncomfortable saying."

"I'll go." Ella popped the balloon of tension. "I can be a little too idealistic."

"A little?" Matt said.

We laughed again.

"Okay, okay." She motioned for quiet. "I'm serious though. My idealism doesn't end with romance and relationships. I'm really hard on myself. If I can't do something perfectly the first time, I don't want to try again. I can't stand messing up. At all. Not even a microscopic mistake no one else can see. If Gavin doesn't 'ooh and ahh' over a meal I cooked I shrink inside. If someone tells me a picture on the wall would look better three inches to the right, I feel like I'm stupid. If I don't co-sleep with Adelaide, or if I do, either way I feel wrong, like the world's worst mother. I feel like I'm never good enough for myself."

I nodded. I could relate.

"I'll say one," Lydia said. "I have that too, but I also have this fear of death. Especially suffering. I don't know if I believe in God or not. Heaven and hell. I want to believe something exists after this life, but I don't know. Falling asleep and being worm food without ever opening my eyes to another day ... that scares me."

"You never told me that," Matt said.

"What's the one that made you uncomfortable?" Ellla said.

"I can't say right now." She knelt down on the floor with Ella and the babies. "Maybe another day."

"Will you tell me?" Matt said. "When we leave?"

"If you promise not to get mad."

"I won't."

"Well, thanks guys," I said. "I'm still so nervous though. There's so much pressure now. Before, we were just friends. Our time together felt natural. Now it's all weird. I'm genuinely afraid that he might kiss me."

Ella laughed. "This coming from the girl who had more dates in one year than I did in my entire life."

"I'm not that girl anymore." She started to speak, but I kept going, "I know you're going to say I'm still the same person underneath, but I'm not. I don't want to date for fun anymore. If I let someone in I don't want to let him out. Ever."

Gavin stood up and put his hands on my shoulders. "Take a deep breath." He exaggerated as he inhaled. "Then back out." He blew the air back out. "Now. Go get ready. Be yourself. Go out with your friend and have fun."

FOR THE FIRST TIME SINCE THE ACCIDENT I THUMBED through my old wardrobe. Every piece of clothing brought back a memory of my life before. I relived a few sunny memories for a few minutes, then pulled out a long black dress. I wore it to a wedding a few months before the fire. If I threw a cardigan over it maybe I'd feel less self-conscious about my chest.

It still hurt sometimes to get dressed and undressed. Another reason I felt silly going on a date. Honestly, I felt like a ninety-nine year old woman going out. What's the point?

The point, I reminded myself, is that you love him.

I finally got into the dress, put a red cardigan over it, then looked in my new mirror. Not too bad.

I stepped closer and touched the scars on my face. Maybe they were right. Maybe I did focus too much on the negative things.

I turned my face and analyzed the scars. I guess it wasn't that bad. Could be worse, I thought.

I imagined the flames again. The intense heat surrounding me as I covered my face with my arms. James screaming my name over and over as I tried to bite my way out of the fabric. The smell. The horrid smell and knowing it was me. It was my life melting away.

But now I had a chance to mold it into something new.

I stepped away from the mirror and thanked God for my life. For everything.

It wasn't that bad at all.

ELLA GASPED WHEN I WALKED DOWNSTAIRS. "SARAH!"

She hurried out of the kitchen with a wooden spoon still in her hand.

I smiled. Felt like prom day only fifty times better and more important.

Ella waved the spoon between us. "It's ... I can't believe it."

"What?" I said. "Is it too much?"

"Not in the slightest." She touched my hair. "You curled it."

"And makeup too."

"So much for being real." She winked and went back to the kitchen.

I leaned on a bar stool. "I knew you'd say that."

"I'm kidding."

"I know. It's not like I'm trying to conceal flaws. Pretty much impossible to do that anyway. Who knows if I'll ever be able to wear foundation again. They told me not to even go in the sun for two years."

"Already broke that one."

The doorbell rang. My knees buckled. "I can't."

"You can," Ella said, waving a dish towel. "Go on."

I walked to the door with my hands held out at my sides, resembling a Disney princess. My stomach, queasy as can be, made me feel sick. I turned the doorknob and waited a second. Then slowly, I opened the door.

Vasili grinned. His intense eyes looked more beautiful than I'd ever seen them before. Even his cheeks were flushed.

I turned back to Ella. She smiled and waved with her wooden spoon. I waved back and closed the door.

Vasili kept trying to say something, but never succeeded. I motioned toward the car and he nodded. We drove into the city, barely saying a word, then walked into the Fulton Theatre.

It's lovely staircase enchanted me as I ran my hand along the railing. We finally reached the second tier. I followed Vasili to our seats, down in the front on the very right.

"What's playing tonight?" I said, looking at the curtain on stage.

He mumbled so low I couldn't hear.

"What?"

He moved closer so his breath touched my neck. I closed my eyes and shivered inside. Oh dear. I still didn't hear what he said, but I knew as soon as the conductor came out that it was the Lancaster Symphony Orchestra. I saw them once in Philly with Ella. Fantastic performance.

The music began within minutes. Soft and melodic, a subtle wintry sound.

I leaned into Vasili and whispered, "I don't feel beautiful enough to be here."

He tilted his head back so his lips almost touched my ear. "Don't focus so much on looking beautiful. Just be beautiful."

I straightened in my seat and listened to the symphony ebb and flow until finally bursting through the room. I could feel it in every fiber of my being. Every note. Every instrument.

I closed my eyes and smiled, picturing gorgeous landscapes and happy people. At some point, during a more suspenseful sound, I even pictured Sherlock Holmes. The Benedict Cumberbatch one, of course. The only one in my mind.

I kept my eyes closed the entire time, letting the music lift and descend me to various places and memories until it stopped and the theatre thundered with applause.

I opened my eyes, disappointed that Vasili was standing. I guess some part of me hoped he'd been staring at me. I laughed inside. Ella ruined me. She absolutely ruined me.

He looked down and smiled at me, then pulled me up too. "Now that," he said. "That proves beauty isn't just for the eyes."

WE SAT IN HIS CAR, PARKED IN FRONT OF ELLA AND GAVIN'S house. He tried to keep the conversation light and friendly, but every time I allowed myself to look at him I thought of Natalie. She should have been on a plane to Paris with the man beside me. But she was home. Single. With a lovely white dress to sell.

I imagined myself in her place.

"I should get going," I said.

He nodded, then turned the music off. "What's going on in that brain of yours?"

"What do you mean?"

"I've watched you for the last few months. You've smiled and laughed even in hard times. Now things are looking up and you seem depressed."

"Oh."

"Oh?"

"Want the truth?"

"Always."

"I'm thinking of Natalie. I feel so bad for her."

"Natalie and I grew apart a long time ago. She's happy. Relieved, even. I think of you as a gift. A last-minute wake up call." He paused and waited for me to respond. When I didn't, he went on, "You can't glue yourself to the past forever. Yesterday I almost made an awful mistake, but that's ten years ago for all I care. Yesterday is so far gone. It's never coming back. Today. Today is it. You and me. There's no more yesterday and tomorrow is only a hope. We have each other right now, but I need your help. I want this to work. It's gotta work." He tapped my knee. "Help me out here. This doesn't have to be so awkward."

I turned my gaze toward the house as the living room light turned off. Vasili reached for my hand, but I pulled away.

"It's me, Sarah," he said.

"I know it's you. That's the problem. You're too good for me. Don't you see that?"

"No. I see the opposite."

"I don't want empty flattery."

"You think I'd lie to make you feel better? You're the one lying to yourself."

"This isn't going to work."

"I'm not letting that happen." He loosened his collar and unbuttoned his shirt.

I looked away.

"Look at me." He put my hand on his bare chest.

My eyes were closed, but I knew the feeling well. Patches of skin, far from soft and smooth.

"Open your eyes."

I did. His chest looked so similar to mine. Pinched and rippled and discolored in places. Our eyes met. The intimacy between us transcended every kiss I'd ever had. No heated passion or sensual tension needed. Only two people being real. Being honest. I couldn't have planned a more beautiful moment if I spent a year trying.

"I could care less about your body." He touched the scars on my face. "If you want to know the truth ... I think a woman who can smile through suffering is way more beautiful than a photoshopped face." He tucked my hair behind my ear. "But it doesn't matter what I think. If you want to judge people by their skin, you'll never allow yourself to be loved."

"I'm scared, Vasili. I'm scared of kissing you. Of marrying you. Of being naked around you. Of going to a beach with you. What if I can't have kids? What if you regret this? What if I need too many surgeries and you waste your life taking care of me? What if we—"

"Stop."

I exhaled. "I'm living in tomorrow now. Yesterday. Tomorrow. How do I find today?"

"This is what you do." He smiled, a charming little smile that turned up the corners of his eyes. "You go to bed. You wake up. And you say to yourself, 'Vasili and I are just friends. I don't have to kiss him or have babies with him. I just want to call my friend and see how he's doing today.' Can you handle that?"

"Friends." I raised my eyebrows. "Okay. I'll try." I opened the car door.

"Goodnight ... friend."

He laughed. "Night, Sarah."

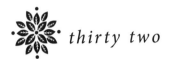 *thirty two*

Trust me, I know it's weird, but his little idea helped. Considering him a friend took away the pressure and replaced it with the natural chemistry we always had. We were good friends simply molding into best friends. Yes, I could handle that.

Or at least I thought so.

We spent the next week talking on the phone or texting throughout our days. In the meantime I found an apartment I liked, nestled in a pretty little street on the west end of Lancaster. I put down a security deposit and planned to move in on June 1st.

Vasili supported the idea fully. He also got pushy with my doctor appointments. I had already postponed my skin graft surgery twice, but he insisted that I do it before May. So I rescheduled it for the last day in April. Only one week to go.

Ella beamed like a Lite-Brite on steroids every time I headed for the front door. "No," I'd say, "I'm not seeing him today." But this time I walked into the kitchen as she danced around while making her famous scones and I said, "Getting together with Vasili today."

"Have fun ... friends." She laughed and handed me a scone.

"No, thanks. Maybe later with some tea. We can watch *Downton* reruns when I get back."

"No ... *Sherlock*."

"Can't argue with that." I looked around the kitchen. "Do you know where I put my keys?"

"I found 'em on the dryer. They're on the table by the front door."

"Thanks." I walked over and picked them up. "I'm having coffee with Natalie first."

Ella spun around. "What?"

"I need to talk to her and make sure she's okay."

"Not many women would care so much about the ex."

"I've never been interested in being part of the majority." I opened the door. "If all goes well, I have a weird, but necessary date planned for Vasili. I'll tell you about it later."

I SAT DOWN BY THE WINDOW AT RACHEL'S CREPERIE. WHILE I waited I bought Natalie her favorite salted mocha drink and got myself a coffee with cream, no sugar.

She walked in and smiled. I stood and greeted her with a warm hug. The kind that lasts a few seconds longer than most. We sat down and I didn't waste any time with small talk.

"Natalie, I am so sorry. I haven't been able to sleep."

She swirled her creamy drink and licked her finger. "It's for the best. I saw it happening before you came, but didn't want to admit it. Not even because I didn't want to lose him. I mean, that too. But mainly I didn't want to be rejected. Since I was the one that ended it, I feel a lot better. Plus, there's this ... well, never mind that. If I'm honest, it's because I didn't want to lose my pretty two-carat ring and my big day to be a bride." She noticed my wide eyes and continued, "I know. Two-carats is a lot. That's what he said, but he let me pick out the ring I wanted and I loved that one."

"Was it embarrassing? Calling off the wedding while the guests showed up?"

"Nah." She laughed. "My dad told everyone. Vasili and I had a really good talk. Kind of awkward now that I think of it. Sitting there in our wedding attire talking about our futures without each other."

"What will you do now?"

"Gonna take that job in California. Moving in July. Starting the job in September." She sipped her coffee.

I sipped mine.

"What about you?" she said.

"I'm moving into my apartment in June. On this side of town. About three blocks that way." I pointed behind her. "Getting back into photography. Not quite ready for weddings, but I can do some engagement shoots and family sessions. Low key stuff."

"That's awesome." She smirked. "What about Vasili? Are you guys together?"

"No." I fidgeted in my seat and looked at my coffee, hoping I'd disappear into it. "We're friends."

She crossed her arms and leaned back. "Friends?"

"This is so strange." I picked at a stray thread on the hem of my shirt, still avoiding eye contact. "I never wanted to be the girl who stole the groom. Looking like this, I'm not even sure why I am."

She uncrossed her arms and pointed her finger at me. "You're an interesting one."

I sighed. "I wish people would stop saying that."

"I saw pictures of you before the fire. I can't imagine what it must be like to lose that kind of beauty. You were gorgeous."

I slapped the table. "Thank you. Oh, thank you, thank you, thank you, for being the first person to admit that I'm no longer that girl."

She twirled the ends of her hair. "Vasili always got upset at me for being honest. He said I always say the wrong thing at the worst time."

I laughed under my breath. "Sometimes you say things out of emotion or you speak a fleeting thought aloud. I think that catches people off guard, but honesty is going to hurt some people either way. I can vouch for it."

"I know it must be hard for you to fall in love again. As a cosmetologist, I think I put even more emphasis on looks. If a romance movie has a female lead that isn't pretty to me, I can't even watch it." Her eyes darted back and forth. "That sounded much worse than I meant it. See, there I go again."

"No, it's true. Our culture is obsessed with appearances. Most people would take a great looking guy over an amazing actor any day. But," I added, "there is Benedict Cumberbatch. Phenomenal actor. I truly think he's the best of our time. Normal looking guy, but his fame and Sherlock character has got women swooning over him. They'd probably roll under moving cars to win a date with him, then be disappointed when he sparks intelligent conversations they can't keep up with. They want a sex god, not a real person with a brain."

She laughed.

I thought for a minute as she ordered a refill.

"I wonder if I'm the only woman who fantasizes about deep conversations of life and art with a man," I said. "Instead of fantasizing about his fingers on my skin."

"You may be in the minority." She smiled. "You really do that?"

"Yeah." I laughed. "There was this one time in high school. I went to a party with a friend. I was in the living room having philosophical discussions with quite a few guys, while my friend had fun in the pool. One after another a guy would leave and come back. When we left she told me she had sex with every guy there. Huge smile of victory on her face. I was disgusted. Seriously."

"Oh my gosh. What did you say?"

"I told her she may get a trophy in the form of Chlamydia if she keeps it up."

"Wow," she said. "I do like a good celebrity crush and steamy romance, but I keep it in fantasy land."

"Not me. I'd rather live such an amazing life that I don't need fantasies. It's hard to figure that out now. What an amazing life is, exactly. Sex has never been on my bucket list though. No fleeting pleasure ever has, especially now. Not to say I won't enjoy it and all, but after this I've realized life isn't about pleasure. The more I tried to force it into that mold, the more unfulfilled and depressed I became. I'm done with that feeling."

"I really admire you, Sarah." She ran her fingers along her necklace. "I mean that. Vasili and I have been friends for a long time, but I never ... I don't know ... he's so simple. I want more out of life. Traveling, great adventures, fame. Truthfully, I thought he was boring and constantly tried to wake him up, but now I can see that he's just different. We have different passions and needs." She twirled her hair again. "I love him, but I think we would've grown to despise each other."

"Why did you wait until the wedding to end things?"

She pressed her necklace pendant—a small square with diamonds—into her chin. "This is horrible, but he has a lot of money. And I mean"—her eyes widened—"a lot."

"You loved him because of the money?"

"No, I fell for Vasili back when he was Prom King. Before ... well, anyway ... I just held on so long, trying to convince myself that it would work, because I knew I'd have a good, stable life financially. You know he paid for my schooling?"

My body temperature elevated. I looked down at the thread I completely pulled from my shirt. Every sound, even the slightest creak in my chair, bothered me. How could she be so selfish?

She pushed her empty cup into the center of the table. "I gotta get going. Heading out to New York with some girl friends of mine." She winked. "Maybe I'll meet this Benedict Cumby guy."

I nodded. My thoughts were too scattered to formulate words.

She hugged me. I tapped her back with the tips of my fingers and pulled away.

"Did I offend you?" she said, clutching her purse as though it would shield her from me.

"No worries. Enjoy the Big Apple."

"Thanks," she said. "Enjoy Vasili."

She pursed her lips to withhold a laugh and rushed to leave. Before the door closed she was already pressing buttons on her phone.

I shook my head and paid for her refill, then texted Vasili. *Can you meet me at 3?*

He responded by the time I turned my car on. *Work till 5.*

Me: *Tomorrow at 3?*

Vasili: *Why not tonight at 7?*

Me: *Needs to be daylight. Tomorrow is supposed to have an overcast. Even better. Tomorrow at 3?*

Vasili: *K dear.*

A few seconds later another text lit up my screen.

I mean ... K friend.

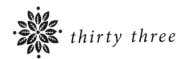

lla ran after me as I dashed out the front door without stopping to explain. Out of breath, we both stood in front of the baby bird. "I woke up and saw these baby birds." I leaned on my knees and caught my breath. "They were in a nest in the flowers outside of my window. Next thing I know this one fell out."

"Well, what are we supposed to do?" She reached her hand toward it.

"No!" I pulled her arm. "If we touch it the mom may not accept it. Let's get it into a box and I can put it back in the nest."

Ella left and returned a few minutes later with a shoe box. I tucked an edge under the little guy and scooted him into the box without touching him.

"He's so adorable." Ella pressed her hands to her cheeks. "There's something about baby animals."

"Okay, let's take him back inside."

Ella carried the box inside and set it on the kitchen counter while I answered a text message from Vasili.

You sure you can't get off work? I wrote.

Vasili: *I'm so sorry. He called out and I need to fill in for his patients, but I'm completely off free tomorrow.*

My heart slowed. *Ok. Tomorrow I have a photo shoot in the morning around sunrise. Can you meet me at 2?*

Vasili: *Yes. I'm really really sorry. I have something planned too. See you tomorrow. I'll call tonight at 9.*

"What's wrong?" Ella said, still smiling at the bird.

"He can't get together today. It's been a while since I've seen him."

"Do you look like that when you don't see me for a few days?"

"Why, of course. I have a photo shoot tomorrow that I wasn't supposed to tell you about, but I need an assistant and Derek said I could ask you."

"My brother?"

"He's proposing tomorrow at sunrise. He wanted to do it on the island he took her to before, but it didn't work out. So he's doing it at Rock's State Park in Maryland. It's going to be outrageously gorgeous at sunrise. There's a cliff that's super high and overlooks all the trees."

"My brother? He's afraid of heights."

"I don't know. That's the plan."

Birds chirped outside the open kitchen window loud enough to distract us. We looked at each other, then walked to the window.

I leaned into the screen and peered around outside. Nothing. Ella slid the back door open and walked out to the deck.

I followed.

She pointed to the window sill. "Look."

"They are looking for the baby."

"Wow. I can't believe it."

Two birds flapped down, chirping frantically, and swooped right into the kitchen. Ella and I ran inside after them.

"Watch out!" I ducked and pulled Ella down as the birds flew around the kitchen.

Eventually they calmed down and landed on the counter. The baby tried to jump out of the box a few times, but failed.

Gavin appeared from around the corner. He pressed Adelaide into his chest and looked back and forth from us to the birds. "What the—"

"Shh..." Ella shooed him away.

He shook head. "What's going on?" He stepped closer and the birds flew back outside, leaving the wee one to fend for himself. "You're not keeping a bird, are you?"

Ella laughed. "Quick, Sarah. Take him back to the nest." She shut the back door and smiled at me. "I've never seen anything like that. I guess when you're meant to be with someone you'll find a way."

"Oh, nice try." I held the box in front of me and took the bird back to his nest. Within seconds the mama bird came back.

For a half-hour I sat by the window and watched them. Chirping and hopping around. So cute. Somehow within that time their simple lives, bundled up in their roofless home, inspired me to fly from my nest and help others.

I left the house a few minutes later and drove to the city. Without a destination, I walked and smiled at every stranger without wondering what they'd think of me. I twirled around street signs, skipped down the brick sidewalks, and stopped to smell every single flower along the way. Every homeless person I passed begged me for a dollar, I gave them each twenty and stopped in a sandwich place, bought a few lunches, and passed them out to the same hungry people. Before I was too concerned about whether they'd spend my money on drugs instead of food. This time I tossed all that aside and gave everyone all I had.

I wore a hat to shield my skin from the sun, but at certain points I tipped my head back to soak in the rays of warmth.

It felt so good. So, so good.

Before getting back into my car, I walked into a cute Asian restaurant and peered around. I spotted a young family with four kids climbing over and under the table, then went to the back.

"Excuse me," I said to a waitress.

"Yes ma'am?"

I whispered, "I'd like to pay for that family's meal and make sure they get big desserts." I pointed behind me.

She nodded. "You know them?"

"No, no." I smiled. "But that makes it even more special, right?"

She scrunched her face and took my card. "That will be $55.78."

"Charge $100 and tell them to get anything they want for dessert."

The poor girl seemed so confused as she charged my card and fiddled with her apron. I reassured her that I was trying to be kind to others. She nodded her head in an awkward circle as I thanked her and turned to leave.

At the table, the mother sighed as she pulled the baby into her lap and tried to get the others to sit still. When she turned to help one of the children up from under the table, the baby grabbed her plate and flung it off the table. Bits of fried rice landed on my skirt.

"Oh, lands!" she said, standing with the baby on her hip. "I'm so sorry."

I smiled and picked the plate up as a waitress came by with a broom. "Life is messy, huh?" I said. "And it's beautiful that way."

She switched the baby to her other hip and glanced at her husband. He shrugged and looked down.

"Enjoy dessert," I said, then walked outside.

Exhaust fumes battled the fresh spring air as I looked up at the clouds and inhaled. A group of Mennonite girls walked by laughing as a flock of birds flew overhead, their arrow pointing toward the sun. The tall, historic buildings. The perfect blend of people. The vast array of smells. The cars with "I Heart City Life" bumper stickers. Ahhhh ... I closed my eyes and stored the memory in my mind.

"Life, I love you."

THE NEXT MORNING I WOKE UP AT 3:30AM TO THE SOUND OF Ella tapping my nightstand. Two-and-a-half hours later we were hiding behind a bush as Derek and Miranda had a picnic on top of the rocky overlook. Red and white checkered blanket. Orange juice in wine glasses. Baked oatmeal and fruit. All the while, a golden light beamed through treetops. Thousands of trees, full of green life, surrounded them. He glanced our way when she wasn't looking. I nudged Ella, whose grin lit up the scene more than the sun itself.

He knelt on one knee. I zoomed in with my camera, clicking as much as possible, capturing every angle I could. She wrapped her arms around his neck, smiling and crying while he pressed his hand into her back, the ring still in his other hand. With a comfortable grin, his eyes glazed over, but no tears fell. She pulled back and grabbed his hands, then flung her arms around his neck again. He laughed and kissed her cheek until she pulled away and answered his question with a kiss.

Ella bounced up and down, sniffing and shaking her head.

"Let's go," I whispered. "I got plenty of great shots. He wanted us to sneak off and keep the pictures a surprise."

Ella clasped her hands together and brought them to her lips.

"Come on, Cupid. Before you have an aneurism."

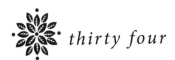 *thirty four*

D

o you know what it's like to spend years building your life, truly enjoying it even amidst the twists and turns, only to wake up one day and realize everything you once knew is gone? Lying there in that hospital bed for months, hearing the pretty nurses talk about their dates and husbands, I began to die. Right there, wrapped up in bandages and unable to move, a piece of me wilted. And another. And another. Until I finally wheeled outside for the first time and prepared to go home—to Ella's house. Dead.

I watched Vasili park his car outside of the coffee shop on Chestnut Street and that hospital experience seemed like another life. Another person. So disconnected from me that I wondered if I really did endure those long nights or if I floated by as an onlooker. How did I get here?

Alive.

I still didn't know how to greet Vasili since we both revealed our feelings, even hugging him made me want to hide under the table. So I stayed in my seat and smiled as he rushed toward me and pulled a chair around so we were sitting close enough to touch elbows. Warmth radiated my body as he rubbed the back of his neck and laughed. I tapped my fingers on the table and blushed.

"So," he said. "How are you, friend? How was the shoot for Ella's brother?"

"Oh, it was perfect." I lit up inside. Most people never asked about my photography sessions.

"Can't wait to see the pictures."

I pulled out my phone. "I saved one on here." I leaned toward him. We both hovered over the screen. "This was my favorite. She reached up to hug

219

him after he asked. I love the way the su—"

"The sun is reflecting on the ring in his hand." He looked closer. "And wow, the way the light trims them both. Oh, and the foreground with the picnic blanket. It looks—"

"Surreal. I know. It's amazing."

"I think it's pretty amazing how we've been finishing each other's sentences since we met. Right ... friend?"

I gently hit his arm and looked down. "Okay, friend. I have a photo shoot planned today for our friendly date. It's really meaningful to me." I pulled an 8x10 picture from my purse. "This is a self-portrait I did when I was living with Ella. She was walking around one day and I caught her as I was heading to the cemetery. I love cemetery photography. We did a few artsy shots of her, then I did this."

He analyzed the picture of me. My long blonde hair curled and sprawled around my head as I lay on the vibrant grass. A gravestone, behind my head, was blurred so you couldn't read the name. I held a pile of dirt in my hand and had sprinkled it around my torso. My face, serene and austere, tilted up toward the camera.

"We did it for fun," I said. "There's no profound meaning behind it, but I feel like it has meaning now. When I took those pictures of Anastasia I thought they were the most beautiful pictures I've ever taken in my life. They weren't photoshopped and manipulated. I didn't smooth over the skin and brighten the eyes. It was so real. A dying child embracing life."

He nodded, probably imagining her face.

"I want that person I was before this to be dead. The more I try to hold on to her and wish I could be her again, the more locked inside myself I get. I feel alive again, Vasili. I feel so good. I want a picture of me, this new me, walking away from the grave."

"I like that idea." He paused and held his chin. "I was just thinking today about how so many people say things like, 'Oh, you're always the same person underneath.' I know I've probably been guilty of saying that, but I don't believe it anymore. I think a person can endure something or meet someone so life-changing that it not only changes his life, but his entire self. Heart, mind, soul—all of it becomes new."

I wanted to wrap my fingers around his and feel his skin against my lips.

Strange as it sounds, the way he talked about life excited me. He awakened so much passion inside of me that I didn't know existed.

Internally, I fanned myself and turned my gaze from his intriguing eyes. Regardless of my flaws and lacking curves, he made me feel like a woman. And I think that made me notice his masculine features even more.

"I have something I want to do with you first." He stood and pulled my chair. "Do we have a few hours before heading off to your grave?"

He laughed at himself. I shook my head and slipped my arms through my jacket as he held it behind me.

"How did you propose to Natalie?" I said as we walked outside.

"Random."

"Yeah. I don't know where that came from."

"She said to me, 'I want that one,' and I bought it."

"Let's take mine," I pointed to my car. "Camera stuff in there. You can drive though." We stood by the passengers door. "But you loved her."

"I did." He sucked in his top lip and took my keys. "Didn't you love James?"

I nodded. "It was more like a friend though."

"Me too." He opened the door and I sat down. "Just like us." He leaned in and winked as he started to shut my door. "Right ... friend?"

He sat down, put the keys in the ignition, and flung a black scarf on my lap.

"What's this?" I picked it up and looked for a hint.

"Put it on."

"Why?" I wrapped it around my neck.

"No." He laughed. "Blindfold yourself."

"Oooh." I placed it over my eyes. "An adventure."

"OKAY." THE CAR FINALLY STOPPED MOVING AND THE RADIO turned off. "Now. In the most friend-ish way possible ... I'm gonna have to hold that hand of yours."

I smiled. "Mmmhmm."

"Wouldn't want you to fall, of course."

No need to worry about that, I thought. Already did.

The car door opened and the sunlight warmed my skin.

"We won't be in the sun for long," he said as I stood.

His hand rested on my shoulder as the door shut. Judging by the sounds of many cars passing nearby, we were around some kind of busy street.

He cupped my hand in his and pulled me into him. I tried to suppress the giddy little girl inside and for some reason that equaled me licking my lips a thousand times.

We walked for a minute or so, up a hill, then he placed my hand on a cool cement block.

"Hold on to that as we walk." He held my other hand.

I wanted to see his face so bad. Cars passed, tossing sharp gusts of air in our direction as we walked. My hair whipped around my face and stuck to my lips.

He stopped and turned me toward the cement wall, then whispered in my ear, "Are we in an ugly place?"

"What do you mean? I don't know where we are."

"Tell me where we are. Listen. Smell. Find a way."

The cars continued to whoosh behind us. When they stopped for a second I listened for other sounds. Birds. Geese. The sound of rustling leaves and a train in the distance. I inhaled. And again. Couldn't place the smell. Somewhat like aged leaves and soil-covered rocks. The breeze tugged at my hair again.

"Is it ugly or beautiful?" he said.

"Beautiful."

"Okay, next place."

WE WALKED UP A SOFT HILL, DOWN A HARD HILL, AND STOPPED. The smell grossed me out.

"Is this an ugly place?" I said, holding my nose.

"Feel it out."

I let go of my nose and held my breath as I took a few steps. "Am I going to trip on something?"

"Free and clear."

I kicked my feet each time I took a step, trying to feel out the ground.

Seemed like pavement, mixed with gravel. Smelled like rotten eggs mixed with cow manure.

He touched my shoulder. "Step up here."

I did, then knelt down. Rows of cool metal lined up beneath us. They seemed to go on for a while.

I stood. "Are we on train tracks?"

"Yep." He took my hand and led me off the bumpy rails. "Wasn't expecting the skunk though."

I laughed.

He escorted me through sticks and rocks and what felt like a dirt path, then helped me sit down.

"Sit here for a while. In silence. Then tell me what you feel."

I leaned back on my hands. The chilly rock under me must've been big enough to hold both of us, because he was sitting beside me. I could feel his arm against mine and it made me want to move closer.

I listened to the bubbling sounds of a rolling brook. Reminded me of Ella's house. Birds chirped and fluttered about. Trees rustled in the breeze. Off in the distance I heard a woodpecker going to town. The sweet earthy scents filled my nose every time a breeze swept by. I inhaled to get more, but I was getting used to the smell.

Nature had its own orchestra. Every sound contributed to a masterful symphony. This place sounded like a soft piano. *Spring Morning*, I'd call it.

Ten minutes later Vasili took my hand and said, "How do you feel?"

"Beautiful." I smiled. "I feel beautiful."

NATURE'S MELODY WAS REPLACED BY A NEW ONE. AS WE drove I listened to the clicking sounds as we drove on the highway. The rush of wind and smell of exhaust fumes. I let my hand sail out the window like the wing of an airplane. The pressure forced my arm back and felt so good.

Taking away my vision made every other sensation more intense. Especially when Vasili touched me. I wanted to kiss him, but I still feared a real future with him.

He parked, then led me to a door and opened it.

"This," he said, "you'll love."

As soon as I entered I heard a blender buzzing. The scent of coffee and books immediately gave it away.

"We're at Barnes and Noble," I said. "The books smell even better today."

I rushed into the store, almost forgetting to let Vasili lead me. I wondered what people would think, but quickly realized I didn't care. He stopped and set my hand on the shelf. It's smooth wood holding hundreds of books. I could see it in my imagination as though my eyes were opened.

"Pick one," he said. "Pick the most interesting story on this shelf."

I ran my fingers along the spines. "Just randomly? How will I know of I can't see them?"

"Ask me to describe them."

I picked one from the shelf, peeled back the cover and sniffed the pages. "Mmmm."

He laughed. "That one is about a lawyer who kills his wife and takes on the case, against the one falsely accused."

I put it back and chose another. The smooth cover and pages beckoned me to smell it again, but I refrained for the sake of maintaining a smidgen of normalcy.

I didn't realize how much I judged books by their covers until now. I couldn't choose one without asking questions about the interior. And even then, it was hard to pick one.

I saw his point.

"Wait there," he said. "Grab that one."

I pulled out a book. "This one?"

"Sociopath nut-job who solves cases with his roommate."

"Awww." I pressed the book against my chest. "It's my beloved Sherlock." I smelled the pages, then stopped myself and closed the book. "I'll take it."

We paid for the book and left the store. He didn't let go of my hand when we reached the car. Instead, he took the book from my hands. I heard it plop into my seat as he held both of my hands.

Don't kiss me, I said inside, hoping somehow he'd hear it. Not now. Don't do it.

His hands touched the back of my neck and his arms rested on my shoulders. Oh, dear. Oh, dear. Oh ... dear!

My pulse skipped beats, creating its own unique rhythm.

Then, he slipped the blindfold off and made a weird face at me. He looked like some kind of angry rat with his head tilted and his brow all scrunched.

I laughed, hiding the disappointment that he didn't kiss me. Yes, even though it would've freaked me out a tad.

"All this time you've been holding this weird guy's hand." He let his face go back to normal. "Amazing how our perspective on life changes when you're blind, huh?"

I nodded, then noticed a glimmer on my chest. I touched the charm. "Did you just put this on my neck?"

"Do you like it?"

I covered my mouth with my hand as my eyes watered. "I ... Vasili ... how?" I let it drop to my chest and searched his eyes. "How did you know?"

"Heard you telling Anastasia one day. You told her not to be afraid to leave the cage." He rubbed his hands together. "Saw it and thought of you."

I held it again. "It's perfect."

The necklace had a special meaning to me. When I was sixteen my first serious boyfriend broke my heart. I caught him kissing Tiffany Jefferson under the bleachers during a pep rally. I pretended I didn't see them and showed up at my house while my parents were talking in the dining room. Mom saw me standing in the doorway and motioned for me to sit. I spilled my heart onto the table, then Dad mopped it up and told me, "Sometimes life shoves you into a cage and locks the door. Don't be afraid to fly again when the door finally opens. Someday it will open again. Courage, my girl. Never lose heart."

During the entire drive to the cemetery I replayed scenes from my life as I cupped the necklace in my hands. A sterling silver cage with small diamonds and a tiny bird further up the chain, flying away. Free.

Vasili would never understand how much this gift meant to me. I'd cherish it forever.

WE SET UP THE CAMERA AND TRIPOD AS THE SUN SETTLED IN an ideal spot. The golden hour. A photographers dream. When the sun casted everything with a picturesque glow, bringing subtle warmth from just the right angle.

I set the timer and stood with my back to the camera, the sunlight hitting my face. Then, I turned my head and looked back toward the grave. A few pictures were snapped, thanks to my timer. Vasili watched me.

He sat against a tree, a content grin across his face. I waved him over.

He walked toward me. Everything seemed to move in slow motion. My throat thickened, preventing all words from escaping. Vasili held my face in his hands and we stayed like that for minutes—or ten very long seconds. Our sun-brushed faces inches from each other. Time froze. It froze and held us there in silence. Like a movie scene that cuts the soundtrack so the only sound you hear is their breathing.

And then time melted.

He kissed my hand and began to put away my equipment. I couldn't move. Still frozen, standing in the puddle of time, I watched him.

I watched every flex of his arms. The slight pulse in his wrists. The way his hair moved when he jerked. His long lashes and piercing eyes. The way he subconsciously rubbed the stubble on his chin. I watched him move and breathe and live. Took in every detail and stored it in my mind. Like the patch of scars right below his collar bone. The slight tug of his shirt around his hips and the loose fit of his jeans. His flushed cheeks and olive skin, and the gentle twitch at the corner of his mouth when he looked my way.

I brought the necklace to my lips and smiled at him. Never would I have imagined life turning out this way, but I guess sometimes life is what we make of it. The good and the bad all rolled into one beautiful mess.

One very beautiful mess.

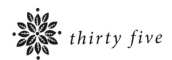

thirty five

I sat by my window, admiring the baby birds as I enclosed my necklace in my hand. Ella sat with me, pointing at the nest and talking to Adelaide. I knew they'd fly any day, any minute, and I didn't want to miss it.

"He hasn't kissed you yet?" Ella said, bouncing Adelaide on her knee. "It's been a while now. I thought for sure he would do it before the surgery, and now look ... you're already back to normal."

I looked around the room at the packed boxes and closed my eyes. Life took me on an interesting ride within these walls, but I was ready for a new one.

"Why don't you make the first move?" she said. "He probably wants to wait until he knows you're comfortable with it."

"That's just the thing." I looked back to the birds. "We're comfortable. He knows I love him. He can see it in my eyes, like I can in his. Not everything needs to be as you imagine. Passion can be a calm meadow just as much as a hurricane."

"Yeah, yeah. I know I'm a hurricane."

"Okay, who am I kidding? I don't know why he hasn't kissed me, Ella. I'm going crazy. At first I wanted to wait. I feared it. This mental battle raging inside of me. Kiss me. Don't kiss me. Kiss me. For the longest time I carried on those mental wars as he stared at me. Now ... now the war has ended. I want to be his and only his. I want our lips to touch and keep touching for the rest of my life." I exhaled and held the edges of my chair. "Wow. I've never felt like this before. It's ... it's so ..."

"Indescribable." She smiled, nodding her head. "Don't even look for the words. No language can describe it."

"Oh, look." I pointed. "He's getting ready."

A baby bird poised himself on the edge of the nest, lifting his wings over and over. I brought my hands to my lips and waited. He gave up and sat back in the nest, then perked up again. A few flaps later, he lifted off and descended to the ground. Ella and I ran down the stairs. Adelaide pointed and babbled as we hurried outside. The little guy was still flapping in the yard, trying his best to get back into the air.

We watched from a distance as he kept trying.

"Come on, little buddy," I said. "You can do it."

Mama bird chirped from the nest, occasionally swooping down to encourage her baby. Ella and I both smiled, bouncing on our feet, hoping he'd get back into the air.

Minutes passed. He flapped his way up, then down, then up again, until finally he ascended higher and higher. Even Adelaide smiled as he made his way back to the nest.

"He did it!" we said, hugging each other.

Ella stopped laughing and looked at me. "Maybe you should kiss him."

VASILI PARKED IN FRONT OF ELENI'S HOUSE AND SQUEEZED my hand. "Ready?"

I nodded, hoping the nausea would subside. Eleni and I never connected much, but thankfully Sophia and Yanni would be at the party too.

"How'd she get such a huge house?" I said as we walked to the door.

"Lives with her boyfriend." He knocked on the door. "He's a brain surgeon."

"Natalie said you have a lot of money."

He laughed under his breath. "She thought I did because I worked to get her anything she wanted. I'm still in debt because of her school loans."

"That's sad."

"I'm fine with it."

"No. I mean that she didn't know your heart."

The door opened.

An older woman with lots of jewelry and makeup looked around us, then called back to through the house, "Tyler!"

Vasili and I looked at each other, hiding smirks.

Bloom

"Hey, Ty." Vasili extended his hand to the man.

"Oh, Mom," Tyler said. "It's Billy. Lenni's brother."

He looked at me. Well, not at me. At my scars.

"This is Sarah." Vasili stepped inside and took my hand. I tried to keep my shoulders high, but they wanted to wilt when I stepped into the house. It seemed more like a museum. And not for the likes of me.

Tyler disappeared around the corner, calling for Eleni. Or Lenni.

"Why'd he call you Billy?" I wanted to lean my head on his shoulder, but settled for standing close enough to smell his hair.

"Most people outside of my family call me that. Vasili is too hard and strange, I guess."

"But Vasili is better."

He squeezed my hand as Eleni rounded the corner and stopped in her tracks. Glancing at our locked fingers, she dropped her shoulders and gave Vasili a glare that a mother gives her disobedient toddler.

I tried to let go of his hand, but he squeezed harder and looked into my eyes.

Eleni huffed and walked away.

The doorbell rang and she returned. Walking around us as though we were part of the decor. Sophia and Yanni entered. They forced a smile when they saw us, but the dark circles under their eyes showed the truth.

Vasili and I took turns hugging them as Eleni disappeared again. Then we all meandered to the patio out back. Classical music played from the speakers as men and women dressed in formal black outfits brought food to guests and refilled their wine glasses. Further down the yard kids splashed in a pool that seemed more like a pond. I tried to ignore the beautiful tan bodies lying beside the pool, but even after we sat down I found myself glancing their way often. Looking at their prominent chests and imagining Vasili kissing my body on our honeymoon.

He tapped my knee and whispered, "We can go if you want."

I shook my head and held my necklace. I'm free, I told myself. Free of caring about what everyone thinks of me.

"Where's the bathroom?" I stood and looked around.

"I'll take you." Vasili stood and turned me around by my shoulders,

229

then showed me the bathroom.

I locked the door and looked in the mirror. "You don't need their kind of beauty," I mouthed to myself. "Close your eyes and see things how they really are."

I flushed the toilet and washed my hands, smiling as I realized how often I retreated to bathrooms to give myself pep talks.

"No way," Vasili said outside the bathroom door. "You have no right to do that."

"It's embarrassing having her here. Everyone is staring and it's taking the attention away from us. This is my engagement party, Billy. Can't you respect that?"

"Oh, now you're calling me Billy? How charming."

"Shut up. Stop making this about you. If you would've told me your date was Sarah I would've said not to bring her. Don't you ever think of others?"

"No. I'm not sure I do."

"Well, maybe you should for once. Did you ever think of how your little experiment may affect others? Poor Sarah thinks you actually fell in love with her when really you just feel bad for her. You're a pig."

"No, Eleni. Your nose is the one so deep in your own fecal matter that you don't even realize why your own mother refused to come today."

"Fecal matter?" She laughed. "Too goody goody to say shit now? Look, I don't have time for this ... fecal matter. Just take her to a nice dinner at Mc-Donalds where you belong. It's bad enough that I have Sophia and Eeyore moping around."

I opened the door in time to see Eleni strut away with her arms glued to her sides.

Vasili smiled weakly. "Did you hear anything she said?"

I shook my head and looked at the painting of the ballerina in front of me. "Can you take me home? I'm hurting." I lied. Well, sort of. I was hurting. Just not physically.

"No." He walked toward the kitchen. "Let's get you taken care of." He pulled a mug out of the cabinet. "Got your pills?"

"No, really." I waved the cup away. "I'm okay. I just need some rest."

Eleni came into the kitchen. "What the—" She snatched the mug from

Vasili. "What are you doing?"

"Getting Sarah some water."

"These are my Audra Winters mugs." She rolled her eyes and put it back in the cabinet. "'They're art. Drinking cups are in the wooden cabinets. Art"—she jerked toward the mugs—"in the glass cabinets."

My heart rate refused to slow down and I knew I'd regret any words said out of anger, but I couldn't help it. "I bet one of those ugly mugs could feed a hundred starving children."

"Ugly?" She gasped. "Look who's talking." She pointed her finger in Vasili's face. "Get. Out."

As we walked to the car two questions repeated in my mind. What on earth did I get myself into and how did I always find the crazy ones?

I FELT BAD FOR HIM AS WE DROVE HOME. I WANTED TO TALK, but I needed time to think and process. He offered to walk me to the door, but I refused.

"I think it's best if we stop holding hands and stuff," I said as I opened the car door. "I don't want want to ruin our friendship."

"I understand." He refused to look at me. "I don't blame you for feeling that way."

That's it? I thought.

"Alrighty then." I stood outside the car. "Have a good night."

Have a good night? Who was I kidding? His shoulders only migrated further south and his lips could barely move for words, much less a smile.

He nodded, then reached toward me as I closed the door. I waited, but his hand retreated back to the steering wheel.

I walked inside and peeked out the window. For a minute or so, he sat there. So still I could've mistaken him for one of my photographs. Then he backed up and drove away.

I turned around and jumped. "Ella. You scared me."

"You're back early. You don't look happy. And you're staring out the tiniest sliver between those curtains. What happened?"

My voice trembled. "I can't do it."

"The party?"

"Vasili. I can't. I'll ruin his life. Just like I ruined James and Abby's dreams of a happy family. I can't. I can't do this again."

"What happened?"

I headed for the back door. "He did it all because he felt bad for me." I swung the door open. "How could I be so stupid?"

Ella stood beside me on the porch. "But he loves you."

"He's never said it. Besides, I don't want to upset his family anymore than I have. Or him. Or myself."

"Truth isn't truth if it doesn't upset someone. You can't please everyone all the time, especially when you're true to yourself. Lies are comfortable. We can hide behind masks our entire lives, but that's not love. Be honest. Tell him how you feel. And whatever happens, happens."

I rubbed my temples. "I'm gonna walk to the creek and turn off my phone. I'll be back after sunset."

She put her arm around me and leaned her head against mine. "No man is a failure who has friends."

I almost laughed.

I HAPPENED TO HAVE THE BLINDFOLD IN MY PURSE. SO WHEN I found a nice rock by the creek, I reclined in the shade and blindfolded myself.

The soothing sounds of water and birds almost lulled me to sleep, but I couldn't relax. Memories faded in and out of my mind. From childhood talks with Mom and Dad to Vasili's conversation with his sister.

The first time my heart got broken I vowed to never let it happen again. The second time, however, Brody Sanders snuck his way in and smashed my fragile heart into so many pieces I thought I'd never heal. But God surprised me with a mended heart and I no longer cared if it broke, but I vowed to never ever hurt another soul the way those boys hurt me.

Ella poked at me all the time. "You're such a people pleaser."

It's true. I earned the title like Michael Jordan earned his MVP during his final days with the Bulls. But is it so bad to want to make others happy? To want to please them at the expense of my own happiness? To do what's right even when it seems wrong?

Does love lie for the sake of maintaining peace?

I thought it did. For so long I lived behind a curtain of lies. Like the great and powerful Wizard of Oz. Only I pretended to smile, to enjoy every moment of self-sacrifice. I became the Queen of Yes.

When I really wanted to go home and spend the evening reading books, James wanted to watch a boring action movie. "Yes, James."

When friends asked for discounts on photo sessions, but I was weeks late on rent. "Yes, of course."

When I fell in love with a man who was engaged and she wanted advice on how to love him better. "Yes, I'll do that, even though it's shredding my heart."

When someone needed a shoulder to cry on, but I needed one more. What did that look like for me? A painted on smile and a resounding, "Yes."

Yes. Yes. Yes.

No.

I listened to the water as it rolled on downstream, like my life. My fake, boring, people-pleasing life. Always going with the flow. Never hiking up my dress and trudging against the current. Playing it safe. Keeping everyone around me happy.

Except I failed.

It didn't work.

I broke hearts and I killed dreams. I ruined ideas and prevented goals.

I lied.

"And no," I said aloud, "that's not love."

I pictured Anastasia's face. Her video. Her regret.

Something brushed against my arm. Warmth radiated my body like springtime sun heated the earth. Vasili?

I kept the blindfold on and enjoyed the comfort of his presence. He touched my hair and chin.

A smile started in my soul and climbed its way to my face. "I love you," I said to him, so naturally, then slipped the blindfold over my head.

But he was gone. Not a person in sight. Not even a squirrel. Only a slight breeze rustling the treetops and a cloud-hugged sun coloring the world pink.

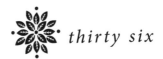

thirty six

So often it's the man. Rushing back to the woman to proclaim his love. Prince Charming searches endlessly for the delicate foot that will fit the glass slipper. Forrest stands from the bus stop and runs to Jenny. In *Notting Hill*, William races through the city to find Anna Scott. Jack dies for Rose as the *Titantic* finds a new home at the bottom of the sea.

Not for me.

I couldn't wait for Hollywood to paint my life with its typical hues. I couldn't wait to gather the pieces of my heart, toss them over my shoulder, and swim upstream. I needed to do it now.

Out of breath, I bursted through Ella's kitchen and tossed my hands in the air. "I'm alive! I'm finally alive!" I yelled, then kissed Ella, Gavin, and Adelaide on the cheek before running out the front door.

Tell me why the longest car rides are the ones you want to jump out of and when you really want to get somewhere, bouncing in your seat and wiping your sweaty hands on your clothes, you hit every red light known to man?

Then, red light of all red lights, I stood on his doorstep, panting and knocking and dreaming of our first kiss, only to see Natalie open the door and shove a detour sign in my face. "He's not here." She wiped her eyes. "I'm glad to see you. I'm sorry for what I did."

"What do you mean?"

"Can you come inside?"

I shook my head. "What's going on?"

"I want him back, Sarah. I made a mistake. I ended things with Vasili for another guy, but I found him in bed with another girl yesterday."

I rubbed my temple.

"Can you help me get him back?"

I covered my mouth with my hand, then covered my eyes. When I looked back to Natalie, she was crying again, but it seemed fake. Or forced.

"No," I said. "I won't help you get him back, because I love him. I love him so much that I could never let him go, not for any reason or any man. He's my home. And there's no place like home."

I turned and jogged to my car, not looking back.

No problem, I told myself, feeling enlivened. Prince Charming had his own detours. I'd find him. Even if it took all night.

After an hour of driving I began to lose my momentum, so I called him.

My phone shook in my hand as it rang.

"Hey," he said.

I hesitated, suddenly speechless.

Then I heard a dial tone.

I called back, but it went straight to voicemail. His phone died. Great. Perfect timing.

Although ... there was one place I didn't check.

I PARKED ON THE STREET INSTEAD OF INSIDE THE CEMETERY, hoping to creep up on him if I found him by her grave.

I passed Sarah Williams who died in 1876. And Lillian Edwards, born 1877 and buried beside Jonathan Edwards. Both died in 1902. So young. I wondered how and why and if I'd die in the arms of my love.

Then I saw him. Lying on the ground in front of her grave. His knees up, highlighted by the bright light from the moon. I thought of our little play. When he pretended to be George and offered to lasso the moon.

I stood about twenty feet away, peering at him from behind a tree. He was blindfolded.

I slipped off my shoes and took one step at a time until I hovered above him. He scratched his neck and put his hand behind his head again. I knelt down as quietly as possible.

He moved his face toward me and I placed my hand on his forehead. "Don't take the blindfold off," I said. "I have something to say first."

A gentle smile toyed with his lips as I asked him to lay his head in my lap.

Minutes passed. I swept my fingers across his face and through his hair. He draped one arm over my knees and held my hand with the other. Although we didn't speak, so much was said. Minutes turned into an hour as I silently told him everything I wanted to say for the last year. No need for words. He understood. I understood.

The summer breeze lifted the hair from my face as a single tear made its way to my neck and soaked into the collar of my shirt. I moved my hand from his hair, over the blindfold, down his nose, then stopped and gently pressed my fingers into the lips I'd been wanting to kiss forever.

"Do you understand what I said?" I brushed my hair behind my ear and leaned toward him. "Did you hear?"

"Actually, I didn't." He took the blindfold off and brought the back of his hand to my cheek. "When someone loves you, there are times when the best way to show them that you feel the same is to just let yourself be loved."

With one hand linked with his and the other over his heart, I leaned closer until our lips barely touched. I prayed God would let me live long enough to die in this man's arms, then closed my eyes and let the world disappear.

As his heart beat under my palm, I smiled, still hovering centimeters from his lips. I tried to remember the exact moment I fell in love with him, but it was impossible. It was as though our love had no beginning or end.

It simply ... was.

epilogue

Vasili and I waved goodbye to everyone as they disappeared down the street. All moved in to my new apartment and only one thing left to do. I linked my arm with Vasili's and led him to the backyard.

"Hopefully this is okay in a city yard," I said, standing in front of the boxes on the patio. "Ready?"

"You sure you're okay with this?" He pulled me into his chest and kissed the top of my head.

We stared at the boxes for a few seconds, until I finally nodded and walked toward the fire pit.

Vasili carried the boxes one at a time, then sat beside me. His eyes asked me if I wanted to stand back while he lit the fire, but I shook my head. I wanted to face my fears. Every last one of them.

He looked at me again before lighting the gasoline covered wood.

I nodded. "One time when I was a kid, I fell off a horse as I was going over a jump. Never happened before. I jammed my finger and the horse almost stepped on my head. My teacher made me get right back on that horse. I was scared out of my mind, but she kept telling me to go over the jump again. Everything inside of me wanted to run and never come back. I was hurt, humiliated, and scared." I tapped the fire wood. "My burns made me feel the same way. I don't want to live in fear. Not about fire or death or getting hurt. I want to live and be honest. I want to be free."

He smiled and motioned for me to sit back. I leaned into my chair and held my necklace in my hands. So fitting. The bird leaving its cage. Finally free.

Vasili struck the match. I flinched, then leaned back a little more as the flames crackled and grew, spreading across the wood and reaching toward the tree branches above us. I stared into the orange and yellow bands of light and nodded my head, remembering the weight of accepting James when he proposed. Feeling guilty for not having butterflies in my stomach and fearing what our marriage would bring. But I suppressed those fears and woke up alone, heat against every part of my body, those flames melting my life away.

Vasili scooted a box toward me. I pulled out my old journals. One at a time, I set them into the flames, careful not to get too close. Then, I rummaged through the other box. Vasili helped. Together, we burned my old clothes, photographs, and dreams.

The smoke curled up and around us. The smoke of yesterday, of my past. Vasili placed his hand on my knee and squeezed. I held his hand to my lips and smiled as my past disappeared in the heat, making way for my new life.

"Do you wish it would've never happened?" Vasili said. "The fire, the pain. Would you take it back if you could?"

"No, I'm thankful." I kissed his hand. "Without the fire, I would've never met you."

He smiled, then pulled me into him. We held each other until the fire began to fade. Then, as the flames finally lost their zeal, Vasili ran his fingers down my cheek, along my jaw, and rested them on my chin.

"I'd die for you, Sarah." He tilted my chin and pulled my lips toward his. "I mean it."

I closed my eyes as he did. Our lips touched. The crickets serenaded us as we kissed, then pulled back, looked at each other, and kissed again. A rush of future dreams scattered across my mind. This was it. Simple, sweet, and free. This was life.

Everything around me vanished and the world went beautiful.

Life, I love you.

Life is what happens while you are busy making other plans.
John Lennon

With a passion for hockey, but disdain for media attention, **Sawyer Reed** tries to rebuild his life after fame by reconnecting with his estranged brother in NYC. While there, he meets an odd girl who won't take no for an answer.

Nora Maddison is doing her best to maintain some level of normalcy while rising to fame quicker than she anticipated. As she disguises herself and meanders about the city, she finds a mysterious man who refuses to give her the time of day.

Eventually, the two find solace in their late night conversations, but when their true identities are revealed they must decide if their hidden romance is worth more than their dreams.

Coming August 2014

When the City Sleeps

chapter one - sawyer

Every Wednesday I requested a table for two, but so far I always sat alone, handing the waiter both menus with an expected sigh. Today I overhead them whispering, wondering if I was being stood up by the same girl every time. I never told them who I was actually waiting for. Figured it would be less interesting that way. But today the young girl took my menu's and said, "The girl over there." She pointed behind her. "She asked if she could sit with you."

I shook my head. "No, thanks."

I didn't look at her. Didn't need to. I saw her come in right after me. Probably wouldn't had noticed her, but she kept smiling at me during lunch. She looked a bit like a freak or a homeless person, but underneath the Yankees hat, frizzy hair, and strange clothing she seemed too pretty to be either.

I looked up and made eye contact with her, then looked down when she stood. Oh great, I thought. Last thing I needed was a whacked out woman in my life.

She sat down in the booth across from me. "Hello."

I nodded and waved to the waitress. When I caught her attention, I mouthed, "Check, please."

"I don't bite," the girl said. "I noticed you wait here for someone every Wednesday, but they never come. Either that's the case or you're too embarrassed to sit here alone, so you pretend like you're waiting for someone."

I took the check from the waitress and shrugged. "Pegged me."

She narrowed her eyes and crossed her arms. "Hm. Good answer."

"Glad I aced your test." I stood and took my copy of the receipt.

"Before you go," she said, standing beside me. "You got change for a hundred? I need four twenties and two tens."

I pulled out my wallet and handed her the cash. She started to hand me the hundred dollar bill, but I saw her name and number inked in red along the edge. Nora.

"Keep it," I said, then walked away, half-regretting the loss of what could've been a friend during one of the loneliest and most confusing times of my life.

The city air hit me like a cloud of second-hand smoke. I couldn't stand New York and if it weren't for my brother I'd stop traveling here altogether. I'm not a city guy, especially this city. Too many memories. Not all bad, but not all good either.

I walked down the street toward my brother's apartment building and saw the strange girl skipping through a crowd on the other side of the street. She turned and waved to me as she rounded the corner. Hands in my pockets, I looked down and reminded myself to pick a different restaurant next week. As much as I didn't want to, I'd be back. Unless he answered the door this time.

I knocked on the door that led to his living room. "Quin, I know you're in there. Come on, Quin. I see your car out front."

I pulled the small mallet from my pocket and banged a tune on the door. He'd recognize it. "Quinton Marshall Reed Junior. Open the door."

I slipped my hands in my pockets and exhaled, wondering why I even bothered. Quin hadn't spoken to me in seven years, but where he lacked loyalty I didn't. I'd come back every Wednesday for the rest of my life, looking like the fool who got stood up every week by some girl when really it was just my brother. Thankfully we fell out of the spotlight years ago, like a one-hit wonder people occasionally surface and say, "What ever happened to...?"

Otherwise I may not had been so keen on The Big Apple. As kids we called it The Big Lemon because we couldn't stand it. Now Quin lived right smack in the middle of it.

Not me.

I hailed a taxi and climbed inside. "Airport, please."

The driver nodded and edged back into the traffic. I stared out the window as people passed in other cars, thinking of the times Quin and I would drive to games and make up stories about people in the cars around us. I watched the people, but they no longer seemed interesting to me. Not without Quin to laugh at the scenarios I'd come up with.

He'd always slap the steering wheel, laughing so hard the car would jerk at red lights, then gather enough air to say, "Where do you come up with these things?"

The taxi pulled into the airport. I handed him double what he asked for and winked. He nodded and thanked me as I turned and looked at the doors to the airport that would take me back to Maryland. I hated flying. Loathed it. Imagined my death every time I boarded a plane. The guys used to call me a pansy. Not sure if I qualify as a pansy or not considering the fact that I played one of the most violent sports in the world--at least you begin to think so after playing it professionally--but pansy or not, I wasn't interested in dying. Which is why Quin had a Stanley Cup and I didn't.

And never would.

The game was his life. For me, it's always been the biggest part of my life, maybe even the deepest, but never the air I breathed. Every hit I took, every slam against those boards, and I'd immediately think of Mom and Dad's grave stones and how I wasn't ready to join them.

Something scratched my back when I walked to the doors. I reached behind my neck to fix my tag, but found a paper instead.

Call me ... if you want. Nora. 555-7859.

She had to know who I was. Probably just wanted an autograph or a few thousand dollars. I crumpled the paper and tossed it in the trash can right outside the door. Another reason I hated playing for The Flyers. Ten times harder to find the right woman when you make millions. And I wasn't interested in the wrong ones. Too shy for that anyway. I left the bedroom to my brother. Yet another area he excelled.

I paid for my ticket and found a seat. Only an hour wait today. I plugged my ears with headphones and watched videos on my phone. Videos of new players. New faces. I studied their every move. And I loved every single second of it.

Out August 2014 - Pre-Order Now

Your Questions Answered

Q. Of all the books in The Unspoken Series, which one do you like the most?

A. That's really hard. I love them all for different reasons. I connect with *Heart on a Shoestring* the most, but I'd have to say that *Bloom* has been my favorite to write so far. I don't know. Honestly, I feel like I say that about each new book as it releases. I have a feeling my favorite is going to be *A Starless Midnight* (Mwenye's story) by the time I'm finished this series.

Q. What kind of music do you listen to as you write?

A. Depends. If you see a song mentioned in the book, chances are I was listening to it while writing. I listen to classical music and nature sounds when I write. My favorite is a nice thunderstorm sound. Is that a boring answer? Haha...

Q. What's the last book you read that you loved?

A. Fiction? Loved? I don't know about loved, but I liked *The Longest Ride* by Nicholas Sparks. Right now I'm reading a bunch of hockey books while I prepare to write book six, *When the City Sleeps*. And believe it or not, I'm really enjoying them.

Q. What's your writing schedule like?

A. I don't have one. I write at least 2,000 words a day. When that happens, who knows. To make time for it I write from my iPhone. Literally. The entire book is written on my phone in between a million other things. So if there are ever weird typos, blame autocorrect. :)

Q. Who is your favorite character in The Unspoken Series?

A. Very hard! Well, in future books I love Asylia (Mwenye's daughter). In the books currently released, that's so hard. I love Vasili in this current book. Miranda is also a lot of fun. Ella will always have a special place in my heart. Can't forget Sarah. I don't know. This is like sticking me in front of all my best friends and asking me to choose only one. I love them all for different reasons. They become real to me.

Q. How can I get free books?

A. Apply for my street team. Details are on my website!

Q. What's next?

A. *When the City Sleeps* is out this summer, then I'm not sure. We'll see what comes after that pretty soon though!

If you have any questions you'd like to see answered in the next book, please email them to Marilyn at marilyn@marilyn-grey.com and we'll select some to answer. You will also receive an answer from her via email. She adores her fans and responds to every email she receives.

Do you love The Unspoken Series?

Don't forget to connect with Marilyn on
Facebook, Twitter, and GoodReads. She is so excited
to hear from fans and talk about the characters
in *The Unspoken Series* with everyone!

Support the Author

Leave a review on Amazon, GoodReads, iTunes, and/or Barnes and Noble!

Printed in Great Britain
by Amazon.co.uk, Ltd.,
Marston Gate.